HEADY

WATERS

John Louis Horan

This is a work of fiction. Names, characters, places, and incidents are products of the author's imagination or are used fictitiously and are not to be construed as real. Any resemblance to actual events, locales, organizations, or persons, living or dead, is entirely coincidental.

Copyright © 2007 by John Louis Horan

ISBN: 978-0-578-06705-6

Chapter 1

"Hey Zelmo . . . ," came the shouted words from the back of the small motor boat, barely audible over the whine of the overtaxed engine and the treble-heavy guitar riffs blaring from the craft's low-grade stereo speakers, "you know what you look like?"

The large-framed brown man on the rear seat was leaning forward to ensure that his rhetorical question did not go unheard by the other three occupants of the boat.

"You look like the big red zit on the ass of that skanky stripper Stiffy was hittin' on last night."

Without turning around, the slightly rotund, shirtless captain of the vessel, whose chunky shoulders and back were fire-engine red from a long afternoon on the river, slowly lifted his thick, heavily-freckled, sun-burnt right arm out to his side, elbow bent, and deliberately extended his meaty middle finger in the air.

Zelmo held his pose several seconds for effect, all the while deftly navigating the boat over the choppy, dirt-brown waters with his left hand, his pinkie finger firmly gripping the steering wheel, and the rest of his fingers maintaining an even firmer grip on a near-empty can of Old Milwaukee.

The brown-skinned man tilted his head back as far as it would go, slowly curled his lips into a wry smile, and let out a gleeful cackle that revealed his great delight at having simultaneously insulted both Zelmo and Stiffy.

"I was *not* hitting on her," the short, hairy passenger in the shotgun seat of the boat protested. "*She* was all over *me*."

"Stiff, was that before or after she told you to 'go blow yourself'?" Zelmo chimed in, never willing to bypass an opportunity to deride their hapless acquaintance of Greek ancestry, whose nickname had been with him for more than a decade, as a result of his misfortune at having popped a spontaneous erection in the shower of the boys' locker room at Riverton Junior High.

Seeing that Stiffy had no retort, Zelmo turned his attention to the front of the boat.

"Cooter, get your ass up, we 're coming in!" Zelmo yelled.

The fourth boater, who was lying face up on the tiny front deck of the craft, with one arm draped over his eyes, twitched slightly in response to the voice calling his name, but otherwise was unmoved.

Cooter's semi-comatose state was the natural physiological result of three straight days of extreme overindulgence in tequila and methamphetamine, culminating at the bachelor party in Riverton the night before.

"I can't believe you let Mikey drink you under the table like that last night," Zelmo continued, knowing precisely which of Cooter's buttons to press to evoke a response.

Cooter barely lifted his arm from his face, turned his head in the direction of the boat's driver, and opened his eyelids just enough to reveal a sliver of his blood-shot eyeballs. "I partied all night," he said, with what little authority he could muster up, before flopping his arm back over his face.

At that, the large brown man at the rear of the vessel, known variously as Chig, Big Chig, or Chigger, for his slanted "Chinese" eyes and dark pigmentation, sprung forward, squeezed between Zelmo and Stiffy, and gingerly got down on one knee, next to Cooter's motionless body, which was clad only in a ratty, holey pair of cutoff jeans, still wet with river water.

"What was that, Cooter?" Big Chig half-whispered in Cooter's right ear, before raising the volume of his voice six levels, "I COULDN'T HEAR YOU!!!"

"Knock it off, Chig!" Cooter squealed as he instinctively flung his arm toward the source of the painful noise.

Big Chig effortlessly grabbed Cooter's arm and began pulling on it, with enough force to jerk Cooter's slender but well-defined body forward, then backward.

In rhythm with each roll of Cooter's torso, Big Chig sang, "C'mon Coot, *crank it up . . . crank it up . . . crank it up.*"

Zelmo and Stiffy erupted in laughter at Big Chig's sarcastic use of Cooter's favorite methamphetamine catch-phrase, which Cooter had exuberantly howled no less than a dozen times over the course of the previous night's festivities.

Having sufficiently bothered Cooter and amused the others, Big Chig released his grip on Cooter's arm and took a seat immediately in front of Stiffy, on the narrow bench seat running along the starboard side of the small boat. Big Chig's dark squinty eyes scanned the familiar, tree-covered terrain along the Nebraska side of the river, until locking onto something of interest.

"Snapper at nine o'clock," he pronounced dryly.

Zelmo and Stiffy immediately turned to their left where, in the distance, a pontoon boat was tethered to the river bank in a small cove. Two well-toned, bikini-clad young girls were sunning themselves, face down, on the large back deck of the stationary boat, while their two shirtless male companions cooled off in the waist-deep water to the side of one of the pontoons, beverages in hand.

Zelmo instinctively eased up on the boat's throttle, affording himself and his passengers several additional seconds of viewing pleasure as the boat pushed northward against the flow of the river. The trio continued to lustfully stare until the contours of the young girls' bodies were no longer discernible.

Zelmo twisted his powerfully plump torso back around towards the steering wheel, tipped his beer can skyward to empty the last of its contents into his open mouth, and shifted the boat's engine back into high gear.

"It *was* good to see Mikey again last night," Big Chig said, to no one in particular, in a rare moment of sincere reflection.

"I told him we was going boatin' today . . ." Zelmo replied, as he cranked the steering wheel sharply to the left, banking the boat in the general direction of the Riverton Marina, with its two narrow concrete ramps descending into the muddy water, separated by a long wooden boat dock hovering just above the water level, "but he said he needed to get back to Omaha for something. Big swinging-dick lawyer."

"Lawyer or not, that dude can still party," Big Chig said, as he bent forward, flipped open the lid on the large, faded red cooler on the boat floor in front of him, and began fishing his muscular brown arm through the frigid waters, in search of one of the few remaining cans of beer.

"If he would have come, we sure as hell wouldn't be drinking this Old Mud shit," Big Chig exclaimed, in reference to the fact that their friend's father was the long-time owner of Riverton's lucrative Budweiser distributorship.

"Grab me one, Chigger," Stiffy stated, suddenly realizing he had not had a beer in the twenty minutes since the foursome had departed the make-shift beach area down-river on the Iowa side.

"Get your own, Numbnuts. I'm not your nigger," came Big Chig's curt response, as he cracked open his beer.

"You look like it," Stiffy muttered under his breath, turning his head towards the boat's driver and speaking loud enough for Zelmo to hear, but taking great care not to allow his comment to come within Big Chig's earshot.

Stiffy reluctantly stood up, reached down to pull the last Old Milwaukee from the still-open cooler, and shuffled his way to the front of the craft, as it sped toward the west shore of the river.

The thick, stifling August humidity, persisting even into the early evening hours, began to envelop the boat as its speed gradually decreased, the artificial breeze created by its brisk journey through the waters dying to a faint wisp.

The high-pitched, rhythmic cadence of the late-summer cicadas, inhabiting the many lush, green cottonwood and willow trees along the river bank, grew ever louder as the boat neared its destination at the Riverton Marina, almost matching the volume and pitch of the searing Bon Scott vocals being spit into the cabin of the boat, courtesy of the vintage AC/DC tape lodged in the craft's cheap, self-installed cassette deck.

Stiffy stood on the triangular front bow of the boat, prepared to disembark, having assumed Cooter's usual role of going ashore to back Zelmo's truck and boat trailer down the marina ramp to the water's edge.

The seven beers Stiffy had consumed that afternoon had convinced him of his ability to replicate Cooter's common practice of leaping from the moving boat to the marina's rickety wooden dock while the boat and dock remained separated by four to six feet of the swift-moving river water.

"Check this out, Zelm," Stiffy said over his shoulder, stepping back with his right leg to gain the momentum necessary for the jump, unopened can of Old Milwaukee still in hand.

"Don't, you dumb-ass . . ." Before Zelmo could finish his admonition, Stiffy was airborne.

His flight ended abruptly, however, when his left foot bounced off the side of the wooden dock, several inches shy of a successful landing, causing his legs to shoot down into the dirty water and his upper body to slam sideways into the edge of the dock.

The force of the collision dislodged the beer from Stiffy's hand and, as he struggled to find a suitable grip on the dock to pull himself up, he caught a glimpse of the can rolling across the bumpy surface of the dock – resembling a maroon and white steamroller – until it dropped off the other side into the water.

Like a parent reflexively diving into a swimming pool to save his drowning child, Stiffy immediately released his grip, ducked his head under the water, and frantically swam beneath the wooden dock, in a desperate attempt to salvage what was the last of the day's beer supply.

The loud thud of Stiffy's body on the dock, and the ensuing jeers from Zelmo and Big Chig, had been enough to rouse Cooter from his stupor, and the three remaining boat occupants peered over the side of the craft, deriving significant entertainment from the sight of Stiffy flailing beneath the dock in futility, searching for an item which likely was well on its way downstream and sinking fast to the river bottom.

But the levity of the moment quickly evaporated as Stiffy's head and shoulders ascended from the water and his hands sprung into view on the opposite side of the wooden dock.

For in his hairy-knuckled right hand, Stiffy clutched not a twelve-ounce aluminum can of cheap beer, but what appeared to be a partially decomposed human head, with a ghostly-gray, waxy complexion and countless tiny perforations in the skin, where hungry fish apparently had been voraciously feasting. Sticking out between Stiffy's hairy fingers were strands of long auburn-brown hair tangled with slimy, bright-green river weeds.

"What the fuck . . .?" Cooter's words succinctly summarized the thoughts of the other two stunned onlookers.

"I think I kicked it loose with my foot . . . when I was under the dock," Stiffy panted, still out of breath from his unexpected foray into the river.

Zelmo reached his chunky red arm out of the boat and grabbed the edge of the wooden dock, holding the boat at arm's length, to get a closer look at Stiffy's macabre discovery.

"Holy shit. That kinda looks like Anna Springer," Zelmo declared.

"No way," Big Chig countered. "Too ugly and no mole over her lip. Anyhow, I heard she left to go back to Washington again."

"Maybe she didn't make it," Zelmo replied.

"Check it out," Cooter blurted, pointing at the head. "Somebody carved the old Motley Crue symbol on the side of her head."

The four river dwellers continued to stare in speechless disbelief at the shriveled disembodied head, considering the possibility of it belonging to the daughter of Riverton's most prominent figure.

The prolonged silence, with only the whir of the cicadas and the chanted chorus of "Dirty Deeds Done Dirt Cheap" ironically playing in the background, was too much for Big Chig to bear.

"Well Stiff, at least you finally found a woman who would give you head," he cracked.

"Shut up, Chig. This is serious." Zelmo's words seemed to hang indefinitely in the thick, late-summer air.

Chapter 2

"You're late, Michael." The Honorable Thomas R. Centers always called Mike Hanigan by his given first name, because that was how it had appeared on Hanigan's résumé when he had first interviewed with the judge for the judicial clerkship position some three years earlier.

"Sorry, Tom. Never happen again," Hanigan stated matter-of-factly as he sauntered into the reception area of the judge's chambers in a slightly wrinkled light-gray suit, with a tabloid newspaper in his hand, and a pair of black Rayban Wayfarer sunglasses occupying their usual morning spot atop his thick, wavy head of dark brown hair.

It was not out of the ordinary for Hanigan to arrive late for work on any day, and certainly not on Monday. But 10:05 a.m. was late even by his usual Monday standards. He made a beeline for the chambers' coffee room.

"So, are you a suspect?" the judge asked, directing his words into the coffee room, in a tone that belied the fact that he had been waiting for several hours to spring the question.

"For what?" Hanigan replied as he emerged from the coffee room into the reception area, steaming cup in hand.

"You were back in your hometown this weekend, weren't you?"

"Yeah. I went to a bachelor party Saturday night," Hanigan said, taking the first careful sip from his coffee cup.

"Oh, you're definitely a suspect then." The judge's svelte, angular body, clad in dark suit slacks, a heavily-starched white dress shirt, and a burgundy tie with matching suspenders, was leaning against the doorframe that connected the reception area with his office, his face expressionless. The judge turned and walked back into his office and out of Hanigan's sight, without further comment.

Intrigued, but slightly bothered by the judge's coyness, Hanigan strolled past the entrance to his own work area, semi-affectionately described by him as "The Cave," for its utter lack of ambience and windows, and instead made his way into the judge's spacious, sprawling office, five times the size of The Cave, with wall-to-wall picture windows and tastefully furnished with a combination of fine, hand-crafted wood pieces, dark brown leather furniture, and Native-American artifacts. The ever-present strains of classical music played softly in the background.

"Alright Judge, you've piqued my interest. What happened in Riverton?" Hanigan asked reluctantly.

The judge gestured toward a large, refinished antique coffee table in front of the chocolate brown leather couch near the center of the office, and the small stack of newspapers located atop the table.

"Maybe if you read something other than the National Enquirer, you'd know," he said.

"It's the Weekly World News, not the Enquirer," Hanigan responded, as he stood over the coffee table and began glancing at the headlines in the Monday edition of the Omaha World Herald, the city's only major daily newspaper.

Immediately, his eyes were drawn to a story appearing on the lower fold of the front page. "Disembodied Human Head Pulled from River," the headline read, with a dateline of "RIVERTON, Neb."

"I'm back from the Clerk's office. Good morning Mike." A silver-haired lady, nattily dressed in a conservative beige women's suit and black under-scarf interrupted, popping her head and shoulders into the judge's office just long enough to utter her greeting.

"Morning Martha," Hanigan said without looking up, as he reached down to pick up the Omaha paper with the same hand that was already clutching a copy of the Weekly World News tabloid. "Judge, I'm going to borrow this."

"We have an exemption hearing at 10:30," the judge stated, now seated at his enormous, well-organized cherry-wood desk, peering through his reading glasses at a single sheet of paper which he held with both of his perfectly manicured hands.

"I'll be ready," Hanigan replied, walking past the judge's desk and towards the back passageway which led directly from the judge's office to The Cave.

Hanigan took a long, cautious drink of his coffee as he walked. The bachelor party in Riverton into the wee hours of Sunday morning had been followed by an all-day gambling and drinking bender at "the boats," Hanigan's shorthand name for the string of riverboat casinos in Council Bluffs, Iowa, directly across the Missouri River from Omaha.

Hanigan knew he would need a significant caffeine jumpstart if his Monday was to be at all productive. And now he had the added distraction of a decapitation in his hometown.

Hanigan nestled into The Cave at his tarnished, hand-me-down desk, which previously had been used by a federal probation officer down the hall from the judge's chambers. He flipped on his desktop computer and eyed the large pile of green court files stacked to one side of his desk, amid a clutter of other documents, past issues of the Weekly World News, and a wooden paddle with a small red ball attached by a long, skinny rubber band.

The top file on the stack was adorned with a large yellow Post-It note, partially obscuring the official United States Bankruptcy Court bald-eagle seal on the front of the file. The note bore Martha's familiar, flowing handwriting and read "Obj. to exemption - 10:30 hrg."

Hanigan grabbed the court file, opened it face up on his desk, and placed the folded local newspaper over the left half of the open legal-sized file, to allow him to skim both the article in the paper and the objection which was to be heard in the judge's courtroom in less than twenty minutes.

Mike Hanigan and Judge Tom Centers had settled into a unique, unspoken code of conduct that governed their working relationship. The judge would tolerate Hanigan's chronic tardiness, morning hangovers, and numerous idiosyncracies, including his penchant for clipping the most outlandish article from each week's edition of the Weekly World News and affixing it somewhere in the judge's chambers, and Hanigan, in turn, would not strive to advance his career by seeking a higher-paying, more prestigious job as an attorney at a large law firm.

Instead, Hanigan would be content to remain as the judge's lifetime law clerk, ghost-writing the brilliant, often-cited judicial opinions and scholarly articles on the intricacies of the Bankruptcy Code, which the judge would sign as his own.

The photographic memory, speed-reading ability, and sharp writing skills which had enabled Hanigan to excel in law school remained in tact, despite the frequent and vicious attacks he would unleash on his brain cells via the vodka bottle. And it was those exceptional talents which had endeared him to the buttoned-up, 52-year-old, oftentimes melancholy bankruptcy judge.

Hanigan took a sizeable gulp of java, and began scanning the newspaper article. Full proper names he had not heard uttered since roll-calls at Riverton High leaped off the page: Edward Anselmo; Curtis Bates; Shawn Lynch; Todd Ralaikas. As Hanigan read the names, he automatically substituted in his mind the appropriate Riverton nickname for each of his high school party-buddies: Edward "Zelmo" Anselmo, Curtis "Cooter" Bates, Shawn "Chigger" Lynch, Todd "Stiffy" Ralaikas.

Hanigan searched the article in vain for the name of the victim, learning only that dental records were being examined by a forensic orthodontist to confirm the identity of the rightful former owner of the partially decomposed head.

Hanigan slumped back in his chair and stared at the drab north wall of his windowless office, which was sparsely decorated with only a few simple black frames containing Hanigan's all-time favorite Weekly World News articles.

As Hanigan gazed blankly in the direction of a faded black and white photo of "The Man Stuck in Steve McQueen's Motorcycle Helmet," he pondered how he very well could have been with the "river rats" when they made their grisly find.

Hanigan had declined an invitation from Zelmo to join them on the river, opting instead to spend the better part of Sunday alone with his thoughts, a steady flow of overpriced, watered-down screwdrivers, and a greasy-haired blackjack dealer at the Mercury-Star casino.

Hanigan's decision to forego the boating excursion was borne of prior experience, which had taught him that lingering too long in Riverton on a weekend could, and often did, yield bizarre and sometimes perverse results. But a decapitation? That was on a different level altogether.

"Mike, the judge is ready for you." Martha's pleasant voice crackled over the intercom speaker attached to Hanigan's phone.

"Be right there." Hanigan abruptly sat up straight in his chair, swept the newspaper aside with his left arm, and began to intently scope the most-recently-filed document in the court file on his desk, picking up enough of the key words to quickly identify the basis for the objecting party's argument that the bankruptcy debtor was not entitled to exempt certain of his assets from the claims of his creditors.

Hanigan dug out a yellow legal pad from the bottom left-hand drawer of his desk, the metal handle to which was dangling for want of one of the attaching screws, and feverishly scribbled down several citations from the governing Nebraska exemption statutes, along with the names of two court cases which, as he recalled them, would address the issues raised in the objection.

Hanigan stood up, tore his page of notes from the legal pad and tucked the page inside the court file. He removed the sunglasses from atop his head and guzzled the remaining coffee from his cup, with the intentness of a newborn sucking its mother's life-giving milk.

"File please, Michael," came the judge's familiar refrain, as Hanigan stepped from the relative dreariness of The Cave into the well-lit reception area.

Judge Centers stood stoic beside the door leading from chambers into the bench area of his courtroom, having donned his long black judicial robe, his arm outstretched, awaiting the file hand-off from Hanigan.

Without saying a word, Hanigan dutifully handed the file to the judge and made an about-face to leave chambers, so that he could enter the courtroom through the "lay person" entrance.

Although Hanigan's assigned seat at a side table in the courtroom was much closer to the bench entrance, the judge insisted that Hanigan use the same entrance as the attorneys appearing before the Court, and that Hanigan be seated at his table a good several minutes before the judge assumed his position at the bench.

Frankly, Hanigan did not mind taking the circuitous route, as it afforded him an opportunity to steal a quick glance at the well-endowed, 30-something with strawberry-blonde hair who manned the reception desk at the U.S. Marshal's office, directly across from the courtroom. She reminded Hanigan of Brenda Fitzgerald, the D-cup Riverton cheerleader over whom he had habitually fantasized in his early high school days.

On this day, Hanigan caught a quick glimpse of the receptionist's tight, powder-blue sweater before turning to pull open one of the heavy, ornately-carved wooden double doors leading into the courtroom. As he did so, his thoughts drifted back to the chilling newspaper account, and he tried to imagine the reaction of the assuredly inebriated boaters as they happened upon the unidentified head bobbing in the filthy river water.

Chapter 3

"I'd make love to you in a New York minute . . . Take my Texas time to do it."

Investigator Steve Fletcher sang along with the twangy voice on the radio, as his blue and white, slightly rusted, older model Ford pickup traveled into the bright, early-morning sunrise, heading east on a two-lane highway from the little village of Dunbar, Nebraska towards the county seat and relative metropolis of 8,500 inhabitants known as Riverton.

Most other mornings, Fletcher would have set out in the opposite direction, on his customary 30-minute westward commute from Dunbar to the Nebraska State Patrol headquarters located in the capital city of Lincoln. But this morning, Fletcher's services as a plain-clothes homicide investigator were needed in Riverton. Due to his proximity to and familiarity with the area, Fletcher had been assigned to handle virtually every suspected homicide in the southeastern corner of the state over the past ten years.

"Take my Texas time to do it." Fletcher sang the chorus as it came around again, the radio reception fading slightly as the truck drove into a valley between two of the many rolling, fertile, crop-covered hills along that familiar stretch of highway, obstructing the signal from the modest tower of KRVT, Riverton's local AM station.

As he sang, a small puff of cigar smoke escaped from the corner of his mouth and intermingled with the line of white smoke streaming up from the thin Swisher-Sweets "breakfast" cigarillo which Fletcher held in his left hand, resting on the door console.

The radiant sunlight beaming in through the windshield revealed the smoke's interesting dance, as it fought both dispersion by the gusts of cold air shooting from the truck's vents and suction from the slight opening at the top of the driver's side window.

As the truck passed the six-mile marker, five minutes from its destination in Riverton, Fletcher ticked off in his mind the facts which had been revealed in the lab report provided to him the day before.

Dental records had confirmed the identity of the victim — Anna Springer. Springer, of course, was the daughter of Phyllis Springer, the U.S. Senator from Riverton who had been elected to the office some ten years before, and was in the early stages of preparing for a reelection bid for a third term.

The politically nimble Senator was both revered and reviled in Riverton. The pork barrel projects she had successfully commandeered into the community – most notably the infrastructure needed to support the expansive facilities of the Trees Are Forever Foundation, a national non-profit foundation at the forefront of environmental preservation and conservancy issues – had certainly brought capital and tourists into the town.

But many long-time residents resented the weekend influx of metropolitan "tree huggers" during the spring and fall seasons, and felt the progressive, environmentalist image bestowed upon the small town was as false and superficial as Phyllis Springer's plastic smile, which she would brandish at every photo opportunity, through her tight, tucked, well-tanned face.

What little Fletcher knew of Phyllis Springer's daughter had been garnered from idle coffee-shop gossip and fishing-trip banter among the Riverton natives. He had heard the elder Springer was pressing her daughter hard to follow in her political footsteps, bringing her to the nation's capital to serve as a Congressional page during her high school summers and grooming her to join the same politically-active college sorority with which the Senator had been affiliated at Washburn University in Topeka, Kansas.

Fletcher had also heard that Anna Springer had dropped out of college shortly after enrolling, returned to Riverton, and become involved in a sexual relationship with Jackie Howell, one of the town's few out-of-the closet lesbians. But Fletcher knew better than to put much stock in the veracity of comments from the ever-active Riverton rumor mill.

Oddly, no missing person report had been filed during the approximately two-week period between the last known sightings of Anna Springer and the date her head was found in the river. Fletcher had learned that, since Anna's hasty and premature departure from college, there had been little contact between Anna and her family members. Senator Phyllis apparently was so livid over her daughter's recent life-choices that she had virtually cut off all ties with her youngest offspring.

The forensics report contained little useful information, due to the fact that the victim's head had been immersed in the dirty river water for approximately four to six days and had essentially served as a fleshy smorgasbord for the hungry fish which had been nibbling away at whatever evidentiary value the head may have contained prior to immersion. However, a microscopic trace of blue-green algae, of the type one would expect to find in a sand-pit lake rather than the free-flowing river, had been removed from one of the ear canals.

Also, just above the right temple were the eroded remains of an upside-down star inside a circle - now known by Fletcher be a form of Satanic symbol called an inverted pentagram - crudely carved into the skin with a small knife or other carving tool.

This certainly was not Steve Fletcher's first experience with a Missouri River-related death. He had personally pulled two other dead bodies from the river during his five-year stint as an Apache County sheriff's deputy, before departing to join the Nebraska State Patrol.

The first such fatality had jumped from the Kennedy Bridge in South Omaha, and had floated the 35-plus miles downstream to Riverton, before the Apache County Sheriff's Department search team spotted the body. Fletcher distinctly recalled struggling mightily, with the aid of a fellow deputy, to pull the lifeless water-logged corpse ashore, only to find other members of the team nonchalantly scouring the river bank area in search of morel mushrooms.

The second river-related death was a Mexican migrant worker who had been stabbed and badly beaten, before being dumped in the river near Council Bluffs, Iowa, his body discovered by two Riverton fishermen, floating face down in a small cove just north of town. Fletcher vividly remembered removing a ring from the victim's hand and watching the flesh slide right off the finger bone along with the ring, like overcooked rib meat at a barbecue.

The stretch of the Missouri near Riverton, with its sharp eastward bend, was strategically located to capture any such human cargo flowing south from Omaha, the state's largest metropolitan area, and Council Bluffs, Omaha's ugly step-sister-city across the river in the neighboring state of Iowa. Those few unfortunate souls who met their untimely demise or had their unceremonious burial in the river seemed destined to be pulled ashore near Riverton.

Fletcher recalled the tale of his grandfather, who grew up in the wooded hills south of Riverton, finding a dead body in a ravine several hundred feet inland from the river, while walking home from country school, at the tender age of nine. As the story went, it was that gruesome experience which had caused his grandfather to speak with a stutter, an impediment which stayed with him until his death at the age of eighty-two.

Fletcher reduced the speed of his truck as it entered Riverton on State Highway 2. He snubbed out what was left of his cigar in the truck ashtray and circled the large, rectangular brick courthouse building near the center of town, with its white steeple top and thick stone placard in the front lawn, pronouncing its status as the oldest public building in the state.

Fletcher pulled the pickup into a spot in the back of the building, alongside two Apache County Sheriff's Department cruisers. Three uniformed deputies casually stood near the garage-level rear entrance into the courthouse building, drinking coffee and smoking cigarettes.

Fletcher stepped from the truck, revealing his scuffed tan cowboy boots, faded blue jeans and an untucked, royal-blue Hawaiian flower-print shirt.

"Mornin' Fletch," two of the deputies said in unison, while the third took a long drag on his cigarette.

"Mornin' boys. Is El-Capitan around?"

"Yup. . . in his office," replied the tallest of the three deputies, whose handle-bar moustache looked familiar to Fletcher, but whose name escaped him, despite the fact that Fletcher had met the deputy at more than one poker game at the Riverton home of Sheriff Bill Rogge over the years.

As Fletcher entered the Sheriff's Department offices, he removed his gold-framed prescription sunglasses, which he always ordered in the darkest possible tint. His neatly-cropped black hair, tinged with slight patches of gray just above the sideburns, and his coarse, reddish complexion looked even darker out of the sunlight. Fletcher liked to tell people he had Indian blood in him, although he was unaware of any facts to actually support the claim.

"William, how the hell are you?" Fletcher said as he strode unannounced into Bill Rogge's office, the walls of which were covered with numerous prize fish mounted on lacquered pieces of wood, hung in no particular symmetrical pattern.

"Hey Fletch," Rogge said in a deep, gruff voice, spinning around in his small leather chair, which seemed to be buckling under the weight of the wide-bodied, burly law officer, dressed in his too-tight tan button-down Sheriff's shirt and dark brown polyester slacks.

"I'm hanging in there. But I'd rather be fishin'." Rogge's face broadened into a wide grin at the sight of his old friend, with whom he had served as a deputy for two years, when Rogge was fresh out of Riverton High School. With his enormous arms folded in front of his wide, brawny chest, his bushy, dirty-blonde mop of hair, and a full beard that was two shades lighter than the hair on his head,

Rogge resembled a cross between a lumberjack and an oversized teddy bear.

"You catch anything lately?" Fletcher asked, as he eyed the walls for any new trophies.

"Nothin' worth a shit. Pulled a few crappie out of Wagon Trail last week."

Rogge lifted one of his huge arms and scratched himself just under the opposite armpit. "But you oughta see my new boat. I got a 20-foot Lund, 175-horse engine, with a 15-horse kicker."

"Whoa, I bet that's got some punch. Where'd you get it?"

"A place up in Okoboji. It's even got one of them GPS deals and a Humminbird depth finder."

"What'd all that set you back?"

"Oh, right around twenty grand, plus a big hit in insurance."

"You mean it costs more to insure a brand new 20-foot fishing boat than it did to insure Old Flat Fanny," Fletcher joked, in reference to the beat-up 12-foot rusted fishing boat Rogge had used for years. "I find that hard to believe. Did you give Ol' Fanny a proper burial?"

"Scrap heap," Rogge replied flatly.

"I heard you got a new Corvette a while back, too," Fletcher continued.

"You win the lottery or something?"

"You think I'd be sitting here if I did? I got a little inheritance money from an aunt who died down in New Mexico."

Rogge shifted his weight in his chair. "So, how 'bout you? You been catchin' anything?" he asked, changing the subject back to their favorite topic.

"Ah, the old lady's been bustin' my ass to finish that new addition to the back of the house," Fletcher answered. "I have not so much as lifted a pole since the Fourth of July."

"How is Connie?" Rogge asked.

"Feisty as ever," came Fletcher's reply.

"She been gettin' into it with Georgette?" Rogge inquired, in regards to the well-known and recurring friction between Fletcher's ex-wife and current spouse.

"Not lately. Just a matter of time, though. Jason will be back living with us once the school year starts, and I'm sure it'll hit the fan again."

"I figured Jase must be living with Georgette for the summer," Rogge commented. "I've seen him out cruising Main a lot of nights with that Reinhold kid."

"He staying out of trouble?" Fletcher asked.

"Far as I know."

"Good. Good."

Fletcher snuck a peek at the clock on the side wall of Rogge's office. "Hey, speaking of trouble, you got any leads for me on this Springer girl? The people down at the marina weren't any help at all and her family claims they hadn't seen her in months."

"I gotta couple angles you might wanna look at," Rogge replied, picking up an orange-colored plastic fly swatter from his desktop, inscribed in black letters with the words "RE-ELECT BILL ROGGE FOR SHERIFF."

"I'm all ears," Fletcher grabbed a county-issue folding chair from in front of Rogge's desk, flipped it around so the back of the chair was facing Rogge, and sat with his legs extended around the back of the chair, waiting intently for Rogge's local insight on the homicide Fletcher had been tasked to investigate.

"Terry Kellogg," Rogge said firmly, before forcefully slamming down the head of the plastic swatter onto the unsuspecting fly near the edge of the desk.

"Nice shot. Is he one of those Kellogg dirtbags in that ugly, neon-green house on First Corso?" Fletcher asked, recalling the stories that his former counterparts at the Riverton Police Department used to relay to him about their almost-weekly domestic disturbance calls to that locale, inhabited by seemingly countless albino-looking, allegedly in-bred misfits.

"Yep. He's Henry Kellogg's oldest boy. He still lives in that same house with the rest of 'em, but now he walks around town all day with that damn Doberman. We've hauled him in at least three times in the last couple years for mutilating livestock. And RPD's busted him once or twice for selling speed to high school kids. He's supposedly into all that Satanic ritual stuff. That same upside-down star that was on Springer's head has showed up before on some of the livestock. "

"Does he have any connection to Springer?" Fletcher queried.

Rogge paused momentarily. "Not that I know of," he answered. "But he didn't have no connection to that poor calf he beheaded at Charlie Sawyer's farm back in April either."

"What else you got?"

"Kellogg's definitely a strong number one. But we could also be looking at a possible jealous lover," came Rogge's response.

"Please don't say Jackie Howell," Fletcher said, raising his eyebrows slightly.

"Jackie Howell," Rogge replied.

"So her and Springer really were licking the beavers?" Fletcher asked, with a hint of disgust in his voice.

"No doubt about it. Ask Cheese."

As Rogge uttered the nickname of one his deputies, Fletcher immediately associated it with the mustachioed officer who had greeted him upon his arrival that morning.

"His nephew was making out with Springer at a keg party one time, gettin' all hot and heavy," Rogge continued. "All of a sudden, Springer stops him, gets up, and takes off into the bathroom with Jackie. Cheese's nephew follows 'em, looks under the bathroom door and sees two pairs of feet facing each other and slurping it up. Apparently, she brought Jackie in to finish what Cheese's nephew started."

"Alright, so the girl was a dyke. How does that make Howell a suspect?"

"From what I hear, they'd been having some knock-down, drag-out catfights this summer . . . supposedly about Springer moving back east or somethin'. And that Jackie, she has a helluva temper. I hear one time she caught Springer in a three-way with two guys up there at her place, and just went ballistic. Screeching and screaming. Busted up a coffee table. Scared the shit out of them two guys."

"Where does Jackie live?" Fletcher asked.

"She rents a little place up on Carnegie hill. Not too far from St. Bonaventure's cemetery. And Springer's vehicle was found parked outside there a couple days after her head turned up in the river."

"Alright, Bill," Fletcher said, as he stood up. "I'll do some sniffin' up there. If you hear anything, give me a holler."

"Will do Fletch. Take 'er easy." Rogge turned back around in his chair and returned to whatever business he was tending to before Fletcher arrived.

As Fletcher departed Rogge's office, he put his sunglasses back on and reached into his shirt pocket for another cigarillo. He stepped into the muggy morning air and effortlessly lit the cigar with one flick of his chrome Harley Davidson lighter.

As he slid the lighter back into his shirt pocket, he pondered which would be the more palatable way to start his day: a meaningful discussion with an albino Satan worshiper, or some quality time with an ill-tempered lesbian. The internal debate continued in Fletcher's head as he climbed into his truck and backed away from the courthouse.

Chapter 4

Even through the dark tint of Steve Fletcher's sunglasses, the florescent-green glow of the old Kellogg house leapt out at him as his truck pulled up in front of the gaudily painted dwelling. Regardless of the number of times Fletcher had seen the home, the same series of questions came to mind.

"What were they thinking? Where did they find that many gallons of paint *that* hideous? Are they missing whatever chromosome it is that keeps normal people from living in glow-in-the-dark houses?"

Fletcher stepped into the unkempt front yard of dry weeds, dirt patches, and blowing scraps of trash, his eyes still fixated on the eery green facade of the home. He took little notice of the pale but dirty toe-headed children running, shouting, and riding garage-sale-grade plastic three-wheelers in and around the yard.

Fletcher looked up towards the second story of the old house as he approached the front step. He surmised that the structure was well-built, as originally constructed, but that a several decade-long drought of any upkeep or maintenance had taken its toll. The sight of the four badly-chipped traditional black shudders around the two second-story windows prompted one last facetious question in Fletcher's mind, as he reached for the doorbell - "What, the paint store was out of hot-pink that day?"

Fletcher could not ascertain whether the doorbell had rung over the din of the playing children. He pushed the cracked plastic button again, this time moving his ear closer to the door.

Fletcher heard no bell, but did perceive an awful noise emanating from within the home, something akin to a dyspeptic elephant blowing its trunk. Now convinced of some form of activity within the house, Fletcher firmly pounded several times on the door with his fist.

No response.

The tortured sound, however, was still perceptible. Fletcher turned to one of the albino children pedaling across the sun-scorched yard on a beat-up Big Wheel, with what appeared to be a mixture of dirt and maple syrup smeared on his chin.

"Hey, is your mom or dad home?" Fletcher said. But the child raced past Fletcher without acknowledging him.

As Fletcher watched the three-wheeler disappear around the side of the house, the florescent-green front door opened to reveal a tall, gangly young man, who appeared to be in his late teens or early twenties, with wildly twisted, uncombed whitish-blonde hair, a pale lifeless complexion, and almost translucent crystal-blue eyes. He was dressed in a pit-stained whitish t-shirt, severely stretched at the neck, and a tight pair of purple cotton gym shorts which starkly revealed that he was not wearing underwear.

The young man stood in the door, holding a shiny trombone and staring at Fletcher with a look that suggested he was not pleased with the unwanted interruption.

"Good morning. My name's Steve Fletcher. I'm with the Nebraska State Patrol," Fletcher briefly flashed the small badge he carried inside the flap of his well-weathered black wallet. "I understand that Terry Kellogg lives here."

"Yeah." The young man's voice was high and raspy, and did not particularly match his appearance.

"Is he around?" Fletcher asked.

"No, he ain't," came the gangly young man's reply.

"Would you happen to know where I could find him?"

"Where's your uniform?" the young man queried, squeezing one eye half shut into a quizzical look, his long white eyelashes obscuring the better part of his almost opaque iris.

"I'm a plain-clothes officer. I don't wear a uniform. Any idea where Terry might be this time of the morning?"

"Not sure. Might be at work. Might be at that church." The young man looked down momentarily at his trombone.

"And where does Terry work?"

"Did he butcher up another animal?" the young man asked abruptly, looking back up at Fletcher.

"No. I just need to ask him a few questions." The tone of Fletcher's voice revealed the faintest hint of agitation. "Do you know where he works?"

"He does some janitor stuff at TAFF?"

"Trees Are Forever?"

"Yeah."

"Okay. And did you say he might be *at a church*?" Fletcher asked, emphasizing the last three words to ensure he had heard correctly.

"He's been hangin' out lately at that little white church south of town."

"The one right off the highway?"

"Mm-hmm," the young man nodded slightly, again looking down at the brass instrument in his hands.

"Alright. Anywhere else he might be?"

"Could be walking Lucy."

"Lucy?"

"His dog," the young man replied, annoyed with Fletcher's failure to grasp the seemingly obvious.

"Is that a Doberman pincer?"

"It's a big black dog that'll rip your balls off if Terry tells it to." The young man smiled for the first time, obviously amused with his response to Fletcher's question.

"Sounds like a Doberman," Fletcher said. "Does Terry leave Lucy here when he goes to work?"

"He don't go nowhere without that dog."

"Fair enough. Well, you've been very helpful, sir. I appreciate the information. And what was your name?"

"Sam."

"You Terry's brother?"

"No. Cousin."

"Alright then, Sam. I'm gonna give you a card with my name and number on it. If Terry gets home before I've had a chance to talk with him, you have him give me a call. Can you do that for me?"

The young man removed one hand from the trombone to grab the card from Fletcher. He looked at the card and half-nodded.

"Thanks for your time, Sam. You have a good day, now." The florescent green door slammed in Fletcher's face just as he finished speaking.

Before Fletcher was two steps down the severely-cracked cement walkway in the front yard, he again heard the faint strains of the awful noise, which he now knew to be the product of Sam's shiny trombone.

Fletcher looked back at the house over his shoulder. Out of the corner of his eye, he saw one of the scruffy children with his shorts pulled down, urinating by the side of the house, behind a gutter downspout.

"Hey, go inside and use the bathroom!" Fletcher yelled. The child looked over at Fletcher, but continued to pee.

As Fletcher started up the engine of the truck, he wondered which description of Terry Kellogg was closer to accurate. Rogge's version, which painted him as an aimless, Satanist amphetamine dealer, or Cousin Sam's version, which depicted Terry as a gainfully employed churchgoer. Fletcher assumed the truth probably rested somewhere in the middle.

Fletcher decided to make his next stop the Trees Are Forever Foundation, ostensibly on the ground that it was closer in proximity to the Kellogg house than the little white church on the highway.

In actuality, Fletcher had a subconscious aversion to churches, visiting them only when absolutely necessary - weddings, funerals, and the occasional infant baptism ceremony. Even those rare visits seemed to evoke a palpable discomfort in Fletcher. The only church visit in Fletcher's memory which had not put him on edge was his own second wedding, conducted in a glittery, heart-shaped wedding chapel just off the Las Vegas strip.

Adding to Fletcher's aversion to the little white church on the highway was his knowledge that one of its ministers was the son of Riverton banker, Ted Sloan.

Fletcher had heard his own father rail for years against the elder Sloan, commonly referring to him as "that rich prick" and accusing his Riverton bank of unfair lending practices in dealing with local farmers, including, of course, Fletcher's father. The way Fletcher saw it, by entering the ministry, Ted Sloan's son was still, in a sense, in the family business - he had simply found an easier way to rob common people of their hard-earned money.

Fletcher's truck snaked its way around the winding, tree-lined road leading to the TAFF complex, with its multi-building headquarters and convention center, surrounded by acres upon acres of forestry preserves and orchards.

Fletcher stopped the truck at the towering, wooden-archway entrance into the complex, overlooking the TAFF facilities in the lush green valley below. He rolled down the truck window to speak with the entrance attendant, who was seated inside a log cabin structure the size of a phone booth. A smiling college-aged girl appeared at the sliding-glass portal to the structure, wearing a dark-green polo shirt with the TAFF tree insignia emblazoned above her flattish left breast.

"Can I help you?" she asked pleasantly.

"Hi there. I'm with the Nebraska State Patrol. Can you tell me if there is a Terry Kellogg working here?"

"I don't know his last name, but there's a guy named Terry who picks up trash around the complex. I saw him earlier today."

"Did he have a dog with him?"

"He sure did."

"Where was he when you saw him earlier?"

"He was over by the visitors' center. But I think he walks all over the complex."

"Will this road take me around the whole place?"

"Here," the girl ducked her head below the portal, before reappearing with a brochure in hand. "This map shows the hiking trails throughout the complex and the system of dirt roads around the perimeter."

"Great. Thanks for your help." Fletcher grinned at the girl and touched the top of the brochure to his forehead in a farewell salute, before driving down the steep embankment road into the complex.

After twenty minutes of slowly navigating the narrow but well maintained dirt roads surrounding the TAFF grounds and peering down seemingly endless rows of apple and cherry trees in search of Kellogg, Fletcher's attention was drawn to something in his rear view mirror.

"Bingo," Fletcher said audibly. He sharply whipped the steering wheel, U-turning the truck, and accelerating back in the direction of a gaunt, wiry male crossing the dirt road with a plastic bucket in one hand, a long wooden poker stick in the other, and a sleek, well-muscled Doberman pincer at his side.

As the truck drew closer, Fletcher could see a number of ugly, bluish tattoos on the young man's pale white forearms, sticking out of the dark green TAFF t-shirt, untucked and hanging over a pair of completely faded blue jeans.

Upon first sight of the oncoming truck, the tattooed man darted quickly into the orchard area. By the time Fletcher 's truck drew even with the row of trees into which the man had ducked, he and his dog were full-out sprinting, cutting over into the next row of trees every thirty feet or so.

Fletcher was in no mood for a footrace in his cowboy boots and knew Kellogg couldn't get too far.

"Just a little jumpy," he thought to himself, wondering if Kellogg had received a text message or cell phone call from good old Cousin Sam, advising him of Fletcher's visit.

"Maybe Rogge was on to something with this guy," Fletcher thought to himself.

Chapter 5

Mike Hanigan stared intently at the double-spaced lines of text on the computer screen in The Cave, his hands intermittently resting on the keyboard and bursting into feverish spurts of skillful typing.

Judge Centers had been asked to submit an article on recent developments in Chapter 12 farm bankruptcy law to the University of Chicago Law Review, for an upcoming special edition on insolvency issues. Hanigan, as usual, was responsible for preparing the first draft. He had cranked out the substance of the article in record time, using only the last two hours of each work day over the past week, but was now struggling to come up with a clever, subtly-humorous title, introduction, and conclusion to tie the article together.

Judge Centers was particularly fond of giving readers the impression that his towering intellect was complimented by a keen sense of wit, and Hanigan knew that a first draft lacking that element would not pass muster.

Hanigan's train of thought was interrupted by a small pop-up box in the upper left hand corner of his computer screen, notifying him of an incoming e-mail message. Hanigan immediately recognized the sender's e-mail address, *genxpastr@ccchurch.org*, as that of Troy Sloan, a friend and acquaintance of Hanigan's since early adolescence in Riverton. Sloan was now a youth pastor at a small non-denominational congregation on the southern outskirts of Riverton, known as Covenant Community Church.

Hanigan's uneasiness with Sloan's avocation as a "man of the cloth" had subsided somewhat in recent years and the two had begun corresponding sporadically over the internet, exchanging e-mails every three to four months, usually on topics such as politics, philosophy, and religion.

The infrequency and unusual depth of their communications mirrored the relationship they had developed during the two-year period prior to their high school graduations, when Sloan would return to Riverton from preparatory school in Connecticut only on extended school breaks and for a few weeks in the summer.

Troy Sloan was the adopted only child of wealthy Rivertonian banker, Ted Sloan, and his martini-drinking, tennis-playing wife. He had grown up in his parents' palatial brick mansion, the largest in Riverton, but essentially had been raised by the family's live-in housekeeper, a frumpy, disheveled woman known simply as "Cin," which was short for Cindy, Cynthia, or maybe Cinnamon, Hanigan was never sure.

As the majority shareholder and chief executive officer of a financial holding company with a controlling interest in a number of banks throughout the Midwest, Ted Sloan had used the Riverton mansion merely as an occasional weekend bed-and-breakfast, before boarding his twin-engine private jet to spend his work-weeks at one of his company's many bank locations in Colorado, Missouri, Iowa, or Nebraska.

As a bored, moderately-attractive middle-aged woman, who craved the attention of younger men, Mrs. Ted Sloan had lived more than half of each year at the family's condominium in Vero Beach, Florida, taking private tennis lessons from the vast array of young, virile pros who worked the condo circuit.

Even when Troy Sloan's parents were in Riverton, he had received little of their attention. His father's relational style was cold and distant, and his mother was capable of showing affection to her child only after downing several high-balls.

On Troy Sloan's rare return visits to Riverton during his two years of prep school, Hanigan and Sloan would sit for hours at night, alone in the mansion, drinking the limited amount of fine, aged scotch that Sloan's father kept outside his always-locked liquor cabinet. They would lament the dysfunction in their families, the bleakness of life in Riverton, and the apparent pointlessness of human existence. They would theorize, postulate, and philosophize on a wide spectrum of issues, usually moving from the profound to the inane as their blood alcohol content rose over the course of the evening.

When his father's available liquor supply waned, Sloan would don a full black tuxedo and drive one of the family's shiny new Cadillacs to a local Riverton liquor store to purchase imported beer. Sloan carried a fake identification card which he had obtained during a weekend trip into New York City, but was rarely called to present it when decked out in the coat, tails, and cummerbund ensemble.

Sloan insisted on this method of acquiring their alcohol, despite Hanigan's standing offer to simply raid the walk-in cooler at his father's Budweiser distributorship. "American hops are substandard," was Sloan's common line in response to Hanigan's offer.

Unlike Hanigan, Sloan had never been comfortable consorting with the town's rough, blue-collar "river-rat" set, largely due to the merciless teasing he had endured at their hands during his formative years, much of which had been engendered by the gaping socio-economic divide between Sloan and his Riverton classmates. Hanigan relished his occasional visits to the Sloan mansion during those two years, viewing them as a much-needed respite from the mindless, alcohol-induced antics of his other acquaintances, and an opportunity to reflect on the deeper issues in life.

Hanigan had heard little of or from Sloan during their college years, with Hanigan at the state university in Lincoln and Sloan attending the Wharton School of Business in Philadelphia. Hanigan fully expected to hear that Sloan had become an investment banker or financial adviser on Wall Street.

When he learned that Sloan had instead bolted to a seminary somewhere in the Bible Belt, he was flabbergasted. Hanigan initially believed it was Sloan's way of slapping his father in the face for all those years of indifference.

Hanigan was equally astonished when he learned that Sloan had returned to Riverton, particularly in light of Sloan's utter disdain for the town's populace. And, of all places, in a church congregation full of "fundies," Hanigan's pejorative term for those of the fundamentalist Christian persuasion.

The incongruity of the silver-spooned, cynical Sloan leading a group of hoi polloi Riverton teenagers in a Bible-thumping session still perplexed Sloan. But he nevertheless enjoyed the renewed discourse with his old acquaintance.

The subject line of Sloan's e-mail was "More Evidence." Hanigan slid the computer mouse across the Irish-flag mouse pad on his cluttered desk and clicked open the e-mail.

> *Hey Mike,*
> *I assume you've heard about Anna Springer. Pretty tragic, isn't it? I can't imagine what her family must be going through.*
> *Everyone is pretty shaken up around here. In my mind, this is simply another piece of evidence supporting my spiritual oppression theory.*

Hanigan paused momentarily and recalled his last email exchange with Sloan, shortly after Easter, during which Sloan bemoaned the slow growth of his church youth group and theorized that it was more difficult to break through with the Christian message in Riverton, because the town had been a long-time stronghold of the "Evil One."

According to Sloan's theory, whereas most small communities in Nebraska were founded and originally populated by a core of sturdy, God-fearing farm families, with solid Judeo-Christian values and belief systems, which were passed down through the generations, Riverton, with its history as an old river and railroad town, was comprised of a citizenry with a lineage traced to a hodge podge of transient traders, trappers, gamblers, and ne'er-do-wells.

Sloan posited, based on a number of passages from the Old Testament, that the current residents of Riverton were under a generational curse, whereby the sins of the 19th century inhabitants of the town continued to be visited upon the succeeding generations, blinding them to the reality of their desperate spiritual condition.

Hanigan did not buy any of this spiritual oppression nonsense and he delighted in critiquing Sloan's ideas, usually countering with some existentialist rationale for the plight of Riverton and its people. He would always close his emails to Sloan with a quote from Nietzsche, Kant, Hegel, or one of Hanigan's other favorite philosophers, so as to mockingly parallel Sloan's habit of signing off with a Bible verse.

Hanigan glanced briefly at his watch, to determine whether he would have time to finish the law review article, respond to Sloan's e-mail, and still make it Duggan's Pub for their Friday Afternoon Club specials. He resolved only to finish reading the e-mail, coax the judge into an extension of time on the article, and hit Duggan's ahead of the after-work rush. Hanigan's eyes flitted back to the closing paragraphs of Sloan's e-mail message.

> *I heard you were in Riverton last weekend. Next time you're in town on a Sunday, stop by the church. Service is at 10:00 a.m. Darcy and I would love to have you over for lunch afterwards (BYOB, of course).*
>
> *Hope to see you soon.*
> *Troy*
>
> *"We are more than conquerors through him who loved us."*
> *Romans 8:37.*

"What the hell does that mean?" Hanigan said out loud quietly to himself, puzzled at Sloan's selected scripture quotation. He motioned the mouse, moving the on-screen arrow towards the top of Sloan's e-mail, and clicked on the print icon.

Hanigan planned to compose his response to Sloan by scribbling it on the printed page over a double vodka rocks at Duggan's. He stood up, pulled the printed e-mail off the laser printer adjacent to his desk in The Cave, and walked back into the judge's office.

"Tom, what's the deadline again on that Chapter 12 article?" Hanigan asked.

Judge Centers was facing the computer atop the large cherry- wood credenza behind his desk, pecking out characters one at a time with his two index fingers.

"What was that, Michael?" the judge asked, with his brow partially furrowed, as he continued to poke at the keyboard, looking down at the keys, then back up at the screen.

"The law review article. When is that due?"

"Need a first draft by Monday," the judge responded.

"What if I told you this thing is so polished, it's virtually in publishable form already?"

"First thing Tuesday morning, not a moment later. And first thing means 8 o'clock, not 10:00. I have several hours that morning I can use to review and revise it."

"Not a problem, Judge. Wait until you see the intro, you're gonna love it. By the way, I need to duck out a little early today."

"Big date?" the judge asked, still peering at his computer screen.

"Yeah. A date with a warm bar stool at Duggan's and a cold glass of Absolut."

"Michael, you know that stuff will rot your liver."

"Thanks, Dad. I'll keep that in mind," Hanigan replied sarcastically. "Are you doing anything exciting this weekend?" Hanigan asked, eager to shift the judge out of lecture mode.

"There's a ballet production at the Orpheum that Margie's been wanting to see," the judge said, finally diverting his attention from his computer and turning his head sideways to face Hanigan. "I suspect we'll attend that Saturday night. And I'll probably get in a racquetball game at the club on Sunday afternoon."

"Activity on Saturday *and* Sunday. You wild man. How do you do it?"

"Good clean living, Michael. You should try it someday."

"I'll wash my Mustang this weekend. How's that for clean living?"

"Wonderful," Judge Centers said without cracking a smile, having grown weary of the conversation. "First thing Tuesday," he stated, as if to clarify that the granting of Hanigan's request for early departure was conditioned upon timely completion of the article.

"First thing," Hanigan repeated, already turning away from the judge, to slip back into The Cave for his suit coat.

He glanced at Sloan's printed e-mail one last time before cramming the page into the right front pocket of his suit slacks.

Chapter 6

"You think he's got any red hair?" Cooter asked expectantly, as he and Zelmo made their way up a rusted metal staircase on the side of the Riverton Fish Market, a dilapidated two-story brick building which had been on Riverton's main downtown street since before it was first paved.

Zelmo ploddingly stepped up to the corrugated metal landing at the top of the stairs and looked eastward, as he did each time he ascended that staircase, to catch a quick glimpse of the river, just four blocks away, where Main Street abruptly ended at the rushing brown waters of the Missouri.

"Zelm?" Cooter said, still wanting an answer from his buddy.

"I don't know, Coot. We'll see," Zelmo responded, slightly out of breath from the short trip up the two flights of stairs.

Zelmo ambled across the metal landing to an unpainted wooden door, balled up his substantial knuckles, and rapped two times, paused one second, then knocked three more times in rapid succession.

Cooter and Zelmo heard the familiar sound of wood sliding on wood, signaling to them that the occupant was moving aside his makeshift peephole-cover.

"Bud-man," came Zelmo's understated, but congenial greeting as the door opened, revealing a barefooted man, with a shoulder-length mane of greasy brown locks commencing at his receded hairline, outfitted in baggy gray sweat pants and a once-black, badly shrunk Nazareth concert shirt from the "Hair of the Dog" tour.

A warm, relaxed smile spread across the man's face, pock-marked and covered with a week's growth of brown whiskers.

"Heeeyyyyy, greetings and salutations, gentlemen," replied Scott "Bud" Graham, in an easy and inviting tone. "Welcome, welcome dudes. Entree."

Graham, whose vernacular often consisted of a strange mix of foreign phrases, cheesy formality, and California surfer-speak, stepped back into his cramped three-room apartment and turned sideways to allow Zelmo and Cooter to enter.

Graham's snug cotton t-shirt accentuated the protruding bulge of his gut, on his otherwise skinny body. The guests made their way into the dimly-lit, cluttered living room, which wreaked of incense, though none was visibly burning.

"Any new fish in here, Bud?" Cooter asked, as he bent down slightly to peer into the 30-gallon florescent-blue fish tank, which was the focal point of the room, occupying the space just across from the 1970's-era green and brown plaid couch, partially draped with a Grateful Dead throw-blanket.

"Nah, man. But unfortunately there is a new one up there," Graham said as he pointed to a semi-abstract seascape painting hanging on the wall behind the fish tank.

The painting depicted a tiny mis-shaped fishing boat being engulfed by what appeared to be dark, foreboding purple-bluish waves. Upon closer inspection, one could discern several dead, dry goldfish and other small aquatic creatures - formerly living tenants in Graham's tank - tacked to the picture with straight pins, an artistic water burial of sorts.

"Little dude in the lower right. I spent last weekend at Shelly's and when I came back, he was belly up at the top of the tank. I got laid, he got laid up. It's a sad state of affairs, indeed."

"How's the tree?" Zelmo asked, cutting right to the purpose of their visit, as he plopped down on Graham's dust-filled sofa.

"The harvest is plentiful. As fate would have it, I was in Omaha yesterday and scored some killer Acapulco Gold."

"You got any red hair?" Cooter asked, looking back briefly at Graham, before returning his attention to a small plastic skeleton head in the fish tank, the top half of which would bob up and down as large water bubbles periodically escaped from its mouth and floated up towards the top of the tank.

"There might still be a few of Shelly's in my teeth," Graham laughed loudly, tickled at his own cleverness, stopping only when he realized the others were not joining in his amusement. He coughed to clear out the phlegm that his sudden burst of laughter had dislodged.

"Aside from that, no Monsieur Cooter, it's either the Gold or some of my prize-winning hydro."

"We don't want that hydro shit. Break out the A.G.," Zelmo stated shortly, not wanting to leave any doubt in Graham's mind as to their level of disinterest in his home-grown hydroponic herbs.

Graham sighed and trudged back into his bedroom, right off the main living space. He re-emerged carrying with both hands a large brass tray, cluttered with an odd assortment of items - an antique cigar box, a yellow-stained plastic Crisco oil bottle, a package of Zig Zag rolling papers, two Bic lighters, a small wooden pipe, several tiny round flat metal screens, and a roll of Bounce fabric softener sheets.

Graham placed the tray on the sturdy oak coffee table in front of the couch and dropped himself into the faded puke-brown easy chair to one side of the table. He lifted the lid on the cigar box to reveal a dozen or more tightly rolled plastic baggies of marijuana, some noticeably thicker than others.

Cooter scurried around the coffee table and took a seat next to Zelmo on the couch.

"Feast your nostrils on this." Graham unrolled one of the plastic baggies, opened the top, and held the open bag in Zelmo's direction.

Zelmo leaned forward and stuck his nose near the top of the baggie. He took a deep sniff.

"Nice. Give me a quarter."

"Quarter bag of Gold -- for you, mi amigo, a frequent-flier discount, forty bones."

Zelmo reached in his front jeans pocket, pulled out two crumpled $20's, and tossed them onto the brass ash tray stand between the couch and the chair where Graham was seated.

"What's up with the Crisco bottle?" Zelmo inquired, as he reached over to grab one of the thicker-sized rolled Baggies from the cigar box.

"It's a bong, man. I hand crafted it myself," Graham replied, lifting the Crisco bottle from the tray and proudly turning it from side to side to reveal its craftsmanship.

"Why would you want to use that piece of shit when you have Big Blue?" Cooter asked, in reference to the three-foot tall blue water bong Graham would typically brandish for his more regular customers.

"It's my creative side, man. I am an artisto. This is my art."

"Let's fire it up," Zelmo said, as he handed Graham a thumb-nail size green clump from his newly-purchased bag, in honor of the house custom of smoking one bowl of the acquired merchandise with the seller.

Graham grabbed the bud and stuffed it into the over-sized metal bowl protruding from the bottom half of the Crisco bottle. Graham had cobbled the stem and bowl of the bong together with metal and rubber components stolen from the Riverton meter plant by Graham's younger brother, Buck, the only of the three Graham boys currently holding down a legitimate job.

Graham sparked up one of the lighters, held the flame intently over the bowl, and began steadily sucking with his lips pressed against the inside top of the Crisco bottle.

Once the greenery began to burn, Graham placed the lighter sideways over the top of the bowl to keep smoke from escaping, the index finger on his other hand patiently covering the makeshift carburetor hole on the side of the bottle, as more and more smoke made its way up the bong and towards Graham's mouth.

The gurgling sound of the water in the bong seemed to set off a Pavlovian response in Cooter, who leaned forward on the couch, "Pass it over here, dude," he directed.

"Who bought the bag?" Zelmo asked rhetorically, extending his right arm and firmly applying pressure to ease Cooter further back onto the sofa, thus ensuring that the bong would come Zelmo's way when Graham had finished.

Graham released his index finger from over the hole and inhaled all of the white smoke hovering inside the Crisco bottle. As he held the smoke in his lungs, he passed the bong to Zelmo, then picked up the roll of Bounce, tore off one sheet at its perforated edge, crumpled it hastily in his right hand and jammed it into one of the ends of the cardboard tube which held the remaining sheets.

"Man, that's a smooth bong," Graham said through pursed lips, still holding the smoke within him. He out-snorted slightly, fighting to hold the smoke in even longer. Finally, after several more seconds elapsed, he raised the Bounce roll to his mouth and blew a tremendous cloud of smoke through the cardboard tube, the sweet pungency of the marijuana smoke being masked slightly by the fresh fragrance of the fabric softener sheet through which the smoke had just passed.

The use of the Bounce sheets was a practice begun by Graham ten years earlier when he first moved into the apartment and wanted to hide his marijuana use from his father, who was the proprietor of the fish market below. Though the original purpose was no longer valid - Graham had long since given up trying to keep his drug use from his parents - Graham nevertheless continued the practice, having grown fond of the aroma it produced.

While the Crisco bong made its way around the coffee table, Graham picked up the small wooden pipe from the brass tray. A small mound of marijuana, brighter green in color than the Acapulco Gold, was already loaded in the bowl of the pipe.

Graham was determined to have his guests sample his hydroponic weed, even if they weren't interested in buying any. He grabbed the other lighter from the tray and began toking hard on the pipe.

After the bong and pipe had cycled around several times, Graham sat back in the easy chair and squinted intently at his guests.

"So, tell me about this Anna Springer deal. That had to be pretty trippy, man. Pulling a rotting skull from the river like that."

"Stiffy pulled it out," Cooter said for clarification, grabbing the pipe from Zelmo in hopes of one last hit.

"It was pretty freaky," Zelmo reflected, looking upward and pulling his shirt away from his chest with his thumb and forefinger, a compulsive habit of his whenever he smoked dope.

"I think her murder is part of a fairly high-level political conspiracy, man," Graham opined, leaning forward slightly in the easy chair, before continuing.

"Phyllis Springer is an up-and-comer in the Republican party and, I'm telling you, those uptight bastards in the party intelligentsia don't take kindly to outspoken gay activists, man. It fucks up their whole 'family values' platform."

Graham looked back and forth between Zelmo and Cooter, looking for any sign of interest in his theory. Seeing none, he nevertheless proceeded.

"I bet it was a well-orchestrated hit by the Republican National Committee to silence Anna, before she really came out of the closet and damaged her old lady's chances of climbing the political ladder. Hell, Phyllis Springer herself may have even been involved."

"Aerial Visine shots!" Cooter shouted, as he stood up from the couch and darted towards the bathroom. Every drug seemingly had the same effect on Cooter, regardless of its classification as a stimulant, depressant or otherwise - uncontrollable exuberance.

Graham now fixed his squinty gaze exclusively on Zelmo, and continued with his theory as to Anna Springer's murder.

"Oh, I'm sure they found some local thug to do the actual throat-slitting, but I guarantee you, this has something to do with dirty politics. I guaran-fucking-tee it."

Zelmo's body was planted motionless on the sofa as Graham spoke. Zelmo's mind, however, which by now was saturated with a powerful dose of THC, was flitting to and fro, half-heartedly attempting to listen to Graham's conspiracy theory, hungering for some fried greasy food, recalling scenes from the pornographic

video he had watched earlier that morning, and finally recoiling at
the limp gaelic-sounding instrumental music wafting through
Graham's apartment.

"This music sucks, Bud. Put on some Zeppelin or Floyd."
Zelmo's directive interrupted Graham in mid-sentence.

Whatever cordiality and deference was due Graham by
virtue of his status as host and narcotic supplier always evaporated
once Zelmo was high. At that point, the parties ' relative positions
on the unwritten Riverton hierarchy of power always manifested
itself in primal ways.

Zelmo was the charismatic ringleader of the tough, hard-
partying "river rat" set, and his ability to throw explosive, face-
splitting punches was legendary in Riverton fight lore. Graham was
a thirty-five year old, out-of-shape, twice-divorced, chronic
marijuana and LSD user, whose father had been a lackie of Zelmo's
father, a generation before.

"You don't like progressive Scottish folk music?" Graham
asked meekly.

"Hell no," Zelmo stated, raising his voice and turning his
head slightly to stare at Graham, but otherwise not moving.

"Alright, man, chill out. I can always go for a little Zeppelin
III."

Graham slowly and reluctantly eased up and out of the
chair and shuffled over to the colossal sound system against the
west wall of the living room. Above the main stereo console hung a
large frayed macrame depiction of Jim Morrison's face, which
Graham himself had made in high school art class - the crowning
achievement of Graham's academic career at Riverton High.

To one side of Morrison was a framed 5X7 color photograph
of a youthful-looking, short-haired and clean shaven Graham,
decked out in camouflage army fatigues and hat, which photo had
been taken during his two-year stint in the U.S. Army. The photo
was oddly out of place among the room's other ornaments, but
Graham liked it displayed as a constant reminder that he was once
a respectable member of society.

"Turn it up," Zelmo barked before the music had even
begun.

As if on cue, Cooter bounced out of the bathroom just as
the first guitar riffs of Led Zeppelin's "Immigrant Song" exploded
from Graham's sound system. Cooter's right hand, which clutched
an economy-size bottle of eye drops, was strumming an imaginary
guitar, his head nodding up and down forcefully to the beat.

As Robert Plant's screeching vocals began, Cooter moved the eye-drop bottle in front of his mouth, clutching it with both hands and wailing into his makeshift microphone — "*Ah -ahh-ahhhhhhhhhhh- ahww. Ahahh -ahhhhhhhhhh - ahww. Come to the land of the ice and snow, where the . . .*"

Realizing he knew no more of the lyrics, Cooter returned to thrashing on a non-existent guitar and slamming his head in time with the rhythm. In his role as Zelmo's court jester, impromptu air guitar performances were fairly common occurrences for Cooter.

Zelmo began bobbing his head as well, though imperceptibly so.

Cooter bounded forward towards Zelmo.

"Visine me, Zelm." Cooter yelled over the blaring music, extending his arm over the coffee table and foisting the eyedrop bottle in Zelmo's direction.

"No, Coot. I'm not getting up," Zelmo replied loudly without expression, pushing the Visine bottle away with the back side of one of his hands.

"Bud-man, Visine me!" Cooter turned his attention to Graham, who had just settled back into the easy chair.

Graham, already feeling buzz-killed over having been hassled with a music change, resisted.

"Cooter, you are so fucking high maintenance, man. Just have a seat, listen to the tunes, and watch the fish."

"Come on, Bud. I need some drops, dude," Cooter pleaded.

Knowing Cooter would not be denied, Graham succumbed. "Alright. Lay down," Graham said as he grabbed the Visine bottle from Cooter and eeked his way out of the chair a second time.

Graham cautiously stepped onto the easy chair, one bare foot at a time.

Once standing atop the chair, he unscrewed the lid to the Visine bottle and turned it sideways, above Cooter's head, which was now resting face up on Graham's filthy avocado-green shag carpet.

Cooter peered upward, his bloodshot eyeballs wide open. He loved the sensation of watching the clear liquid drops as they descended from eight feet above and the challenge of keeping his eyes open as the drop splashed at or near his eyeballs.

Despite the countless number of previous occasions on which Cooter had engaged in this activity, as each drop hit either his face or, less often, his actual eye, Cooter cackled wildly, like a stoned hyena, as if it were his very first time experiencing the sensation.

"C'mon Cooter, let's go get some McTrash," Zelmo stated abruptly.

The "munchies" had clearly overtaken Zelmo, and he felt compelled to make a trip to the dumpster bins behind the McDonald's restaurant in Riverton, in search of individually wrapped throw-away leftovers and mis-orders. A powerful force indeed was necessary to pry Zelmo from his potted position on the sofa, and his hunger for greasy Big Macs and Filet-O-Fish sandwiches was just such a force.

He stood impatiently at Graham's front door with his hand on the doorknob, as Graham squeezed out another eye drop for its lofty descent towards Cooter's face.

"Coot, let's roll!" Zelmo roared over the blasting music and Cooter's gleeful cackle.

Cooter promptly rolled onto his stomach, popped up, wiped the excess moisture from his face and zipped towards the door.

"Later Bud," came Cooter's nonchalant farewell, as Graham's two stoned customers vanished from his apartment as quickly as they had arrived.

Chapter 7

"What's up Troy?" the voice cracked slightly, betraying the speaker's relatively recent voyage through puberty. "This is Cale Bates, that guy I've been telling you about," said Danny Reeves, a scrawny adolescent with a mop of shaggy, jet-black hair hanging in his eyes, as he stepped just inside the office of youth pastor Troy Sloan at Covenant Community Church.

Two paces behind Reeves was another, slightly older teenager, sporting a similarly healthy head of curly, golden-brown locks, but appearing reticent to enter the room. Both visitors were clad in excessively baggy, low-riding jeans and long black t-shirts.

"Hey, come in, come in!" Sloan's voice was welcoming and friendly, with a subtle air of enthusiasm. "So, you're Cooter's little brother?"

Sloan was standing up behind his cheap metal desk, smiling and pointing at the teenager with golden-brown hair still outside the office, attempting by his every word and motion to disarm the obviously-pensive visitor.

"Good old Cooter," he stated again for emphasis.

"You know Cooter?" Cale Bates responded, taking a deliberate step into the office, as if some sort of password had just been spoken, de-activating whatever invisible force field had kept him outside.

Upon entry, Bates immediately began gawking at the walls of Sloan's cramped office, which were littered with posters of hip-looking Christian rock and pop artists and blow-ups of promotional materials from past events of the church youth group which Sloan had dubbed "The Edge."

"Oh yeah," Sloan replied. "Curtis Bates, Riverton Junior High. 'Bout twelve, maybe thirteen years ago. I was there."

Sloan chose his words carefully, not wanting to convey the false impression that he had actually been a close friend of the teenager's eldest brother.

"Nice rat-tail, my man," Sloan said, changing the subject deftly, as he gestured toward the long, skinny, tightly-braided strand of golden-brown hair proceeding down Cale Bates' back, slicing between the two columns of printed concert tour dates on the teen's black Slipknot t-shirt.

"It's faggot-ass," Reeves piped in, just slightly jealous of the attention Sloan was giving his friend. "Oop," Reeves said, as his hand shot over his mouth as quickly as the words had left his mouth. "Sorry, Troy."

"Don't tell me 'sorry.' I'm not the one you just insulted," responded Sloan.

"Hey Cale, check this out." In lieu of an apology, Reeves beckoned his friend to a cluster of digital pictures hung in an intentionally haphazard fashion towards the bottom of the rear wall of the youth pastor's office. "This is MudStock."

"Killer," came Cale Bates' one-word reply, spinning around to peer intently at the snapshots of dozens of mud-covered teenagers, taken at the youth group's annual back-to-school event, held on a quarter acre of farmground owned by a member of the congregation, plowed under and pumped full of 20,000 gallons of water, to create an enormous pit of slimy mud.

"You gotta do it this year, dude," Reeves entreated.

"How much is it?" Bates asked, turning his head slightly back towards Sloan.

"No charge, Cale. All Edge events are free for guests. Danny would just need to sign you up some time during the next two weeks."

Sloan slipped out from behind his desk and stood behind the two teenagers as they continued to look at the images of the muddy bodies. He placed a hand on the Reeves' right shoulder and gave a firm squeeze, letting his prize pupil know he was proud of him.

Danny Reeves had come to the "The Edge" youth group only 14 months earlier, but had shown a keen hunger for spiritual truth and a strong desire to bring others around the church. Sloan had a natural kinship with Reeves by virtue of the teenager's home life which, though substantially less privileged than Sloan's as a teen, was similar in terms of his parents' utter lack of interest in their child. Sloan gathered that a big part of Reeves' attraction to the church was the simple fact that Sloan paid attention to him.

"Who's this hottie?" Cale Bates asked abruptly, placing his right index finger on one of three mud-covered teenage girls wearing shorts and bikini tops, arm-in-arm, smiling for the camera.

"That would be Natalie Westbrook," Sloan answered politely.

"Bounce the eyes, right Troy?" Reeves said, turning his head slightly to make eye contact with the pastor.

"Hey, you were listening," Sloan replied, his voice thick with encouragement.

"Listening to what?" Bates asked inquisitively.

"At the Edge, we've been doing a series called `Sex God's Way,'" Sloan replied. "Last week, we talked about how important it is for guys not to let their eyes linger too long on things that might lead them away from what God has planned for them in the area of sexuality. We called it 'bouncing your eyes.'"

"So when Danny steals one of his dad's Hustlers, he should bounce his eyes off the pictures and just read the articles?" Bates was looking over at Reeves with a mischievous grin on his face, waiting to see if his naughty revelation would evoke the intended response from his friend.

"Shut up, you loser," Reeves yelped as he punched Bates sharply in the right arm, just above the elbow.

"Pastor Troy," a woman suddenly appeared in the doorway of the office, who, by her very appearance, announced to the world that she was a church secretary - conservatively dressed in a thick calf-length wool skirt, which from a distance, looked as if it was made of burlap, accessorized with a pair of 1960's style horn-rimmed glasses, and ugly brown orthopedic shoes.

"I'm sorry to interrupt," the woman said, "but there's a gentleman here from the police and Pastor John is out on benevolence calls. The officer says he would like to visit with one of the other pastors. Would you be able to talk with him?"

"Sure Nettie. No problem."

As Sloan walked toward the doorway of his office, he glanced back over his shoulder, "Danny, you haven't been shooting off illegal fireworks in the church parking lot again, have you?"

The black-haired teenager shook his head firmly in the negative.

Steve Fletcher stood uncomfortably in the "gathering space" of Covenant Community Church, shifting his weight from one leg to the next and checking his watch every 15 seconds or so.

Fletcher 's eyebrows rose visibly above his dark sunglasses as Sloan emerged from his office and approached Fletcher. He surveyed Sloan's ultra-casual attire - open-toed sandals, loose-fitting pastel orange shorts and an untucked, black button-down short-sleeved shirt, splashed with streaks of bright tropical colors and open to the third button. Sloan's hair was spiked with a few bleached blond streaks and he had an earring in his left ear.

"Shit," Fletcher thought to himself, "if I could dress like that, I might actually come to church once in a while."

Sloan extended his hand as he walked towards Fletcher. "Hi. I'm Troy Sloan."

"Oh, so you're Ted Sloan's boy?" Fletcher asked in reference to the Riverton banker Fletcher's father had so frequently derided, trying hard to mask the prejudgment in his voice, as he shook Sloan's hand.

"He may not claim me these days, but yeah, that's right. I'm the youth pastor here," Sloan replied.

"I'm Steve Fletcher, Nebraska State Patrol. I'm conducting an investigation and wanted to ask you a few questions."

"Absolutely. Hopefully it doesn't involve any of my youth kids," Sloan responded.

"Do you know a Terry Kellogg?"

"I know who he is. I think Terry's been coming to Pastor John's Overcomers ministry."

"Overcomers?" A puzzled look slid across Fletcher's face.

"It's a twelve-step ministry for people with substance abuse issues."

"One of those 'higher power' programs?" Fletcher queried, referring to the well-known first of twelve steps.

"You could say that. Although I'm pretty sure Pastor John gets a little more specific about who that higher power is," Sloan answered, smiling warmly at Fletcher.

"Right," Fletcher responded uncomfortably. "How long has Kellogg been in that program?"

"Oh, I think he's been to maybe five or six meetings, but I can't say for sure. That's really Pastor John's deal."

"Do you know how Kellogg got hooked up with your church in the first place?"

"I don't know for sure. It seems to me that maybe drug treatment was a court-imposed condition of his parole or probation or something. Our program's on the court-approved list."

"And when are those meetings held?" Fletcher inquired.

"They've been moved to Tuesday and Friday nights, and I think they start around 7:30."

"Alright, I may stop by tomorrow night and see if I can catch Terry here."

"Is he in some kind of trouble we should know about?" Sloan asked.

"No, we're just conducting a routine investigation and we need to ask him a few questions."

"Does this have anything to do with the Anna Springer murder?" Sloan inquired.

"Why do you ask?"

"Oh, I remember Pastor John saying that Terry was really distraught about that whole situation. Apparently, he knew her from work or something."

"At Trees Are Forever?"

"Yeah. Pastor John helped get him that job."

"Are you sure Anna Springer worked there? Because her family never mentioned that."

"I'm pretty sure she worked in one of the offices there, or something."

"I appreciate the information, uh, Reverend." Fletcher was never certain how to address clergy. "Like I said, I may stop back out on Tuesday night. This Pastor John guy will be here then too?"

"Yep. He facilitates the meetings."

"Gotcha," Fletcher concluded, extending his hand to Sloan in genuine gratitude for the information.

After Fletcher shook hands with the young pastor and began walking out, he stopped and called out to Sloan, who was heading back towards his office.

"Hey, just out of curiosity, do you get to dress like that on Sunday morning?"

"What . . . this?" Sloan motioned with both hands down his attire. "Absolutely. But I might button my shirt up another button."

"Huh," Fletcher murmured as he pushed open the door and exited the building.

Chapter 8

As Mike Hanigan settled into his usual spot at the small wooden table along the side of the courtroom, near the judge's bench, a familiar cast of characters milled about, ten to fifteen yards away in the "gallery" area, just behind the waist-level varnished wooden wall which separated the front and back portions of the courtroom.

The portly, good-humored attorney with a full head of snowy white hair who served as a Chapter 7 Trustee.

The quirky but eloquent lawyer with a lazy eye who sometimes acted as debtor's counsel in large bankruptcies, but who most often represented creditors' interests.

The tall, skinny attorney with a bad comb-over and an outdated, extra-wide striped tie, who specialized in handling Chapter 13 bankruptcies for consumers.

The non-descript, unassuming little every-man in the off-the-rack suit who did nothing but debtors' work of all kinds.

Two well-coiffed, well-dressed counselors from one of Omaha's large "silk stocking" law firms, who no doubt were appearing on behalf of major secured creditors.

And, finally, the aging female lawyer from the U.S. attorney's office who handled creditor matters for the federal government and whose shortly-cropped gray hair and dark-framed glasses made her look every bit at home in the "old boys' club" that was the Omaha bankruptcy bar.

Judge Centers forbade Hanigan to fraternize with the lawyers, on the ground that it might give an appearance of impropriety. Hanigan nevertheless enjoyed observing their interactions with one another from his table, during the time before the judge assumed his rightful place on the bench.

Hanigan could often make out the substance of one of the conversations taking place in a cluster of several of the lawyers, which usually would end in a punchline, followed by a burst of laughter from the participants. It always struck Hanigan that, for a group that dealt constantly with the mundane issues of insolvency, it was quite a jovial bunch.

"All rise. The United States Bankruptcy Court for the District of Nebraska is now in session . . .." The judge's courtroom deputy, an effeminate gray-haired man in his early sixties, always

paused briefly for dramatic flair, before concluding, with a
discernible lisp, "the Honorable Thomas Centers presiding."

The judge marched deliberately into the bench area,
clasping a stack of court files at his side. With military-like
precision, he placed himself carefully into the high-backed chair
behind the bench, turned the chair a perfect ninety degrees to face
the courtroom, and positioned the files in their precise location to
the right of his bench-top flat-screen computer monitor.

As always, he cleared his throat, causing a muffled crackle
over the somewhat-antiquated courtroom speaker system.

"Please be seated," the judge commanded, arching his back
slightly and peering out over the inhabitants of the courtroom's
gallery area, before turning to read from the court file on the top of
his neat stack.

"Our first case this morning is in the matter of Randall and
Rita Baxter, Case No. BK06-43120."

As the judge uttered the first case description, two of the
attorneys in the gallery area stood up and made their way forward,
through the swinging wooden door of the dividing wall, into the
counsel's area, with its two large rectangular glass-covered tables
and numerous thickly padded cordovan leather counsel chairs.

Custom dictated that the table on the right was to be
occupied by debtor's counsel or the Chapter 7 Trustee, and the
table on the left by the creditors' lawyers. And this instance was no
different, the non-descript little every-man turned right and placed
his large brown accordion file, bulging with papers, on the debtor's
counsel table, catching the bottom of his badly stained tie under
the file.

And one of the impeccably groomed secured creditor's
lawyers assumed his place at the left table. With his $1,200
tailored suit and small streamlined leather briefcase, the attorney
looked polished and crisp.

"Counsel, please enter your appearances," the judge said,
looking down at the attorneys.

"Uh, Dale Irwin for the debtors, Your Honor," said the every-
man, slumping as he stood, still pulling papers from his file.

"John P. Wright, Jr., appearing on behalf of Mercedes Benz
Credit Corporation." The creditor's counsel stood perfectly erect as
he formally entered his appearance on the record, holding his $200
Mont Blanc ink pen between both hands at chest level, and
pausing before he sat back down, almost as if he were expecting a
polite round of applause from the gallery after he stated his name.

"We're here on a Motion for Relief from the Automatic Stay, filed by Mercedes Benz Credit Corporation," the judge continued. "Mr. Wright, this is your motion, do you have any evidence you would like to offer?"

The judge proceeded with his standard protocol of permitting the attorneys to submit their evidence in affidavit form, before hearing their oral arguments.

"Mr. Wright, any argument?" the judge inquired, knowing full well there would be.

"Yes, Your Honor."

The creditor's lawyer made his way through a dry and familiar recitation of the legal standards for lifting the automatic stay which otherwise precluded creditors from pursuing collection from their bankrupt borrowers, and detailed why his client should be permitted to repossess its collateral from the debtors in this case.

As he did, Hanigan's attention began to drift. His eyes roamed around the courtroom, from the upholstered blue walls with symmetrical waves jutting out from them, supposedly designed to enhance the acoustics in the room, to the wooden benches in the gallery area which reminded Hanigan of the pews at St. Peter's church in Riverton, to the bronze plaque on the far wall commemorating the fact that the federal building in which the courtroom sat had been built during the administration of Omaha-born Gerald Ford, something that was certainly evident in the 70's-style architecture and decor of the room.

Debtors' counsel was now making his pitch to the judge, in opposition to the creditor's motion.

"At least these debtors' position has some sex appeal," Hanigan thought. Debtors' counsel was arguing that his clients should be entitled to continue driving their brand new Mercedes S500 sedan while they made meager partial payments to their unsecured creditors under a Chapter 13 repayment plan.

"Your Honor, Mr. Baxter is in an occupation that is very status-driven," argued the every-man attorney. "The customers and clients he deals with are sophisticated, high-end consumers, and, uh, they have certain expectations about the people they do business with. It is crucial for Mr. Baxter to have a reasonably presentable vehicle to make sales to the type of clientele that give him business. For that reason, the motion should be denied."

Hanigan knew this argument would not go over well with the judge, who, despite his six-figure salary and healthy federal benefits package, insisted on driving a slightly older-model Volkswagen Passat - nice but not audacious.

Hanigan's foreknowledge of Judge Centers' likely disposition of the motion certainly wasn't arrived at by observing the judge's demeanor on the bench. It always amazed Hanigan how the judge was able to remain so stoic, so reserved - the dispassionate dispenser of bankruptcy-style justice. "He would make a helluva poker player," Hanigan had often thought to himself.

Of course, playing poker would involve a degree of calculated risk, something that to Hanigan's observation, the judge did not entertain.

When written opinions were issued on matters of precedential significance, the judge always entered rulings with an eye toward insuring that his decisions would not be overturned by the district court or the bankruptcy appellate panel.

The judge had gone into the law, as his father before him, instead of pursuing his true love, photography. Safety and security.

On those occasions when the judge's staff would go out for lunch, even the judge's driving revealed his aversion to risk. His car always traveled 3-5 miles per hour under the posted speed limit. And his hands always occupied the textbook 10 and 2 positions on the steering wheel.

The one and only time Hanigan had seen the judge "cut loose" was on one of the Bankruptcy Court's biannual visits 350 miles west to the city of North Platte, Nebraska, former stomping grounds of "Wild" Bill Cody, to preside over adversary proceedings between parties living in the central and western parts of the large, primarily agricultural state.

After the day's court proceedings, the judge, Hanigan, Martha, and other members of the "court family" traveled to a highly-recommended local steakhouse-lounge where they feasted on incredible prime rib from the corn-fed beef produced on ranches in that area and listened to a western band play up-tempo, fiddle-driven songs referred to by Hanigan as "square dancing music."

Over the course of the evening, the judge drank three or four light beers and told stories from his past. He was feeling so good that he was actually convinced by two middle-aged twin sisters in matching western-style apparel and cowboy hats to get up and line dance with them.

Much to the judge's horror, one of the sisters appeared before him the next day as a bankruptcy debtor in a nondischargeability proceeding, thus confirming in the judge's mind that it never paid to "let yourself go."

And back on the bench today, the judge was as stoic as ever. "Thank you counsel. The matter will be deemed submitted, and a memorandum and order will be forthcoming," the judge stated.

Judge Centers closed the court file in front of him and reached to his right for the next file on the well-organized stack beside him, as the two lawyers collected their things and walked back to the gallery area.

"The next matter is In re: Automotive Services Risk Retention, Inc., Case No. BK06-74621."

The judge looked down and peered over the top of his glasses patiently, as the portly, white-haired attorney and the quirky lawyer with the lazy eye advanced to the counsel tables.

"It appears that a section 304 petition has been filed, in connection with a provisional liquidation proceeding down in the British Cayman Islands," the judge began. "We are here today on the debtor's motion for a preliminary injunction. Who appears on behalf of the debtor?"

"Please show the appearance of Vincent Fiala, on behalf of the duly-appointed provisional liquidators of the estate of the debtor," came the lazy-eyed lawyer's response, emphasizing the words "duly-appointed provisional liquidators" so as to clarify the judge's slight misstatement as to who the attorney was representing.

"Thank you," said the judge, unfazed by the lawyer's subtle correction.

"Any other appearances?" he asked, glancing in the direction of the chubby, snowy-haired counsel.

"Joe Stanley, your honor, on behalf of Evelyn Bornemeyer and other similarly-situated creditors."

"Thank you," the judge responded. "Mr. Fiala, it's your motion, please proceed."

"Your honor, Automotive Services Risk Retention, Inc. is a corporation incorporated under the laws of the Cayman Islands." The lazy-eyed attorney removed his glasses as he peeked down at the sheet of notes on the table before him.

"On July 27th, it filed a petition in the Grand Court of the Cayman Islands for an order of provisional liquidation of the company's assets. An order was entered by that court appointing my clients as Joint Provisional Liquidators of the company."

"My clients have now filed with this Court a petition under section 304 of the Bankruptcy Code, and they are requesting that this Court enter an order for preliminary injunction to immediately enjoin actions that might be taken by creditors or other parties against the property of the foreign debtor so that United States creditors do not seize or attach assets or property that should be distributed through the Cayman Islands liquidation proceeding."

"And its your clients' position that section 304 vests this Court with that authority?" the judge asked.

The droopy-eyed counsel argued to Judge Centers that he had the power to halt all U.S. lawsuits against the lawyer's client, in order to foster a smooth liquidation of the company's assets in what was the Cayman-Islands equivalent of a bankruptcy liquidation. Counsel asserted that such an order was necessary to prevent creditors from grabbing any of the company's assets located in the U.S.

The lazy-eyed attorney turned and took a small step to his right, before again facing the bench.

"Judge, if the debtor is required to employ the services of counsel in the United States in various state and federal jurisdictions to defend contract and tort lawsuits, such as the one commenced by Mr. Stanley's client in this district, it would be extremely irreparable harm upon the debtor's liquidation process in the Cayman proceeding. For these reasons, my clients respectfully request that the Court grant their motion for preliminary injunctive relief."

"Thank you, counsel," said Judge Centers. "Mr. Stanley?"

"Yes. Thank you, Your Honor." The portly lawyer had to push his chair back considerably to make it possible for his girth to come to the upright position.

"My client, Ms. Bornemeyer, has filed an objection to the motion on behalf of herself personally and all persons similarly situated to her. Ms. Bornemeyer is the lead plaintiff in a class action lawsuit against the debtor pending in federal district court here in Nebraska."

Stanley described the tort and fraud claims asserted in the class action as arising from the Cayman company's failure to honor its obligations under countless vehicle warranty service contracts.

He then argued that the defendant company is "Cayman" in incorporation papers only because it is registered as an 'exempt' company in the Caymans, is prohibited from doing any business there, and has done all of its business in the United States since the day it was created.

"Until a few weeks ago, all of the company's financial interests were right here in Nebraska. Then, sometime in early to mid July of this year, the debtor transferred approximately $48,000,000 to banks in the Cayman Islands," Stanley asserted.

"All of the entities for which it provided insurance, its members, are located in the United States. All of the Vehicle Service Contracts which it administers and for which it has provided insurance to its members, were entered into in the United States and are subject to the laws of the various states in this country."

"In short, Judge, it is my client's position that the debtor is really not a foreign entity and therefore the Cayman proceeding is not a 'foreign proceeding,' nor are the joint Liquidators 'foreign representatives' as those terms are used in section 304."

As the snowy-haired attorney wrapped up his legal argument, Hanigan was busy trying to conjure up a way to parlay the case into a trip to the Cayman Islands.

Chapter 9

Steve Fletcher's body sank back in exhaustion into a heavily-padded wooden bench running along the inside of the outer wall of the enormous, stained wood deck that surrounded two and half sides of Fletcher's modest country home, which sat atop the crest of a small hill in the rolling agricultural fields outside the tiny village of Dunbar.

This was one of those rare late-summer evenings when the muggy, humid Nebraska air gave way to a light, dryer breeze that carried with it just the slightest hint of the milder, more enjoyable autumn evenings to come.

The deck was Fletcher's pride and joy and he often proudly shared with visitors that it actually had more square footage than the main level of his house. Fletcher and his brother had built the deck on a scorching summer weekend three years earlier. The original roughed-out plans had called for the deck to be only half its current size.

But as the work progressed, fueled by the steady consumption of ice cold Miller High Life from Fletcher's garage refrigerator, either one or the other of the two Fletcher brothers would suggest that the deck be made yet another foot larger. By the time the sun had set on the weekend, the deck extended so far into Fletcher's yard that it had engulfed two good-sized maple trees planted 25 feet from Fletcher's home, for which large round holes had to be cut through the deck itself.

As Fletcher lit a full-size dark brown cigar, he contemplated the unfinished trim work on the new addition being added to the back side of the house. He pondered whether the Springer homicide investigation would afford him enough time to finish the trim before the cold weather set in.

Fletcher stretched his long Levi-clad legs and rested his feet on one of the detachable padded deck chairs he had built. He noticed that his right big toe was just starting to poke through one of the well-worn loafer "boat shoes" that his wife, Connie, had bought him three years before at the Riverton outlet mall.

"Looks like I need some new boat shoes," Fletcher said to his wife as she slid open a glass door and stepped out from the home onto the deck, using only her left elbow to glide the door open, since both hands were occupied with short round glasses of Windsor Canadian and Squirt.

"I've been telling you that all summer, Fletcher." Connie always referred to her husband by his last name when she wanted to make a point. She handed one of the drinks to Fletcher and assumed her usual position at the small built-in wooden picnic table protruding from the side of the deck.

Fletcher had begun courting Connie shortly after the divorce with his first wife, Georgette, had become final, but before Connie had informed her first husband that she wanted out of their marriage.

Fletcher and Connie came to each other not unlike two abused puppies, both beaten down by their first spouses' repeated marital infidelities. Their spouses' indiscretions, it seemed to them, were the inevitable result of the couples' involvement with the middle-aged party crowd in Riverton.

In each other, Fletcher and Connie had found a common desire to retreat to a calmer, simpler, more stable existence, detached from the Riverton bar scene.

It had been Connie who convinced Fletcher to leave his job with the Apache County Sheriff's Office and accept a position with the State Patrol, as a means of gaining further separation from their circle of party-happy Riverton acquaintances. Relaxed country living suited them both now – hard work, home-cooking, good whiskey, and easy conversation.

The only real issues of contention between the couple during their fifteen-plus years of marriage had been Fletcher's now-teenage son from his first marriage, Jason, who lived with them during the school year, and Connie's occasional propensity for blowing money at the Riverton Keno parlor.

But through it all, Fletcher's relationship with Connie remained solid and their commitment to one another unwavering.

"So how was the Manor today, hun?" Fletcher asked, in reference to the nursing home in Riverton, where Connie had served as a nurse's aid for the past eight years.

"Oh, it was fine. A usual Monday. But we did have another escape attempt," Connie answered.

"The old farmer again?"

"Yeah, Wilbur Davis. Judy found him a block and half away, heading down 11th Street in his wheel chair."

"Where was he going?"

"We have no idea. He can't speak, so he can't tell you nothing. His wife, you know, is in a different ward at the Manor.

They don't even stay in the same room. He's got no other family in Riverton."

"Maybe he was heading to the bar," Fletcher quipped, turning his cigar sideways in front of his face to see how it was burning.

"Maybe," Connie said, as she took a sip of her whiskey sour. "You know, one of the wheels on his chair was partially locked and he was still able to get all the way down there, with just his one good arm."

"Did he lose part of an arm in the service or something?"

"No, he had a stroke a couple years ago. He can't use that whole side of his body. And that's why he can't talk. But you know, he's got more strength in that one arm than some of our little gals up there have altogether."

"Farming all those years. It'll make you strong. Them gals better never piss him off."

"Oh believe me, we tick him off every time we bring him back from one of his escapes. He was madder than a hornet today."

Fletcher rolled the ice around in his glass with one hand as he drew a sizeable amount of smoke into his mouth from the cigar in his other. "Any prizes in today's mail?" he asked.

"Nothing," Connie answered, having grown well accustomed to Fletcher's daily query regarding possible sweepstakes winnings.

Each morning, Fletcher would spend nearly an entire hour filling out entry forms from several special sweepstakes catalogs to which he subscribed. Over the course of his marriage to Connie, a seemingly endless stream of prizes had arrived periodically in their mailbox. While most of the items were relatively cheap trinkets -- plastic visors, baseball caps, foam footballs, childrens' videotapes, Fletcher's beloved Harley Davidson lighter -- every few years Fletcher would win big.

In the fourth year of their marriage, a $5,000 set of decorative China had arrived by UPS. Since that day, Connie had never again complained about the amount of time and postage Fletcher "wasted" on his sweepstakes hobby.

But Fletcher's occasional winnings did not stop his co-workers at the Patrol from ridiculing the practice, often comparing him to a little old lady clipping coupons. Fletcher's standard reply had remained constant – "It's cheaper than playing the lottery," knowing that most of his fellow law enforcement officers would spend anywhere from $10 to $50 a week buying various forms of lottery tickets and pickle cards each time they stopped for a donut or coffee at a convenience store, "and my odds are a helluva lot better," he would always add.

"You gotta go back to Riverton tomorrow?" Connie asked, after a long but completely comfortable silence.

"I got some reports to file in Lincoln in the morning, then I'll drive back to Riverton. I'll be late getting home. I got a evening meeting. Rogge's gonna bring in that Kellogg kid for questioning, and I also need to try and track down Jackie Howell some time."

"Jackie Howell the lesbian?"

"Yeah."

"You know her half-sister works at the Manor," Connie offered.

"Really?"

"Yeah . . . Linda Turley. She was talking the other day about how Jackie has a new girlfriend."

"Wow, that was a quick rebound," Fletcher replied. "She must not be too broken up about losing Anna Springer."

"Apparently it's the high school volleyball coach in Riverton."

"You gotta be kiddin' me," Fletcher said incredulously. "They got a lezbo coachin' a bunch of teenage girls running around in skin tight shorts. What the hell are they thinking?" Fletcher took a small gulp of his drink. "Makes me glad I don't have a daughter." Fletcher looked over at Connie, with subtle apprehension etched on his face.

"Only ten more days until we get Jason back."

"Don't remind me," Connie said.

"Now, come on. It won't be that bad," Fletcher responded. "It's his senior year. Hey, and at least I'll have somebody to mow this place for me the next couple months."

"Oh boy. That gets me excited," came Connie's sarcastic reply.

"Speaking of getting you excited, what do you say we make good use of every last night we have alone, starting tonight?" A sly grin crept across Fletcher's lips, still partially wet from his last swig of whiskey sour.

"I'm pretty tired, Steve."

"I know your pretty. That's why I want to take advantage of you."

Connie smiled with one side of her mouth, in a way that let Fletcher know he would get his wish. As that fact registered, he could feel a hint of activity in his groin area, as a whiskey-aided flow of blood began to push into that region.

Fletcher swallowed the remaining contents of his glass, snubbed out his lit cigar, and reached across the wood deck table to grab Connie's hand. They left the glasses on the table and headed into the home.

Chapter 10

The late-morning sunlight spread itself across Mike Hanigan's bedroom in his apartment on the eighth floor of a newly-renovated 1920's era brick warehouse building on the east edge of Omaha's downtown Old Market area.

Despite Hanigan's best efforts to block the sun's intrusion with thick, dark blue velvet curtains, the light somehow managed to invade the room from above, below, and between the slightest cracks in the curtain fortress.

Hanigan groaned and rolled over onto his stomach, clutching his pillow behind his head to shield his eyes from the unwelcome intruder.

On a typical Tuesday morning, the bright light would not have been deemed such a mortal threat, but because this Tuesday, Hanigan would be "working from home," he had taken the liberty of drinking just under a fifth of vodka and several beers during a rousing game of Texas Hold-Em the night before, with three former law school classmates.

Judge Centers was in St. Louis attending a three-day judicial conference, and another provision of Hanigan's unwritten code of conduct with the judge permitted Hanigan to occasionally work from home on such occasions.

Just before noon, clad only in a pair of silky black boxer shorts, Hanigan rolled from his blanketless, sheet-covered bed, and started the coffee maker he had strategically located on the computer desk in his bedroom. He pulled a bottle of generic ibuprofen from the top drawer of the desk, effortlessly popped the top with his thumb, and poured precisely two tablets into his mouth, grinding them with his teeth as if they were chewable aspirin for children, before washing them down with a gulp of room temperature water from a half-empty bottle of Dasani.

He sat back down on his bed, to regain his equilibrium, and reached forward to push the "on" button on his laptop computer. He had resolved to check his office email first thing in the morning. As it was not yet 12 noon, Hanigan felt he was complying with the spirit of his resolution.

The email program loaded quickly on Hanigan's screen, and through his sleep-encrusted, semi-blurry eyes Hanigan immediately noticed an email from Jenny Berg, amid the clutter of other work-related and junk messages.

As in his professional career, Hanigan tended to underachieve in his social life, preferring to date women who were above average in attractiveness but near the bottom of the socio-economic ladder - the types of women who frequented the working-class bars and taverns Hanigan favored. As a rule, Hanigan didn't like to invest the work required to court attractive, upwardly-mobile professional women.

But there was something about Jenny Berg that made him want to put forth the effort. Berg's father had been a well known trial lawyer in Omaha before becoming a respected state district court judge. Berg was being groomed to be a tenacious litigator in her own right.

She had won the national moot court competition with her two-person team from Creighton University School of Law in Omaha. Well before graduating from law school, she had received offers of employment from the most prestigious firms in the Midwest, but she opted to briefly defer those opportunities in favor of a two-year clerkship with a federal magistrate judge, primarily because she wanted to immerse herself in the pretrial practice aspects that such a position would afford her. Berg would leave no stone unturned in her quest to become the quintessential litigation practitioner.

Hanigan was keenly aware that Berg's strange pull on him was based in large part on the polarity of their approaches to life. Hanigan was laid back, largely indifferent, and generally preferred the path of least resistance. Berg was spunky, self-motivated, fiery, and full of life. Behind her soft straight blonde hair, cute features, and petite figure lied the tenacity of a pit bull who would not back down from any challenge.

When they had first met at a social mixer function for federal law clerks, it had actually been Berg who had sought Hanigan out, having heard of his storied achievement of acing the standardized law school entrance exam – purportedly the only person in the state to have ever done so.

While she didn't mention it to Hanigan, Berg was equally impressed with the fact that a law review article Hanigan had written as a second year law student at Creighton was used by esteemed constitutional-law professor Dawson Cordova as a teaching aid in subsequent years' classes, including Berg's class.

After a few minutes of their initial conversation at the mixer, however, Berg was visibly disappointed that Hanigan did not share her enthusiasm for discussions about all things legal.

Over the course of the past year, Hanigan had learned in his conversations with Berg to initially humor her with several minutes of semi-serious jurisprudential dialogue, before talking about other non-legal topics, which Hanigan found eminently more interesting.

Actually, Hanigan's reluctance to talk about legal work was not isolated to his conversations with Berg. During his frequent visits to South Omaha's taverns, he never talked about his work, either with whatever male drinking acquaintances were present or as part of his pick-up routine on the women Hanigan may have been pursuing. The few times the topic had come up, he simply described himself as "working for the federal government."

With as much eagerness as his hangover would allow, Hanigan guided his computer's mouse to Berg's email entitled "Dumbfounded," and clicked it open.

> *Okay, Mr-Cordova-con-law-guru, see if you can crack this one: What could possibly possess a prisoner civil rights plaintiff to claim that state-actor defendants have violated his ELEVENTH AMENDMENT rights?????*
>
> *To be fair, that may be more of a psychological question than a constitutional law one. You know, time and again I'll catch myself thinking I know this section 1983 civil rights stuff in and out. Guess I have more to master.*

Hanigan smiled at the notion of a prisoner deriving rights from a constitutional amendment routinely used by governmental employees to defend against civil rights lawsuits on the grounds of qualified immunity.

Part of him secretly wished he could trade jobs with Berg for the sheer entertainment value of reviewing the frivolous civil rights complaints and habeas corpus petitions filed by incarcerated litigants, prepared without the aid of any professional legal counsel.

Berg would often regale Hanigan with stories of actual lawsuits filed by prisoners seeking anything from softer toilet paper, to harder pillows, to plastic surgery and sex-change operations.

Hanigan reached over and poured some steaming coffee into a badly stained white mug bearing a red "Budweiser - King of

Beers" emblem. The mug at one time had been part of a set of six
from his father's vast collection, but had dwindled to only one
through breakage, loss, theft, and unknown causes.

Hanigan pecked out a quick facetious response to Berg's
email:

> *You must have missed that day in Con Law. I vividly
> remember Cordova discussing a 1985 plurality opinion from
> the Supreme Court, authored by Justice Blackmun, which
> read the Eleventh Amendment as creating in all
> whiny-ass prisoners a liberty interest in remaining free from
> even the slightest annoyance perpetrated by a government
> official. It was quite a controversial piece of jurisprudence at
> the time.*
>
> *Frankly, I'm disappointed in you. Perhaps you should
> forward all future section 1983 cases to this lowly
> bankruptcy clerk, as I was clearly the
> more attentive constitutional scholar.*

Berg's reply to Hanigan's email came quickly, suggesting
she was attentively working at her computer in the Magistrate
Judge's chambers, even over the noon hour. Her reply bore a
revised subject line of "Round 2."

> *Okay Wonderboy, since you're on a roll, try your head at this
> stumper:*
>
> *Each morning I consume a carton (8 oz) of skim milk with my
> Total cereal and banana. The milk carton informs me that 0
> calories come from fat, total fat = 0, and saturated fat = 0.
> Then the carton reads that the milk contained therein has 5
> mg of cholesterol. Is it truly possible to have cholesterol in
> foods containing no fat? How so? I always thought cholesterol
> is derived from animal fats: eggs, cheese, cream, meats, etc.
> . . . all of which contain fat obviously.*
>
> *Have you read any obiter dicta on the subject?" (And don't go
> running to Google!)*

As it seemed to Hanigan that his intellectual prowess was
the thing Berg found most appealing about him, he wanted to

dazzle her with an accurate and immediate answer to her query, but still abide by her closing admonition against internet cheating.

He pulled a well-worn Webster's collegiate dictionary from the bottom drawer of the computer desk and flipped to the definition of "cholesterol."

Using the information contained in the lengthy definition and whatever little knowledge he had himself on the subject, he composed his response to Berg, and pressed "Send" - less than fifty seconds after opening her email.

> *Cholesterol occurs not only in animal fats, but also in animal oils, bile, gallstones, nerve tissue, blood, and other tissue. Moreover, the cholesterol referred to on your milk carton is most likely the commercial form of the compound C_{27}-H_{45}-OH, which is used chiefly for synthesis of vitamin D.*

> *Now, if you would just look at the pictures of the missing children, like most normal people, you wouldn't have to worry your pretty little head about such things.*

Within seconds, Berg's reply appeared on Hanigan's screen again with a new subject line - "AMAZING."

> *You're either a walking encyclopedia or a very quick manual researcher. Did you fabricate the compound id or are you a mad scientist in cognito?*

> *Hey, I thought I would write Prof. Cordova and personally invite him to the Omaha Bar skating party (to be held Sunday, 8-28, at Aksarben from 2-4 p.m.). May I photocopy for him your very funny retort or do you claim it as privileged work product?*

Berg's final email set off a flurry of thoughts in Hanigan's mind.

First, he was thoroughly pleased that his cholesterol answer had further bolstered Berg's overinflated view of his mental largesse.

Second, he wondered how he could be so interested in a woman who would not only consider spending part of a weekend roller skating with a bunch of lawyers, judges, and law professors, but would even go so far as to invite others to such an event.

Third and most importantly, the inclusion in Berg's email of the date, time, and place of the skating party was very intriguing to Hanigan.

Perhaps this was Berg's subtle way of inviting him to the party or at least letting him know where he could find her if he was inclined to see her outside the work environs of the federal court.

After several minutes of reflection, and three or four healthy gulps of coffee, Hanigan convinced himself that Berg was in fact opening the door for him to ask her out. Hanigan had never asked a woman out via email, but something deep within him compelled him to make the move.

While his usual tendency would be to procrastinate on such a decision, he knew he needed to act on this one now, before the murky alcohol remnant departed from his head and he lost his nerve.

But he certainly did not want his first date with Berg to occur in the context of a lame legal skating party. Hanigan wanted to get Berg away completely from the legal community and, if at all possible, get a few drinks in her.

Hanigan boldly typed up a solicitation for Berg to join him for drinks at a local pub the following evening and sent it sailing over the information superhighway, from his bedroom to the federal courthouse just nine blocks away.

He sucked down the last of his cup's content and waited.

Chapter 11

Steve Fletcher's truck sped past the clusters of fast food restaurants and small outlet stores which now lined both sides of Highway 75 through the southern half of Riverton.

His destination, the Pizza Hut restaurant on the southernmost edge of town, had been the very first nationally-franchised eating establishment to open for business in Riverton, some 25 years before. But with the growth of the Trees Are Forever Foundation, the related tourist boom, and the general national trend in favor of drive-through dining, the fast food business had since proliferated in Riverton.

As Fletcher pulled into the almost-empty parking lot of the pizza place, a good hour after the Tuesday dinner rush had subsided, the sight of the building's distinctively sloped red roof evoked alternately clear and cloudy memories of his first-ever visit to the restaurant, during its initial year of operation.

Fletcher, as a wide-eyed sophomore in high school, had tagged along with his elder brother for an after-hours trip to "The Hut" to visit his brother's best friend, Pete Beacheau, pronounced Bo-Shay, then a 20-year-old natural-born-storyteller nicknamed "Bullshit," who would falsely explain the derivation of the off-color moniker by stating that his surname was actually French for the word. Beacheau had somehow convinced the restaurant's owner that he was capable of serving as a part-time weekday manager for the fledgling business.

Fletcher recalled stepping into the restaurant with his brother late that evening, after the restaurant had closed, and seeing Beacheau putting his managerial skills to work: ordering one employee to close the curtains on the windows and lock the doors; directing another to put a large Canadian bacon and sausage pizza in the oven; and guiding a third as he carefully carried three full pitchers of draft beer out from behind the counter and placed them on a table in the center of the restaurant.

Beacheau then dug a hand into his tan polyester Pizza Hut slacks, pulled out a shiny silver coin, and smiled at the Fletcher brothers - "Quarters anyone?"

Ninety minutes later, the 16-year-old Fletcher found himself doubled over next to the air conditioning unit at the outside rear of the restaurant, violently discharging the contents of his stomach –

beer and semi-digested pizza morsels – all over the parking lot pavement. His introduction to the popular Riverton drinking game had been a rude one indeed.

Fletcher wondered how many managers had come and gone at the Pizza Hut between Beacheau's short-lived stint and the restaurant's current manager – Jackie Howell.

Though Fletcher had never met Howell, as he stepped into the restaurant this evening, his eyes immediately drew a bead on a mannish-looking female talking on the telephone behind the counter, who he was certain had to be her.

With her pronounced square jaw, her near crew-cut hairstyle, and the short sleeves of her Pizza Hut manager shirt rolled up a couple folds to reveal a pair of fairly well-defined biceps, the only slight hint as to Howell's actual gender was the pair of dangly pink and black earrings hanging from both her lobes.

Fletcher waited patiently at the counter as Howell took down the details of the pizza order from the person on the other end of the phone line. He squinted slightly to make out the name on the silver-plated nametag just over her left breast - "Jacquelyn Howell - Manager."

In one swift motion, Howell hung up the phone, spun around to slide the order ticket into a metal clip behind her, and looked back over her shoulder at Fletcher, "Did you have a take-out order?"

"No, ma'am. I'm with the Nebraska State Patrol. I wanted to get a minute of your time to ask you a few questions."

"Sandy, cover the register," Howell's voice sounded surprisingly feminine, before she intentionally dropped it a half-octave lower, "I'm taking a quick break."

As she stepped out from behind the counter and brushed past Fletcher, she looked at him with a piercing cold stare, as if she despised his very existence.

Fletcher followed Howell out the north exit of the restaurant.

"Damn, she could be a man," he thought to himself, observing her masculine gait from behind as she made a left on the elevated concrete sidewalk running along the north side of the building, heading toward the situs of the Fletcher's adolescent vomit- session.

"Boy, this brings back some memories," Fletcher mused in a casual, friendly tone, attempting to break the tension.

"You're probably too young, but do you remember a guy named Pete Beacheau?"

Howell was looking down, digging a lighter from the flour-splashed black pouch in front of her.

She ignited the menthol Marlboro Light dangling from her lips and drew hard, finally looking up to meet Fletcher's eyes.

"He was one of the first managers here," Fletcher continued, undaunted by Howell's failure to acknowledge his question. "Funny guy. They called him 'Bullshit'."

"Did you guys find the sick bastard who killed her yet?" Howell asked sternly, crossing her semi-muscular arms in front of her and nervously tapping the butt of her cigarette against her left elbow.

"Assuming you're talking about Anna Springer, we *are* workin' on it," Fletcher said. "You and her were pretty close, were you?"

"I fucking loved her." Howell bit her lower lip and looked past Fletcher.

"I'm very sorry for your loss," Fletcher replied. As a State Patrolman, he had consoled countless relatives and loved ones over the loss of those near to them, but never a decedent's gay lover. He wasn't sure the same rules applied.

"I'm very sorry," he said again. "How long had you been together?"

Fletcher wanted to ease into the topic he had come to discuss.

"Off and on for the last year and a half."

Howell clenched her jaw and took another intense drag on her smoke, appearing as if she was fighting to hold back tears.

"Had you and Anna been having some problems recently?" Fletcher braced himself for Howell's response.

"The only problem we ever had was her bitch of a mother," Howell replied, her voice seething with obvious hostility.

"Senator Springer caused you some problems?"

"I swear to God, that cunt is pure evil. She didn't give a shit about Anna's happiness. Her only concern was *her own* image and *her* career."

Two large veins were beginning to bulge from the sides of Howell's neck as she spoke.

"She was always pushing Anna into things she didn't want to do."

"What kind of things?" Fletcher asked.

"Everything." Howell forcefully flicked the barely-smoked cigarette several feet away with her right middle finger, with all the machismo of one of Fletcher's hunting buddies.

"She wanted her to go to college. She wanted her to spend her summers in Washington. She wanted her to date rich fraternity guys. And she did *not* want Anna seeing me. Everything was image with her. Miserable fucking hag."

"Did Anna ever date any guys that you know of?" Fletcher held his breath in anticipation of another outburst from Howell.

He had long theorized that, in every lesbian couple, there was one more masculine partner who was completely sold on the gay lifestyle, and one more feminine, generally more attractive partner, who was perhaps more prone to "swing both ways." Based on the stories relayed to him by Bill Rogge and Fletcher's initial observations of Howell, he had Anna Springer pegged as the "switch hitter" in this couple.

"Like I said, we were off and on. When we weren't seeing each other, I'm sure the old bitch made her go out with some wealthy members of the Young Republicans."

"Any that you know of recently?"

Howell pinched the top of her nose, rubbing the corners of her eyes with her thumb and forefinger. She closed her eyes as she rubbed.

"I hadn't even seen her for almost three weeks before she turned up dead." Howell's voice cracked slightly. As she opened her eyes, Fletcher could see they were beginning to water.

"She said she was going back to Washington for a couple weeks to interview with some lobbyist groups or something, but . . . I *do* think she was seeing some guy."

"What makes you say that?" Fletcher asked.

"You think because I'm a woman, I don't know when I'm gettin' sloppy seconds?" Howell looked at Fletcher with the same icy venom in her stare as when he introduced himself, but this time through puffy red eyes.

"So, who was he?" Fletcher inquired.

"I don't know." Howell's voice now sounded fragile and broken, and tears were freely streaming down both cheeks. Howell seemed genuinely hurt. She covered her eyes with both hands and sniffed loudly.

Fletcher paused. For the first time, he felt deeply sorry for the masculine woman breaking down in front of him. He thought perhaps the rumor Connie had conveyed to him about Howell dating the high-school volleyball coach was untrue. He decided to avoid that topic altogether on this visit.

"I know it's difficult for you, Ms. Howell," Fletcher softened his voice noticeably, "but it could be very important in helping us find who did this. Any ideas at all as to who she might have been seeing?"

"Maybe someone she met in Kansas at college." Howell whimpered slightly as she spoke into her hands. "Maybe someone at the Foundation. I don't know."

She jerked her head from out of her hands and turned abruptly away from Fletcher, walking further towards the back of the restaurant parking lot, in an apparent attempt to regain her composure. From behind, Fletcher could see her take a deep breath, hold it momentarily, and puff out her chest.

"But she had told you she was going to Washington, D.C.?" Fletcher raised the volume of his voice slightly, in order to span the distance created by Howell's walk-off. "When was that?"

Fletcher's question was interrupted by the ring of his cell phone. He quickly yanked the phone from his belt clip, and flipped it open.

"Fletch here," he answered.

"Fletch, it's Bill," the distinctively rugged voice of Sheriff Bill Rogge emanated from the phone. "We just got a call from the Cass County Sheriff. They pulled an arm out of the river south of the Lake Wa Con Da area. It's probably Springer's. And get this, it has a bunch of what looks like canine bite marks on it."

"Kellogg?" Fletcher asked.

"I bet you anything," Rogge said with certainty in his voice. "We got him in custody already."

"I'll be right there."

Chapter 12

"What's the story, Bill?" Steve Fletcher asked a street-clothes-clad Bill Rogge, whose substantial presence filled a wide space in front of the reception desk in the Apache County Sheriff's office, where he stood surrounded by uniformed deputies and a short, heavy-set female dispatcher.

The office was certainly more bustling than usual for this hour of the evening, Fletcher thought. The latest break in the Springer investigation obviously had stirred things up.

"You familiar with the Lake Wa Con Da area?" Rogge replied, looking up from the handwritten report he held in his enormously stout right hand.

"It's been awhile since I've been up there," Fletcher said, recalling a Labor Day boat outing a number of years before at the residential lake community located about halfway between Riverton and Omaha, just off the Missouri River.

"There's a couple small inlets down towards the southeast corner of the lake," Rogge began, "they drain out to the river several miles downstream.

Some kids was down there in the inlet waters with hip waiters on, catching tadpoles, and one of 'em ran his net along the bottom and it bumped into a few fingers sticking out from under the mud and silt."

Rogge turned toward the reception desk and continued with his briefing.

"They pulled it out and there it was. Here, I'll show you the pictures they faxed down to me," Rogge said, as he stepped around behind the reception desk to grab a small stack of black and white photographs.

Rogge held out the photos one at a time over the desk for inspection, and Fletcher began with the obvious observations concerning the severed arm.

"Definitely a female. No rings. No bracelets, No tattoos. Not real hairy. Traces of dark nail polish on a few of the nails."

"And doggie bites," Rogge added, as he turned to the next photo showing the underside of the arm.

"Got into her pretty good it looks like. Did they send the arm to Lincoln to run the forensics?" Fletcher inquired.

"That or Bellevue, I'm not sure which," Rogge answered, in reference to the Omaha suburb.

"Anything else of interest near the site?" Fletcher said, pulling one of the photos from Rogge's hand for a closer look.

"Nothing yet. Them Cass boys are still scouring the area. I bet old Terry wasn't smart enough to cover his tracks very well. They'll turn up something."

"Where is he now?"

"We got him in the holding cell downstairs with Elmer," referring to the Riverton town jailer, who had been manning that post for nearly thirty years.

"We're holding him on suspicion of trafficking narcotics and contributing to the delinquency of a minor, based on an old complaint from the high school principal. We haven't mentioned nothing about the murder."

"Good. Mind if I have a crack at him?"

"It's your show, Fletch. He's all yours."

"Still gotta take the back stairwell to get down there?" Fletcher asked.

"Oh, hell no, we're all handicap accessible now. We got an elevator and everything. We wouldn't want to discriminate against all them crippled criminals out there. I been trying to get the County Commissioners to give my deputies raises the past three years, and they can't afford that, but they somehow came up with 40 grand to put in that friggin' elevator."

"Let me check it out," Fletcher strode towards the exit to Rogge's office.

As Fletcher and Rogge stepped off the new elevator into the basement of the Apache County Jail, Fletcher saw from behind the familiar bald head of Elmer Guess, whose gray hair around the bottom perimeter of his head was even sparser than the last time Fletcher had seen him, some three or so years before.

Elmer was seated at the jailer's desk, scouring the farm sale ads in the Thrifty Nickel newspaper and circling those of interest to him.

"Howdy Elmer." Fletcher's greeting seemed to startle the elderly man, suggesting he had not even heard the elevator doors open just fifteen feet away from him.

The old man at first look puzzled, then smiled in recognition of the man who many years before had talked to him on a daily basis about the weather and the state of the local farm crops.

"Just waiting for that pension to kick in," Elmer replied, mistakenly assuming that Fletcher had asked him how he was doing.

"Mr. Kellogg giving you any trouble?" Fletcher asked.

"None at all," Elmer scratched the top of his bald head with the hand holding a dull yellow No. 2 pencil and released his other hand's grip on the folded newspaper section. "But he's asked me three or four times about his dog. 'Where we keeping him?' 'What are we feeding him?' 'Will he get out for a walk?' I keep telling him the city pound'll treat the dog every bit as good as we're treating him."

"Mind if I go in and have a chat with him?"

"Course not," Elmer started to slowly lift himself out of his chair.

"I got it, Elmer," Rogge placed his large right hand on Elmer's shoulder and gently pushed him back into the seated position.

As Rogge and Fletcher approached the holding cell, Fletcher could see, through the small square window near the top of the interrogation room door, the profile of the pale, wiry young man who had previously run from him in the orchards of TAFF.

Terry Kellogg's greasy blonde hair was pulled back into a small pony tail sticking out of the middle of the back of his head.

"How we doing this evening?" Fletcher asked as he stepped through the door, closing it behind him, leaving Rogge on the other side.

"I'm okay." Kellogg was seated on a hard-backed wooden chair behind a sturdy but badly scuffed oak table. He was gnawing hard on what little was left of his right thumbnail.

"Elmer taking good care of ya?"

Kellogg shrugged his shoulders without looking up at Fletcher and without ceasing his veracious chewing.

"Terry, my name's Steve Fletcher. I'm with the Nebraska State Patrol. We're hoping you can help us out with an investigation we're conducting."

"Whatever it is, I didn't do it," Kellogg responded quietly, still not looking up, but switching over to chew on his left thumbnail. "I'm a new creature in Christ."

Fletcher ignored Kellogg's religious pronouncement.

"Actually Terry, I tried to meet with you a few days ago at your workplace, when I pulled up in my truck . . . in the orchard area at the Foundation. But you took off running. What was that all about?"

"That was you in the blue Ford? I thought you was Larry Totten. He told me he was gonna run me and Lucy over next chance he got."

"Floyd Totten's boy? Now why would he wanna do that?" Fletcher asked, with noticeable disbelief in his tone.

"I don't know. I even went out to tell his old man I was sorry for what I done to their hogs. Pastor John said I needed to do that as part of my recovery."

"Is that right?"

"Yeah, that was Step 9. I'm up to Step 10 now."

"What's Step 10?"

"I gotta take a personal infantry."

"You mean inventory?"

"Yeah. I need to figure out what I'm still doing wrong."

"What have you come up with so far?"

"They tell me I got anger issues," Kellogg answered.

"Have you ever gotten angry with anyone at the Foundation?"

"No." Kellogg looked down at the concrete floor of the holding cell and ran his right hand up and down his scrawny and veiny left forearm, which was covered in jagged scars and poorly-done blue and black tattoos of what appeared to be occultic symbols and rock band names like Black Sabbath, Danzig, and Sepulchur.

"Did you know Anna Springer?" Fletcher asked.

"I didn't have nothing to do with her being killed." For the first time, Kellogg raised the inflection in his voice and looked Fletcher in the eyes.

Fletcher noticed Kellogg's eyes were nearly identical to those Fletcher had seen in Cousin Sam, the young man who had answered the door at the fluorescent green house.

"Now, Terry, that's not what I asked. I asked if you knew her."

"She worked in the office. I work outside all day."

"So you did know who she was?"

"The only time I'd see her is if I went inside to the cafeteria to get a pop. I'd walk by the office where she worked, and I could see her in there. And sometimes I'd see her drive off in her car."

"They got outdoor pop machines all over that place. Why would you need to go inside to get a soda?"

"I like the fountain kind. And they don't got Mountain Dew Code Red in the machines."

"What kinda car did she drive?" Fletcher asked, wanting to see if Kellogg's answer matched the information he had received from his other sources.

"A little silver thing. Foreign. I don't know what it is."

"You sure it's silver?" Fletcher asked, having received information indicating that Springer drove a yellow Mazda.

"She'd park it right down by the VIP spots."

"You sure that was her vehicle?"

"It's the only one I ever seen her drive."

"Did Ms. Springer ever do anything to upset you?"

"I never even talked to her."

"Did she ever talk to you?"

"Never."

"Did that make you angry?"

"I'm used to chicks ignoring me."

"But it made you mad when Anna ignored you, didn't it?"

"Not really."

"Terry, we know you were working at the Foundation the last day she was there - July 20. Do you remember seeing her that day?"

"I don't remember one day from another. I might have seen her. I might not have. I don't know. I ain't seen her in quite a while. Like I said, I didn't have nothing to do with killing her."

"Terry, I'm gonna shoot straight with you. We found an arm we think belongs to Anna Springer, in the river south of Lake Wa Con Da. You been up in that area lately?"

"I ain't got a car. How could I even get up there?"

"Just so you know Terry, they found a bunch of dog bites all over her arm. If they belong to Lucy, we will find that out. And if we find that out, we'll get a warrant to search your entire house. So, if there's something you need to tell me, you should do it now, while I can still help you out."

"Lucy wouldn't bite no one unless I told him to."

"Lucy's a 'him'?"

"Yeah."

"What's with the name?"

"It's short for Lucifer. I was gonna change it, but Pastor John told me it actually means 'Light One,' so I figured I'd keep it the same."

"So, did you tell Lucy to bite Anna Springer?"

"No!" Kellogg yelled, before slumping back in the chair and again compulsively biting one of his fingernails.

"Well Terry, again, if them dog bites match Lucy's teeth, it ain't gonna be pretty. In fact, it'll be lights out for old Lucy."

"Lucy didn't do nothing!!" Kellogg stood and pointed his bony white finger in Fletcher's direction. "If they hurt him, so help me God I'll . . .!!!"

Kellogg stopped abruptly and slammed his posterior back down into the wooden chair, as if suddenly remembering one of his Step 10 resolutions. He re-commenced chewing his left thumbnail with a decided vengeance.

"The only sure way to protect your dog and to help yourself out is to tell me everything you know about Anna Springer."

Fletcher had played the role of the "bad cop" before, but never the "bad dog catcher." He hoped his new tack would open something up inside Kellogg.

"I told you everything I know," Kellogg's voice had returned to a more dulcet tone.

"When are they gonna let me see Lucy?"

"You don't got any other information that might help us out with our investigation?" Fletcher asked.

"Go talk to Pastor John. He'll tell you I'm a different person now. The old has gone, the new has come."

Kellogg sounded to Fletcher as if he were repeating lines he had heard spoken on numerous occasions and had rehearsed in an attempt to convince himself of their truth.

"I may do that," Fletcher replied. "But if you decide you have more to say about this, you tell Elmer to get a hold of me. Okay?"

"I got nothing more to say."

"Suit yourself."

Chapter 13

"Someone's been sitting on my throne," Judge Centers said as he entered The Cave, fresh back from his judicial conference in St. Louis.

In his hand, the judge held a glossy 3X5 photograph of Mike Hanigan, bedecked in the judge's long flowing black robe, but seated on the toilet in the judge's private in-chambers restroom, pretending to read from a large, hard-bound copy of the U.S. Bankruptcy Code, with an ultra-earnest look on his face.

Hanigan veered his eyes away from his computer screen and towards the photo, grinning with pride at his handiwork.

"It's about time you developed that," Hanigan said. "You must be losing your passion for the lens. That shot was taken over a month and a half ago."

"And who, pray tell, was your accomplice in this little endeavor?" the judge asked.

"I work alone," Hanigan replied, turning his attention back to the computer screen.

In actuality, Hanigan had convinced one of the building's friendly old security guards to snap the shot, after a failed attempt to talk Martha into it. The photo had been taken using one of the judge's own cameras, which he maintained on a shelf in his office.

It was just the latest in a series of practical jokes Hanigan had orchestrated, but was also intended as a form of humorous protest against the judge's jealous protection of his private restroom, which he forbade anyone else in the chambers from using.

"This is violative of chambers protocol on about five different levels," the judge whined, only half in jest, holding the photo closer to his eyes to check for additional details.

"If it's any consolation Tom, I didn't use any of your precious toilet paper."

"I suppose you used my robe instead."

"No, but I gotta tell you, it's very liberating going without pants under a robe like that. You really should give serious consideration to the possibility of some judicial free-balling in the future."

The judge frowned. "Tell me again why I keep you around here?" he asked.

"Because I make damn good coffee," Hanigan quipped, raising his mug as a toast, before swilling a sip of chocolate raspberry - his personal favorite.

"Have you made any coffee for Jenny Berg yet?" the judge asked coyly.

"What's that supposed to mean?" Hanigan asked, with a noticeable wrinkle creasing his forehead.

"Well," the judge began, "Martha heard from Judge Bartlett's secretary that you and Ms. Berg have been seeing each other. So, I just wondered, in this day and age of equal rights, who makes the coffee in the morning?"

The judge was looking down sheepishly at his right foot, which was making a small circle on the well-worn short-napped carpet in The Cave.

"I knew it wouldn't take long for word to get around, but this is ridiculous," Hanigan said, obvious disgust in his tone.

"We've had one date and we're going out again tonight. I swear, this place is worse than a small town. Everyone thinks they need to know everyone else's business." Hanigan was shaking his head back and forth slightly.

"Well, Michael, you've never been shy before when it comes to talking about your love interests. So, I didn't think you'd be offended if I brought the subject up. Especially since I actually know this girl. Her father was a few years ahead of me in law school. Good lawyer. Good judge. Great guy."

"I'm glad to know I've got your blessing, Your Honor," Hanigan said sarcastically. "I don't think I could sleep at night if you weren't comfortable with my date's family pedigree."

"Who knows, if you don't run her off, maybe she can straighten you out," the judge continued.

"To be honest," Hanigan began, "I'd rather not talk any more about this, because inevitably, whatever I say in here will wind its way through half of the federal judiciary and get back up to Jenny."

"Fair enough, Michael. I respect that. You must be pretty serious about her."

The judge waited for a reply to his statement, but none was forthcoming, so he changed topics.

"You know, Michael," the judge paused briefly, tapping the long edge of the 3X5 photo repeatedly against his open palm, "I have to say, this doesn't quite measure up to the phony lawsuit."

"You're right, it's hard to top that," Hanigan smiled, recalling the last significant practical joke he had played on the judge – drafting a fictitious but authentic-looking civil complaint and having it served on the judge in chambers by the U.S. Marshall.

The fake legal document had convinced the judge that he and his wife had been sued by their snobbish neighbor, who just months before had unsuccessfully contested the Centers' application with the City of Omaha for permission to use their stately home as an occasional bed & breakfast.

The judge had resisted but then reluctantly given in to his wife's prodding to undertake the venture, and service of the bogus summons and complaint was enough to send him into a nervous tizzy of regret.

"So much planning. So much attention to detail."

Hanigan was smiling broadly now and looking up towards the ceiling, reliving in his mind the moment he signed the fake complaint by forging the name of a local plaintiff's personal-injury attorney who Hanigan had previously heard the judge lambaste for his tacky, tasteless television ads.

"So much waste of federal taxpayer dollars," the judge retorted, though he was now smiling too.

"Thank God you let me in on it before I told Margie we'd been sued. She would have had an aneurism."

"How is the bed & breakfast business these days?" Hanigan asked with a modicum of genuine interest in his voice, taking another sip of coffee.

"Tolerable, I guess. We had a Pakistani physics professor over last month. He was in town for a weekend giving a lecture at Creighton. Fascinating guy."

"I'm sure he was," Hanigan said, unable to forego his natural sarcasm for too long.

"In October, we're having Wyoming's state poet laureate for two nights. He's coming in for a regional poetry symposium. He's called the 'Cowboy Poet,' so I'm not real sure what to expect."

"Oh, just watch a few Bonanza re-runs before he shows up, and you'll be fine."

"Actually, I thought I'd show him some of the nature shots I took when we were in Jackson Hole last year. So if he ever publishes a book of his cowboy poetry and needs some accompanying pictures, he'll think of me."

"You never stop looking for that one big break, do you?"

"Oh, Michael, you know I could never give this judgeship up. It would pain me too much to see you unemployed."

"Don't worry about me, I'd go into the car warranty business and re-locate to the Caribbean," Hanigan said, pointing to the text on his computer screen.

"I've been working on this Cayman Islands case. Those guys had quite a racket going . . ."

"Are we going to have to boot the case on jurisdictional grounds?" the judge interrupted.

"I don't know yet. I've gotten a little sidetracked reading all about this company and what it does. It's a Cayman corporation, but its principal place of business is in Omaha. It was formed pursuant to a piece of U.S. federal legislation, the Liability Risk Retention Act, but it's regulated by the Monetary Authority in the Caymans," Hanigan turned from his monitor to face the judge, before continuing.

"The company basically formed a giant insurance pool to cover warranty claims made against car manufacturers and dealers, funded by premiums paid in by the people buying the cars. They transferred $48 million in cash to the Caymans, just before filing their liquidation proceeding down there."

"And they filed the Cayman proceeding primarily to put the brakes on a class action filed against them upstairs?" the judge asked, referring to the federal district court, located just one floor directly above the bankruptcy court offices.

"That, and they got in a big pissing match with their reinsurance carrier about who was responsible for covering a good-sized chunk of warranty claims. But the class action was brought by a bunch of consumers who got stiffed on their warranty contracts. They just got certified as a class before the Cayman proceeding was filed."

Hanigan opened the court file, as if looking for something.

"It's interesting, though," he said, "you should see the list of the company's officers and directors. It's quite a who's who of scumbags. You remember Jerry Remlinger?"

The judge's blank stare gave Hanigan his answer, so Hanigan continued.

"He played football for the Huskers back in the late 70's, but got kicked off the team for *allegedly* accepting a car and a bunch of money from a booster. Anyway, he's the Chairman of the Board. And Ken Bertrand, from the Federated savings-and-loan scandal–he's on the Board also."

The judge nodded, acknowledging his recollection of the Bertrand scandal.

"And this strange mobster-wanna-be from Riverton, Carl Talbot, whose family ran a couple hotels and a restaurant down there," Hanigan said. "Back when I was in high school, this Talbot guy was in charge of the bus boys at the nice steakhouse his parents owned. A buddy of mine worked under him and said the guy would show up for work sky high on coke and, every now and then, would just walk face-first right into a wall, but then nonchalantly go about his business as if nothing happened."

"Sounds like a real winner," the judge responded.

"Anyhow," Hanigan continued, "the Board of Directors conveniently voted to pay themselves and other key officers their annual salaries and director fees in advance, about a month before the Cayman proceeding was filed."

"Sounds like there's got to be an avoidable transfer somewhere there," the judge said.

"You're probably right, *if* U.S. bankruptcy law applies," Hanigan opined. "But who the hell knows what the Grand Court of the Caymans might do with it under their liquidation scheme. The insolvency laws down there look quite a bit different than our Bankruptcy Code."

"Well, see what you find on the issue of whether relief is even appropriate under section 304," the judge instructed. "It may turn out to be a short opinion."

"I hope so," Hanigan replied.

"Michael, don't let your aversion to hard work color your judgment," the judge kidded, as he headed back towards his own office via the back passageway.

"Your Honor, I think you need to take another look at that picture you're holding. That's not the sports section or a People magazine I'm reading there.

Hanigan waggled his finger in the judge's direction.

"Even as I was defiling the Holiest of Holies, I was reading and memorizing the Advisory Committee Notes to every Code section in Chapter 11," he said. That's the epitome of hard work and dedication."

"More like defecation," the judge said as he disappeared from The Cave.

"Good one, Judge," Hanigan leaned sideways in his chair to project his voice after the judge. Hanigan was thoroughly pleased with the judge's growing willingness to trade barbs with him. Three years ago, such an exchange would have been unthinkable.

"I need to start planning my next prank," Hanigan thought to himself, as he flipped through the stack of documents next to his computer.

Chapter 14

Steve Fletcher sat alone at the sprawling dark maple-wood table in the executive conference room of the main office building at the Trees Are Forever Foundation, tapping his chrome lighter softly on the layer of thick glass covering the table, in rhythm with the chorus of the Hank Williams Jr. song still circulating through his head from earlier that day.

Fletcher peered around at the Adirondack-style timber and stone support posts and log cross beams that framed the room, before noticing a quotation etched in one of the wood panels running along the top of the wall to his right - *"The best friend on earth of man is the tree." Frank Lloyd Wright.*

"Poor Frank must have never had a dog," Fletcher thought to himself, dropping his gaze down to the double doors leading into the conference room, just as an overweight, round-faced, but professionally-dressed and nicely-groomed woman was entering, with two other people immediately behind her.

"Hi, Mr. Fletcher, we're so sorry to keep you waiting," the round-faced woman was bubbling with enthusiasm even in her apology. "My name's Donna Chitwood."

She walked towards Fletcher, arm extended, her short, chubby hand peeking out from the sleeve of her light blue business suit. "I'm the director of human resources here at the Foundation."

Fletcher slid the lighter into the breast pocket of his aqua-colored Hawaiian-print shirt and stood up to shake the hand of the round-faced H.R. director.

"This is Gail Thompson, a Senior Administrator and accountant in our planned giving department." As the H.R. director spun around to introduce the woman following closely behind her, she inadvertently struck her on the shoulder.

"Oh, I'm sorry, Gail," she offered, as she made two quick strokes with her chubby hand on the area of the woman's shoulder that had been struck.

The accountant, stern-looking with plain but attractive facial features, reached past the round-faced woman to shake Fletcher's hand.

"Gail was Anna Springer's immediate supervisor during her time in the planned giving section," the H.R. director continued with her introduction.

"Nice to meet you." Fletcher said, smiling. The stern-looking woman grudgingly reciprocated with a conservative, tight-lipped grin.

"And this is Doug Moles, the head groundskeeper."

The H.R. director stepped further back away from Fletcher as she introduced a well-built middle-aged man in a dark green short-sleeved TAFF shirt and long khaki-colored grass-stained shorts. His face was well-tanned but obviously weathered from innumerable hours spent under the hot Nebraska sun, and the portion of his scalp revealed by his receding hairline was a significantly lighter tone than his face and arms, suggesting that he favored wearing a hat when outside.

"Howdy," the man blurted in a loud voice, a byproduct of spending long stretches of time on a noisy lawn tractor.

"Good to meet you, Doug," Fletcher increased the intensity of his grip on the man's hand, trying to match the tight, vice-like squeeze being put on his own hand by the groundskeeper. "The place looks great out there."

"It keeps me hoppin'," the man replied, still with more volume than the setting warranted, before finally relinquishing his exceedingly strong grasp on Fletcher's right hand.

"I bet it does. How many acres is this place?" Fletcher asked with interest.

"Oh, if you include the orchard lots, 260," the groundskeeper replied.

"No kiddin."

"Why don't we go ahead and sit down?" the H.R. director said, seemingly eager to regain control of the conversation. "And I'll see if we can get some coffee brought in."

"None for me, thanks. I'm all coffeed out for the morning," Fletcher said as he sat back down at the conference room table.

"Oh, okay," came the round-faced woman's reply, pulling out a chair for herself, apparently not interested in retrieving coffee for her two co-employees.

"Well, I've told Gail and Doug that you are looking into Anna's death and that you have some questions about Anna and possibly Terry Kellogg."

"That's right. And I do appreciate you taking time out of your work schedules to talk to me."

"I get paid just the same," the groundskeeper said, finally lowering the tone of his voice to an acceptable indoor level, oblivious to the nasty look the H.R. director was shooting in his direction for his flippant comment.

"Why don't we start with Anna Springer," Fletcher continued. "How long did she work here?"

"We hired Anna on a part-time basis about two years ago when she was still in high school," the H.R. director began. "Originally, she was in our public relations department, but within a month or so, we moved her to planned giving."

"Why was that?" Fletcher asked.

"As I recall, that was at her request," the H.R. director answered.

"She never wanted to work in P.R.," the stern-faced accountant spoke for the first time. "That was something her mother had arranged."

"We did not give any special consideration to who Anna's mother was when we hired her," the round-faced woman said defensively, in reference to Senator Springer and the position she had held for years on the Board of Directors for the Foundation. "She was hired based on a number of a very good references, and there was a real need for help in public relations at that time."

"So, for most of her time here, she would have been working with you, Ms. . . . uh. . . Thomas, is it?" Fletcher inquired.

"Thompson," the accountant corrected, not noticeably offended by Fletcher's failure to accurately recall her name. "Yes, I supervised Anna after she transferred into planned giving. When she left to go to college, I basically gave her a standing offer to return any time she wanted."

"She did a good job for you, then?"

"Anna was excellent with numbers. She obviously inherited her dad's acumen for accounting," Ms. Thompson said, in reference to Anna's father, a quiet, reserved CPA with a successful tax practice at a two-man accounting firm in Riverton, who had always taken a backseat to the forceful, outspoken politically-active matriarch of the family.

"When did she come back to work then?" Fletcher asked.

The accountant looked upwards thoughtfully, "It was . . ."

"About six months ago," the H.R. director interrupted.

" . . . March 14 of this year," the accountant finished her sentence with the precision expected of someone in her profession. "It was right in the middle of our busiest time. About a month before tax day."

"You guys get quite a few donations, do you?"

"As of the end of the last fiscal year, the Foundation passed the million-member mark," the accountant began. "So, when you factor in multiple-member families, you're taking approximately

750,000 giving units. Now granted, not all units will donate above minimum membership levels in every fiscal year, but even if only a third of the units give some time during the year, that's over 250,000 units to track and process." The accountant paused briefly. "That's probably more information than you wanted."

"No, that's fine." Fletcher was jotting a few notes on a small tablet. "You mentioned that Ms. Springer had left to go to college. Any idea why she came back to Riverton in the middle of the school year?"

The round-faced woman opened her mouth as if to speak, before realizing she had no information germane to Fletcher's question.

"I gathered she was pretty miserable at Washburn," the accountant offered. "I think she decided she just wasn't sorority material."

The tone of the woman's voice suggested that she considered herself similar to Springer in that respect.

"Did she ever have any problems with anyone here?" Fletcher asked.

"She was a model employee," the H.R. director bubbled. "We never had any problems with her."

"But did she have any problems with other employees that you know of?"

Fletcher looked intently at the accountant, hoping to momentarily silence the bubbly H.R. director.

The stern-faced woman rubbed her bony chin thoughtfully, gazing up above Fletcher's head, as if calculating a series of long division problems in her head.

After several seconds, she shook her head.

"Not really." She paused for several more seconds.

"But I do recall her saying that the trash guy gave her the creeps."

"Terry Kellogg?" Fletcher asked.

"I don't know his name," the accountant responded. "The young man with all the tattoos that had been picking up trash outside the building."

"That's Terry," the groundskeeper half-shouted, as if startled awake from a deep slumber.

"Did she say why he gave her the creeps?" Fletcher asked.

"He would walk by the office every so often and stare at her through the window," the accountant answered.

"Did he ever say anything to her?"

"I don't believe I've ever heard him speak," came the accountant's reply.

"Terry ain't much of a talker," the groundskeeper pulled his chair closer to the table and sat up straight, as if preparing to fully engage in the conversation now that his underling had become the topic.

"And when did you hire Terry?" Fletcher inquired, looking in the direction of the groundskeeper.

"*I* didn't hire him," the groundskeeper placed one of his well-tanned hands on his chest and began rocking back and forth in his chair.

"Terry was hired at the beginning of the summer, as part of our community reinvestment program," the H.R. director offered.

"What is that?" Fletcher asked.

"It's a program where we make a number of seasonal jobs available for people who may otherwise have difficulty finding gainful employment."

The H.R. director's voice contained a hint of altruistic pride.

"Okay." Fletcher continued to scribble notes in his pad.

"But we do a substantial amount of pre-screening before we hire anyone for that program," the H.R. director said defensively. "And Mr. Kellogg had no history of violent crime . . . at least against people. In accordance with the protocol for the program, I did discuss the nature of his criminal record with the executive director of the Foundation and got his approval before we made the hire."

"Is that Sheldon Steinhart?" Fletcher asked, from his general recall of who held that post.

"No, actually, Richard Talbot replaced Mr. Steinhart almost a year ago," the H.R. director responded.

"One of Gladys Talbot's boys?" Fletcher asked.

"Yes, God rest her," came the H.R. director's reply.

"Any other incidents with Kellogg?" Fletcher inquired.

"I've had to tell him several times to clean up after his dog," the groundskeeper offered, glancing at the two women at the table, in a manner that suggested he would have made a different word choice had they not been seated there.

"Anything else?" Fletcher asked.

All three TAFF employees shook their heads in the negative, and Fletcher began flipping through his note pad.

"Did Ms. Springer ever mention a Jackie Howell?"

"She would talk on the phone sometimes to someone named Jackie," the accountant offered. "But I never knew who it was.

Anna did not talk much about her personal life. She was always very business-like in the office. And that's the way I preferred it."

"I've seen her with Jackie Howell before down at the Wheel-House," the groundskeeper boomed, smiling sheepishly, in a way that implied he was proud to be privy to some information his female counterparts were not.

"They looked pretty chummy, if you know what I mean." The groundskeeper winked in Fletcher's direction.

"Was this Jackie a boyfriend of Anna's?" the stern-faced accountant asked, sincerely clueless to Springer's homosexual predilections, eliciting a sharp, abrupt laugh from the groundskeeper.

"Actually, Ms. Thompson," Fletcher said, looking down at his notes, "Jackie Howell is a woman. And she claims to have been having a relationship with Ms. Springer."

The accountant gasped and threw one of her slender hands in front of her mouth.

"Did you know this?" she asked, turning towards the round-faced woman.

"The Foundation is an equal opportunity employer. We do not discriminate on the basis of race, gender, religion, or sexual orientation," the H.R. director spoke as if reading from a cue card.

"But Ms. Howell does seem to think that Anna may have been involved with someone else as well," Fletcher continued. "Are any of you aware of any relationships Ms. Springer may been involved in?"

"No," the round-faced woman answered, almost before the question had left Fletcher's mouth.

"One of my lawn guys talked about asking her out," the groundskeeper said, as he scratched the balding spot on his head, "but I don't think he ever did."

"What's his name?"

"Oh, Eric Christensen. But Eric's a good guy. He wouldn't hurt a fly."

Fletcher scribbled in his notepad one last time before shutting it, and slipping into his breast pocket, behind his chrome lighter.

"Did Ms. Springer have an email account here?"

"Yes," the accountant replied.

"You mind if I take a look at her in-box?"

"Fine with me," the accountant said, looking toward the H.R. director to make sure it was acceptable to her.

"You are certainly free to," the H.R. director said, "but we just had the entire computer system overhauled and upgraded two weeks ago, so there may not be anything in there."

"What was the purpose of that?" Fletcher asked.

"Oh, we do that periodically, you know, to keep up with all the changes in technology."

"Terry didn't have access to any email," the groundskeeper volunteered.

"I'd like to take a look at it anyway." Fletcher closed his notepad, but then quickly flipped it open again. "One last thing - did Ms. Springer have a reserved parking spot?"

"Oh, certainly not," the round-faced woman said, the bubbliness in her voice giving way slightly to a hint of indignance. "Only upper management employees have specially reserved spots. Everyone else parks in the general lot."

"Really?" Fletcher made a quick note. "Because Terry Kellogg seems to think she would park a small silver, foreign-model vehicle in one of the VIP spots."

"Well, he must be mistaken," the H.R. director said confidently.

"There is that little silver hybrid thing we got from Trianta that usually sits in the VIP lot," the groundskeeper said.

"The Envi? Anna wouldn't have been driving that," the tone of the round-faced woman's voice had degraded into condescension, and her dislike for the groundskeeper was palpable. "That's considered a company car and again, only executives would have access to it."

"Just the same, I'll want to visit with whoever controls access to that vehicle."

"That won't be a problem," the H.R. director replied, seemingly forcing the bubbliness back into her voice.

Chapter 15

"Your gut doesn't have that golden brown tan it usually does this time of year," came Mike Hanigan's good-natured jibe, as he sat pool-side enjoying a beer and glancing at his father's bulbous pale belly, covered in curly, reddish-brown hair, hanging heavily above the waist line of a pair of navy blue swim trunks.

"I haven't gotten out much this summer," Donny Hanigan replied to his son, looking down towards his own belly, in front of which he held in both hands a single twelve-ounce bottle of Michelob Light, sheathed in a crisp new red Budweiser Koozy.

He tapped the very top of the bottle lightly against the edge of the glass table at which they were seated, just a few feet from the pool in the backyard of the Hanigan residence in Riverton.

"Been watching a lot of the Golf Channel on the satellite."

"You don't even golf," Mike said, chuckling.

"So . . .," Donny Hanigan stated in his rough, gravelly voice, as he took a swig from his beer bottle, "it's relaxing to watch."

"You got an outdoor pool and a hot tub, and you're spending your summer sitting in that dark basement rec-room watching guys chase a little white ball around all day?" Mike asked incredulously.

"What do you got against golf? I thought all lawyers were required to take that up as their official pastime."

"I'm not a real lawyer, remember?"

"Oh yeah," the elder Hanigan responded. "Believe me, I've given up trying to explain to people what it is you do. I say you're a clerk, and they cither think you stand behind a store register all day or that you work in a bureaucrat's cubicle somewhere filing documents."

"Well, since you're all into this golf thing now, just tell em' I'm like a caddy for the judge. I research the course for him, warn him of hazards, tell him which clubs he should use and . . .," Mike paused for effect, "occasionally wash his balls. And he gets all the credit."

"Whatever it is you do, I'm sure your mother would be very proud of you," Donny Hanigan offered.

Mike had wondered how long it would take his father to bring up the topic of Karen, his dearly departed wife, who had passed away four years before, almost to the day, following a lengthy battle with cervical cancer.

Mike had made a point of visiting Donny Hanigan around this time of the year ever since her passing, knowing it was a particularly difficult time for his father.

It had been Mike's mother who had constantly encouraged, prodded, and cajoled him to put his exceptional intellectual gifts to use. She was thrilled when Mike announced he would be attending law school. Mike never had the heart to tell her that his primary motivation for the decision to pursue a legal education was to delay entry into the "real world" for another three years.

"You ready for another beer?" Mike said, rising from his straight-back patio chair and pulling his own empty Michelob Light bottle from its red sleeve.

"No, I'm good," his father replied, looking down at his beer bottle again.

When visiting his father, Mike always drank the family merchandise, forgoing his preferred hard liquor, partly as a means of bonding with the old man, and partly because he never forgot the near-rage his father flew into on one occasion during Mike's high school days upon finding an empty Coors Light "tallboy" can on the floorboard of Mike's vehicle.

The irony was not lost on Mike at the time that, instead of being upset about Mike's underage drinking and driving, his father was livid about what he deemed to be a breach of loyalty to the family business. "We are a Budweiser family!" Donny Hanigan had fumed, "We drink only Budweiser products!"

"I've started seeing a new girl," Mike said as he returned to the glass table, fresh beer in tow, hoping to keep his dad's spirits from spiraling downward after the mention of their lost loved one.

"Really? Anyone I know?"

"No, this chick has class."

"Very funny, smart ass. What's her name?"

"Jenny Berg. She clerks for one of the other federal judges up there. She's a real fireball. I think you'd like her."

"Why didn't you bring her down with you? You ashamed of the old man?"

"No, I'm afraid she'd get one look at those sexy abs you're sporting and dump me for you," Mike tipped a healthy mouthful of brew between his slightly parted lips, and swallowed.

"Actually, she does seem kinda intrigued by Riverton," Mike continued. "She's an Omaha girl and she has this delusion that small towns are these quaint little charming places. I told her I might bring her down here tomorrow. I'm a little worried that Riverton may blow her whole perception to pieces."

"Oh, Riverton's a nice town. It's been good to us."

As he spoke, Donny Hanigan panned his eyes around the backyard at all the luxuries that operating a beer distributorship in an alcohol-drenched community had afforded him - the pool, the hot tub, the satellite dish, the four-car garage filled with shiny new vehicles.

"But you know, Mike, I'm seriously thinking about getting out of the game."

"What do you mean?"

"The company's requiring a lot of its older distributorships to upgrade their facilities. They want me to buy some ground near one of the new commercial developments west of town and put up a $4 million facility."

"So take out a loan. What's the big deal?"

"This operation's been 100% debt-free since for more than a decade. We own all the assets free and clear. And I don't know if I have the energy for that kind of project. Now may be a good time to cash out."

"What would do with yourself if you sold out?"

"I don't know . . . move to California and take up tennis . . . or golf."

"Knock, Knock!" Two familiar faces suddenly appeared over the top of the five-foot stained pinewood fence which surrounded the Hanigans' pool. "We were cruising by and saw the Mustang in the driveway," Big Chig announced.

"You're in town on a Saturday night and you don't look us up," Zelmo added. "What, you too good for us now?"

"Much too good," came Mike Hanigan's deadpan reply, never willing to let Zelmo play his guilt-trip games. "Come on in, guys."

Big Chig and Zelmo pushed their way through the wooden fence gate, both slovenly dressed in casual shorts, tank tops, and sandals, and looking as though they probably had spent most of their Saturday on the river.

"Grab a beer," Mike offered, pointing his Michelob Light bottle in the direction of a large stainless steel refrigerator, next to the deluxe barbecue grill on the sizeable pinewood patio leading into the Hanigan residence.

"Beer Man!" Big Chig shouted to the seated Donny Hanigan, as he shuffled past the glass table towards the refrigerator, a baseball cap turned backwards atop his dark black head of hair. "How are you?"

"Fat, old, and tired," Donny grumbled, "but otherwise dandy."

After retrieving two Budweiser longneck bottles from the fridge, Zelmo and Big Chig pulled two patio chairs up to the glass table, between Mike and his father.

"So, you guys are celebrities now. Front-page Omaha World Herald celebrities," Mike noted, recalling the cover page article on the Springer murder.

"I never saw that," Big Chig replied. "But I did see Zelmo was in the Riverton News-Press last week for his third DUI."

"That was only my second, douche bag. And at least I've never been written up for public indecency," Zelmo retorted, in reference to the time Big Chig was caught by a Riverton police officer having sex at 2 a.m. on a wooden playground structure at one of Riverton 's elementary schools, with a haggard, middle-aged woman he had picked up at the Wheel-House bar.

"That was well worth it. I'd do that again in a heartbeat." Big Chig's mischievous smile revealed a full mouth of white teeth and a perverse pride in his accomplishment.

"Something tells me that isn't a story I want to hear," the elder Hanigan said, as he pushed his chair away from the glass table, and began walking towards the sliding glass door leading into the house. "You guys have a good night."

"Where you going?" Mike asked.

"I'm gonna catch the third round highlights of the PGA Championship."

Donny Hanigan slid the glass door closed behind him before Mike could fire off any sarcastic remarks.

Five years earlier, before his wife's death, Donny Hanigan would have sat outside with Mike and his buddies for hours, drinking beers and telling stories of the early days of his Budweiser distributorship, including his numerous trips to St. Louis to party with August Busch III, members of the St. Louis Cardinals baseball team, and the legendary sports broadcaster Jack Buck.

It was as if the death of Mike's mother had drained away all of Donny Hanigan's lust for life and the charismatic prideful bluster which had made him such an engaging figure.

"You wanna blaze this?" Wasting no time after Donny Hanigan's departure from the table, Zelmo pulled a healthy-sized joint from the faded, river-worn waist pack affixed to the side of his shorts.

"I can't," Hanigan responded. "I think there's a health insurance renewal coming up soon at work and they usually take a piss test. You guys go ahead."

"C'mon Mikey. A couple hits ain't gonna hurt nothing." Zelmo could never resist an opportunity to apply peer pressure to one of his acquaintances.

"You guys toke away. I wanna hear about this Anna Springer murder. Any idea who did the deed?"

"Bud Graham thinks her old lady had a hand in it," Zelmo offered, through the side of his mouth that was not wrapped around the tightly-rolled marijuana cigarette, as he sparked a lighter and maneuvered the tip of the joint into the flame.

"Now, there's a reliable source," Hanigan replied sarcastically. "What's his basis for saying that?"

"I don't know. Some shit about a political conspiracy." Zelmo was now holding the hit of smoke within his lungs and passing the joint in the direction of Big Chig.

"She's gonna kill her own daughter for political advancement? Graham's such a burn-out," Hanigan scoffed.

He was not buying the half-baked theory of the fully-baked town druggie.

"Last I heard," Mike continued, "that new debate-team teacher was trying to indoctrinate Anna into the gay lifestyle. What was the story with that?"

"Licky Mikki?" Big Chig said frowning. "That's old news, dude. It was Anna that split Mikki and Jackie Howell up a couple years back. Anna and Jackie had been mowing each other's lawns ever since. But now I heard Jackie and Mikki might be back together again. One dyke gets pushed off the Pussy-Go-Round, and another one jumps back on."

"There's your motive for murder, right there," Hanigan stated. "Jilted lover."

"Nah, I heard some guys at the bait shop saying Terry Kellogg was the prime suspect," Big Chig offered, as he brought the joint to his full dark lips.

"The speed dealer?" Hanigan asked, trying to recall in his mind what that person actually looked like. "Why would he kill her?"

"He's gotten into some pretty weird shit lately," Big Chig responded. "Devil worship. Cutting himself up. And he was working at the same place she was. He could've been stalking her."

Big Chig took a tiny sip from his beer bottle, as if to chase down the marijuana smoke still in his lungs. He nudged the joint near Hanigan, hitting him on the knee with the back of his hand, as the smoke streamed upward from his fingers.

"Oh hell, I suppose I can drink a gallon of orange juice in the morning to mask this," Hanigan said, succumbing to the tempting smell of the marijuana smoke rolling off the cigarette, as he took the hand-off from Big Chig.

"Mikey!" Zelmo cheered encouragingly.

"Where's Cooter tonight?" Hanigan asked before he began to toke on the joint, as if there were some logical inconsistency in drugs being ingested without Cooter being present and partaking therein.

"Probably paying a visit to the Orchard *Ho*-tel again," Big Chig answered, placing primary emphasis on the "Ho" syllable.

"What's that mean?" Hanigan coughed slightly as he spoke, it having been awhile since he had taken a healthy hit of marijuana smoke into his lungs.

"You haven't heard about the *Ho*-tel?" Zelmo asked, with noticeable surprise in his voice.

Hanigan shook his head in the negative, coughing again into his hand.

"The old Orchard Inn, south of town." Zelmo paused momentarily to make sure Hanigan was tracking. "On the weekends, they get strippers from that dumpy little joint over in Hamburg who come and turn tricks at the motel."

Zelmo reached across the glass table to grab the still-burning joint from Mike's hand.

"Yeah," Big Chig continued the story, "you call the front desk and ask for the special reservations attendant. They transfer you over to someone else. Then you ask for Room 169 if you want a half hour of action, 269 if you want a full hour, or 369 if you want 90 minutes. Give 'em your credit card number and a phone number where they can call you back and confirm at. They give you the room number, you show up at the appointed time, and 'boom,' it's on."

"Oh and get this," Zelmo chimed back in, "if you want four lines of coke in your room waiting for you, you tell em' you would like ice in your room. They just take the charge off your card."

"You're shittin' me." Hanigan was genuinely amazed that such activity could be carried on at a legitimate business establishment in the small community. "How do they pull that off?"

"It's part of The Syndicate," Zelmo answered, compulsively pulling his tanktop away from his chest, in his patented post-dope-smoking maneuver.

"The Syndicate?" Hanigan said, chuckling.

"That's what they call Carl Talbot's under-the-table operations," Big Chig interjected.

"Carl Talbot, huh?" Hanigan asked rhetorically, scratching his scalp with the hand that wasn't occupied with a Koozy-sheathed Michelob Light. "That guy's been busy lately. I just saw his name in some documents up in bankruptcy court. He's on the board of this foreign company with a bunch of other shady characters."

"Here we go, Chig," Zelmo said. "Now he's gonna start going into all this lawyer bullshit, to try and impress us."

"If he wants to impress me, he should go find that big bad beer bong and let me slide about twenty ounces of the King of Beers straight down into my gullet."

Big Chig winked at Hanigan and grinned, fondly recalling the many times in summers past when he would stake his rightful claim as "Beer Bong Champion," by allowing others to pour mass quantities of brew through a funnel and tube contraption as he stood in neck deep water in the center of the Hanigan's pool, always outlasting any other competitors in the game of drinking submission.

"I think it's hanging on a hook in the garage next to my dad's Expedition. Help yourself, Chig," Hanigan offered.

"Don't mind if I do." The large brown man nimbly scooted out of the patio chair and trotted towards the garage, leaving Zelmo holding the joint out with no ready recipient to claim it.

Something told Hanigan he wouldn't be getting rid of his house guests any time soon.

Chapter 16

As Fletcher stepped out of his truck onto the faded asphalt parking lot of the Riverton Marina, he spied Bill Rogge in the distance, removing the white leather boat cover from the shiny new 20-foot water craft still on the trailer behind Rogge's extended-cab long-box Chevy Silverado pickup truck.

Fletcher had not been fishing with Rogge in nearly five years, and he was surprised when Rogge had asked him, on just two days' notice, to join Rogge on the river for an early Sunday-morning fishing excursion.

Fletcher guessed that Rogge was anxious to show off his new boat to anyone who would look at it.

And Fletcher was all too happy to oblige, as he could feel his summertime fishing opportunities slipping away.

Besides, Fletcher reasoned, Connie was working all day, he would still have most of the afternoon to work on the house addition, and being on the water was usually an excellent way for him to clear his mind during a difficult investigation.

Fletcher reached into the bed of his Ford truck to grab his favorite fishing pole and the large red-and-brown tackle box he had won three years earlier as a prize in a Field & Stream magazine sweepstakes.

Fletcher was decked out in an army-green, wide-brim fishing hat, his dark prescription sunglasses, an older, more well-worn version of his usual Hawaiian-print shirt, a long slightly-baggy pair of khaki-colored fishing shorts covered with numerous pockets and pouches, and a brand-spanking-new pair of tan boat shoes recently purchased by Connie at the Wal-Mart in Lincoln.

As Fletcher sauntered toward Rogge's new boat, the brawny law enforcement officer looked up and smiled.

"Mornin', Fletch. Hey, give me a hand with this, would you?"

"You bet."

Fletcher laid his gear down under a large willow tree in front of Rogge's truck and walked around to the side of the boat opposite his friend.

Fletcher began popping open the dozens of stainless steel snaps on his side of the boat, which fastened the cover snugly around the top of the craft.

"You wasn't kidding, Bill, this *is* a big boat."

"Yeah, and the bigger the boat, the bigger of a pain in the ass it is to get into the water," Rogge offered.

The two men continued to unfasten their respective sides of the boat cover, working their way toward a meeting near the back-end of the craft.

"Where's Slim?" Fletcher asked, in reference to Rogge's brother-in-law and erstwhile fishing companion.

"I didn't invite him. I thought we might need to talk a little about the Springer case, and I didn't want an extra set of ears on board."

"Since when are you worried about talking shop in front of Slim?"

"Oh, I don't know, this Springer thing's just a little higher profile. Until we get somebody charged, I'd just as soon keep the information as tight as possible."

Rogge gathered up the cumbersome boat cover between his burly arms, and squeezed it inwards like a giant, unwieldy accordion. "How close are we to nailing Kellogg for it?" he asked.

"It doesn't look like we're gonna get a definitive match on the dog bites. So we don't got a whole lot to go with," Fletcher said, as he walked back around the boat toward the front of Rogge's truck.

Fletcher reached down for his fishing pole and tackle box with his right hand, placing his left hand over his shirt pocket to keep his lighter and cigars from spilling onto the pavement.

He stepped towards the boat to hand his fishing equipment to Rogge, who had jumped up inside the vessel.

As the hand-off was being made to Rogge, Fletcher gave his honest assessment of the current evidence, or lack thereof, against Kellogg.

"We got no eye-witnesses. No murder weapon. No confession. No other physical evidence linking Kellogg to the crime."

Rogge placed Fletcher's pole and box on the floor of the craft and shuffled toward the rear, pulling the bunched-up boat cover off the back flank and inside the boat, where he began tucking it away inside an under-seat storage compartment.

"Fletch, we both know this guy's a major dirtbags who gets off on killing things." Rogge's voice was straining slightly, as he pressed hard on the cover to jam it into the compact storage area. "Cutting up the animals just wasn't doing it for him anymore, so he graduated up to something more interesting."

"You may be right, Bill, but the evidence just ain't there yet. And, I don't know why, but something in my gut just tells me he's not our guy."

"I betcha anything if we could get into his house, we'd find all the evidence we need," Rogge pressed.

"That *is* the next step," Fletcher responded. "I gotta talk to the County Attorney about whether we got enough to at least get a search warrant."

"Hell, there oughta be enough for that." Rogge jumped down from atop the boat, and became more animated in his speech. "He worked with her. He was hassling her. He's the only person in town who's ever beheaded anything. She had that Satanic symbol on her head. And her arm was covered in dogbites. I've seen Sherman issue warrants on a helluva lot less than that before," Rogge said, in reference to the long-time local district court judge.

"I'll talk to Pete about it tomorrow," Fletcher said, using the popular nickname of Roy Peterson, the Apache County Attorney.

Rogge and Fletcher climbed into the cab of Rogge's truck, and Fletcher immediately rolled down the passenger side window, reaching into his shirt pocket for a cigar.

"You know what's strange, Bill?"

"What's that?"

"Just before she disappeared, Springer told everyone she was going to Washington D.C. for two weeks. But none of the airlines have any record of her buying a ticket during that time."

Rogge put the truck in reverse gear and looked back over his right shoulder, "Maybe she was gonna drive there."

"Not likely," Fletcher responded, removing the plastic wrap from his cigar.

"She would usually fly even when she was only going back to college in Topeka."

After backing up a bit, Rogge caused the truck to jump forward, and looped around the lot in a half-circle on his way toward the cement pathway which led down to the Marina's two concrete boat ramps.

Suddenly, he stopped the truck at the top of the pathway and slammed the vehicle into park.

"Fletch, I'm gonna tell you something I should have told you when we first talked about this case."

The fact that Rogge had stopped the truck in a location which would block any incoming or outgoing traffic from the boat ramps suggested to Fletcher that what Rogge was about to say must be important.

"Right after the head was found in the river, I got a phone call with an anonymous tip from someone claiming to have inside information. They said they know for a fact that Kellogg done it."

"What?" Fletcher asked rhetorically, removing the unlit cigar from his mouth. "Why didn't you tell me that before?"

"Ohhh . . ." Rogge growled and rolled his head from side to side. "The guy insisted that I not tell anyone about the call. So, I . . . I just thought I'd see what kind of evidence we came up with before I mentioned anything about it."

"Any idea who it was that called?"

Rogge paused and wrinkled his forehead. "No. And I asked him several times who he was, but he sounded real scared about the whole deal, and said he just couldn't tell me."

"Did you run a trace on the call to see where it came from?"

"As I recall, it was from some unidentified number outside of Riverton."

"Huh," Fletcher said audibly, making a mental note to himself to ask the Sheriff's office for the phone records from that time period. "Anything else you remember from the call?"

"Nah, he wouldn't give me any details. But he was insistent that Terry Kellogg had done this."

"Well, that and a plug nickel will get you a hot cup of diddly squat," Fletcher mused, stealing one of his father's favorite corny sayings. "But I guess it might help us get that warrant."

"There you go," Rogge said. "Let's go fishing." Rogge abruptly pulled the gear shift down into drive and lurched the vehicle forward.

As the truck bumped along the rough pathway leading down to the water, an uncomfortable silence, big enough to fill the extended cab, crept into the space between the driver and passenger.

Fletcher pondered why Rogge had withheld the seemingly innocuous fact of the anonymous tip from him. Rogge had always been a straight-shooter with Fletcher in all their professional dealings.

Even more curious to Fletcher was why Rogge chose to disclose the information to Fletcher when he did. Was the subtle deception eating at big Rogge so badly that he arranged for a special fishing trip with Fletcher just to come clean?

"River's low this mornin', ain't it?" Rogge's question broke the awkward silence.

"Mm hmm," Fletcher responded affirmatively, still considering what had just transpired in the truck.

Rogge pulled the truck forward in the flat concrete area just above where the marina's two cement boat ramps began their descent into the filthy river water.

He reached his burly right arm over and grabbed the head rest just behind Fletcher's head, looking back with intentness towards the river, as he expertly maneuvered the trailer down the ramp and into the surging brown waters.

Rogge placed the truck into park, then popped open the glove box in front of Fletcher, grabbing from within a small key ring with two brass keys on it.

"Fire it up, Fletch." Rogge dangled the keys above Fletcher's lap, before dropping them into Fletcher's open extended palms.

Chapter 17

"Do you always drive this fast?" Jenny Berg asked from the passenger seat of Mike Hanigan's three-year-old, silver Ford Mustang, as it zipped southward in the passing lane of Interstate 29, on the Iowa side of the Missouri River.

"Only when I've been drinking heavily," Hanigan deadpanned.

"You're kidding, right?"

"As far as you know," came Hanigan's expressionless reply.

Hanigan had acceded to Berg's request to take her to his hometown, and they were now speeding their way on a Sunday afternoon drive toward Riverton.

While State Highway 75 provided a shorter, more direct route from Omaha to Riverton, Hanigan did not particularly care for that narrow, two-lane highway due, in part, to his penchant for swerving into the opposite lane during frequent CD changes.

It hadn't occurred to Hanigan that, with Berg along for the ride, he would have a companion who could tend to the music selections. But Hanigan also preferred I-29 for its view, with the dark, shadowy, heavily-forested river bluffs off in the distance to the east, rising up behind the perfectly flat rows of green Iowa corn in the fertile river bottoms area.

"Did I tell you the judge is struggling again with The Envy?" Berg asked, trying to keep herself from continually looking over at the speedometer.

Hanigan knew Berg was referring to the malady occasionally suffered by both of their bosses, an affliction Berg had dubbed "Article III Envy."

Whereas federal bankruptcy judges and federal magistrate judges are appointed by the judiciary to limited renewable terms of years, pursuant to Article I of the Constitution, their more esteemed colleagues in the federal judiciary are appointed by the President to lifetime tenures, pursuant to Article III of the Constitution.

With that distinction came less job security, less compensation, less prestige, and, oftentimes, an inferiority complex, for the Article I judges - hence "Article III Envy."

"What brought it on this time?"

As he spoke, Hanigan reached down to forward the classic Frank Sinatra disc to the next track. Of the diverse selection of CD's in his six-disc changer, which included several obscure independent label metal releases, an Irish tenor disc, and a classic Ramones LP, Hanigan felt the Sinatra disc gave him the best chance to set an appropriate, romantic mood.

"Oh, this time it was triggered by someone repeatedly referring to him in an appeal brief as 'the Magistrate,' instead of the Magistrate Judge. He hates that."

"Of course. Who wouldn't?" Hanigan said with sarcasm dripping from his voice.

"And so that led him into his usual diatribe about how they should change the name of his position altogether, to dissociate it from any ties to the lowly clerical magistrates under the old system which, of course, bear little resemblance to highly-empowered magistrate judges under the current system who, in reality, can function, for all intents and purposes, as full-fledged district court level trial judges."

"*If* the parties are kind enough to grant them such power," Hanigan added, in reference to the fact that federal magistrate judges can preside over civil trials only if all parties to the lawsuit give their consent, and otherwise are relegated to handling only pretrial matters.

Hanigan was thoroughly amused with Berg's rant. He loved it when she got on a roll and spoke in long, quick rambling sentences without so much as taking a breath.

"I know once I'm out practicing, I will never consent to let him preside over any case I'm handling," Berg said. "And it's not because he isn't a damn good trial judge. It's because I know he'll bend over backwards to avoid any appearance of giving favorable treatment to his former law clerk."

"Isn't there some prohibition against appearing before the judge you clerked for?" Hanigan asked.

"Yeah, but only for the first few years after the clerkship ends. After that, there's no prohibition."

"In my case, Centers would probably take it upon himself to extend that for twenty years, just so he wouldn't have to deal with me," Hanigan joked.

"Aren't those the `Risky Business' sunglasses?" Berg inquired, taking on Hanigan's usual role of shifting the conversation away from work, as she leaned forward to turn the stereo volume down slightly.

"The Rayban Wayfarers," Hanigan began, placing his right thumb and forefinger above and below the right lens of his glasses and deliberately lifting the frames up, before allowing them to drop back down on the bridge of his nose.

"Made famous by John F. Kennedy in the early 60's, brought back into style by Tom Cruise in the 80's, and soon to make another comeback, thanks to yours truly."

In actuality, Hanigan gave very little thought to fashion trends. Truth be told, he had found the glasses on top of a urinal late one night at a Bellevue bar five years ago and had worn them ever since. Most of the rest of Hanigan's wardrobe was put together with a similar lack of forethought.

Berg's question about the sunglasses, in fact, had been posed in hopes of opening up an opportunity for Berg to tactfully suggest a wardrobe makeover for Hanigan. But she apparently decided to take the conversation in another direction.

"JFK, Tom Cruise, and Mike Hanigan - three devastatingly handsome Roman Catholic men of power and influence," Berg chided, tongue in cheek.

"I thought Cruise was a Scientologist," Hanigan said.

"Yeah, but he was brought up Catholic. I'm sure at some point he'll return to the Church. Did you know he thought about becoming a priest?"

"How do you go from considering a life of celibacy to sleeping with some of the most beautiful women in the world?" Hanigan asked rhetorically, trying to visualize the famous actor in a priest's collar.

"When I was a little girl, I thought I wanted to be a nun," Berg offered, looking intently at Hanigan to gauge his reaction.

"No way," came Hanigan's disbelieving reply.

"Seriously. I wanted to be like Sister Eleanor, my second grade teacher at Cathedral Elementary. She was such a neat lady."

"So, what happened?"

"I decided I liked to argue too much."

Hanigan stuck his lips out and nodded his understanding. "I can see that," he said.

"Pretty much from fifth grade on, I've known I wanted to be a trial lawyer."

"I cannot relate to that," Hanigan confessed earnestly. "I still don't know what I want to be."

"You have so much talent and potential, Mike," Berg stated encouragingly. "I think you could be a tremendous litigator."

"I'm actually fairly content where I'm at." Hanigan shifted in his seat and reached down to turn the volume of the stereo back up slightly, obviously uncomfortable with Berg's compliment and the implied suggestion that he should be doing more than clerking for a bankruptcy judge.

"You and I should recruit a couple other ambitious federal clerks and start a small litigation boutique in Kansas City or Minneapolis or somewhere."

"Do you have any idea the amount of work and hassle that would be involved in starting your own shop?" Hanigan asked, thinking through in his own mind all of the reasons why such a move would never make sense for him.

"If I ever decided to practice," Hanigan continued, "I'd probably just go to some mega-firm, work my ass off for a few years, save a bunch of money, then take a year off and chill out somewhere in the tropics."

"All of the big firms are in their hiring cycle right now. I've got four interviews next month. You should get your résumé out there," Berg offered.

"See that exit there?" Hanigan was gesturing with his right hand toward a green highway sign which read 'McPaul Thurman.' "That' s the exit for Crystal Lake. Outstanding party spot, with the exception of the occasional nasty shard of broken beer-bottle glass in the sand."

Berg, visibly frustrated with Hanigan's attempt to sidetrack the conversation, looked towards the exit.

"Mike . . ."

"We'd take a 16-gallon keg over there, start a bon-fire on the beach, and party all night. Sometimes even skinny-dip. You ever been skinny-dipping?"

"No, I haven't," Berg huffed, "but you can put that down as one of your outside interests when you update your résumé to send out to all the same big firms I'm interviewing with."

"Jenny, the judge hired me based on the understanding that I would be a *lifetime* clerk. It wouldn't be fair to bail on him after only three years."

"I bet he'd give his blessing in a heartbeat. He has to know he's holding you back."

"Thanks a lot," Hanigan's voice betrayed a slight hint of hurt, as he looked away from his passenger, in the direction of the rolling bluffs to the east.

"That's a compliment to you, Mike, not an insult," Berg reached over and placed her left hand on Hanigan's right thigh.

"Let's talk about something else," Hanigan said, dropping his right hand from the lower part of the steering wheel and laying it atop Berg's hand, intertwining his fingers with hers. "You've been dying to see Riverton. So let's talk about what you can expect today."

"Alright, what do you have planned for me?"

"I thought we'd start with a leisurely stroll through Arbor Meadow."

"Okay."

"Stop off at an apple orchard for some home-grown Riverton caramel apples. Spend an hour or so at one of the notable historical sites in the area, then have a few drinks before dinner."

"Sounds great," said Berg, perking up in her seat. "And who are these people we're having dinner with?"

"A friend of mine from high school days and his wife. Brace yourself - he's a preacher at a fundamentalist Christian church in Riverton. But, believe it or not, he's actually a pretty cool guy. He's about the only person I could think of in Riverton who would be able to provide you the kind of stimulating, intellectual dinner conversation you're accustomed to."

"What's his wife like?"

"I've only met her a couple times. I get the sense she's pretty into the wife and mother thing."

"Oh great, we should have a lot in common," Berg commented facetiously.

"Relax, you can always break out your nun story. I'm sure she'll relate to that."

Hanigan turned the Mustang off of the Interstate at the Riverton exit and accelerated westward towards the concrete bridge which extended across the Missouri River, leading into Riverton.

A green highway sign welcomed those crossing the bridge to the "Good Life" in Nebraska, which, for a discerning mind like Hanigan's, carried the implied suggestion that the quality of life in the state the traveler was just leaving must be less than satisfactory.

Chapter 18

"So, how did you two meet?" Jenny Berg asked Troy Sloan and his wife, Darcy, across the cloth-covered table in a dimly-lit Riverton steakhouse, wasting little time after the couples' cordial exchange of pleasantries to probe for the answers that her inquisitive nature always seemed to demand.

"We met while I was in seminary in Tennessee," Troy responded. "Darcy worked in the library there, at the circulation desk. To be honest, I probably wouldn't have graduated without her."

"Oh, Troy," Darcy Sloan replied quietly, looking down at her table cloth, visibly embarrassed by her husband's comment.

"It's true," Troy continued. "I was so clueless in terms of theology. The professors would throw out terms like eschatological hermeneutics and dispensational premillennialism, and I'd go running to the library after class looking for a book to figure out what they were talking about. Darcy was always there to help me."

"That's so sweet," Berg said.

"Sounds a lot like our relationship," Hanigan interjected, glancing at Berg. "Jenny reads these lawsuits filed by psychotic serial killers on death row, and comes running down to my office so my diabolical mind can interpret what they're asking for."

"So, is it true you didn't have a very religious upbringing?" Berg asked Troy, still intent on satisfying the natural curiosity sparked by Hanigan's earlier description to her of Sloan's unlikely path to his current vocation.

"I was raised as a CEO Presbyterian," Troy replied.

"CEO, what's that?" Berg asked.

"Christmas and Easter Only," Troy replied smiling.

"How about you, Jenny?" Darcy Sloan asked. "What's your church background?"

"I'm a practicing Roman Catholic," Berg responded.

"Did you catch that, Troy?" Hanigan asked. "She added the word 'practicing' to distinguish herself from me – the *nominal* Catholic. Yep, that's pretty much my M.O. I'm an attorney, but not a *practicing* attorney. I'm a Catholic, but not a *practicing* Catholic."

"Both of those things can easily be changed," Berg offered, grinning at Hanigan.

"No thanks," Hanigan said curtly. "Ma'am, could I get another drink here?" he asked, raising his empty cocktail glass for inspection by the waitress walking past their table.

"We actually have a fair number of Catholics that attend our church," Troy offered.

"Really?" Berg asked, frowning. "How is that?"

"And Methodists and Lutherans," Darcy added.

"We like to think of our church as non-denominational, open to people from all religious or non-religious backgrounds," Troy explained.

"But technically, we *are* part of the Kansas-Nebraska Baptist Convention," Darcy said, a slightly corrective tone in her voice.

"Yikes, that's scary!" Hanigan said loudly, throwing his hands up in the air. "That's like one step away from snake handlers and tongue speakers."

"Mike," Berg lightly scolded, in a manner that suggested she was not completely in disagreement with the gist of Hanigan's comment.

"No, that's fine," Troy said. "That kind of reaction is exactly why we changed our church name from Covenant Baptist to Covenant Community. 'Baptist' is a negative buzzword that turns off a lot of spiritual seekers. Back in the day, I know I never would have set foot in a Baptist church."

"But we hold fast to the core Biblical beliefs of the Baptists," Darcy explained.

"To the Baptists!" Hanigan said, raising his just-acquired vodka tonic in a mock toast, before taking an enormous first gulp of the clear liquid.

"So, then, does that mean you don't believe in infant baptism?" Berg asked, leaning forward over the table intently.

"Uh-oh, here we go," Hanigan said, leaning back away from the table, drink in hand. "Never discuss religion or politics at dinner," he murmured.

"We have something similar to that. We call it baby dedication," Troy stated, seemingly ignoring Hanigan's admonition. "But we do also practice baptism by immersion for adults."

"Well, as I recall it, our catechism teaches that infant baptism is necessary for the remission of original sin," Berg stated.

"Hey, speaking of original sin," Hanigan said in a hushed tone, lunging abruptly forward with his one free hand cupped to the side of his mouth. "Do you see Carl Talbot standing over there by the bar?"

"Sure," Troy replied, after glancing behind him in the direction of the restaurant's lounge area. "In the short-sleeve black shirt. He manages this place."

"Did you guys know he's running a little prostitution ring out of one of his family's motels?" Hanigan whispered.

"You're kidding," Troy said, leaning in closer to the table.

"I shit you not," Hanigan replied, raising the volume of his voice slightly.

"The Orchard Inn, south of town. They call it the *Ho*-tel." Hanigan looked over at Darcy to see if his comment had its designed effect.

"That's only a few blocks away from the church," Darcy gasped. "That can't be true."

"First-hand testimony from satisfied customers says it is," Hanigan said, hitting his drink one more time.

"I knew the Talbots were having some financial troubles, but I have a hard time believing they could sink to that level, especially with Richard holding such a high-profile position at Trees Are Forever," Troy offered.

"What kind of financial troubles?" Hanigan asked.

"Who's Richard?" Berg asked, almost simultaneously with Hanigan's query.

"Richard Talbot, Carl's older brother," Troy said, opting to answer Berg's question first. "He's the Executive Director at the Trees Are Forever Foundation. Their mom, Gladys Talbot, was on the Board there for years, but she passed away a little over a year ago."

"The story is," Sloan continued, "when she died, she funded some kind of trust with a ton of money, which could be gifted to the Foundation, but only if Richard was named the director. And sure enough, he got the job."

"What kind of financial troubles?" Hanigan persisted.

"Last year, after Gladys died, the motels and this place were on the verge of being foreclosed on by some big Omaha bank, but my dad's bank stepped in and refinanced their whole operation," Troy answered.

"That's strange," Hanigan offered. "The old lady had enough money to buy her son into the top spot at TAFF, but couldn't operate her businesses in the black."

"That story about why Richard got the director position is just a rumor," Darcy said. "Troy shouldn't have said anything about it."

"You're right, Darc," Troy responded, a hint of shame in his voice.

"What do you think old daddy Ted would do if he knew his borrowers were running a *Ho*-tel on bank-financed property? You suppose his loan documents have a no-prostitution clause in them?" Hanigan joked, as he sucked back another mouthful of mixed drink.

"If it's true, it would probably cost Charlotte Talbot her job at the bank," Troy surmised.

"That's right, I forgot she worked over there," Hanigan replied.

"Charlotte is Richard Talbot's wife," Troy explained to Berg, anticipating her next question. "She's a loan officer at the bank that my dad owns here in town."

"You think she had anything to do with convincing Ted to bail out the Talbot businesses?" Hanigan asked.

"Honey–," Darcy interrupted, in a tone that implied she was not pleased with the direction of the conversation and did not want her husband to answer the question.

"I think so, but really don't know for sure," Troy responded, seemingly resigned to abide by his wife's desire to end that topic of discussion.

"So, if old Ted finds out a bunch of skanks are turning tricks at the *Ho*--tel, Charlotte's ass is grass," Hanigan said, not willing to let the topic die.

"Actually, the sad reality is, as long as they stay current on their loan payments, my dad probably couldn't care less how they do it," Troy said.

"Oh, here comes our food," Berg said, looking at the waitress coming up behind Hanigan with a large tray weighted down with a half-dozen large and small plates and dishes.

"The *Ho*-Tel kinda fits in perfectly with your whole Riverton spiritual oppression theory, Troy," Hanigan offered, unfazed by the food server's presence at their table. "You should run that one past Jenny."

"Spiritual oppression?" Berg asked.

"Yeah," Hanigan continued, "Troy thinks Riverton is under a voodoo curse from back in the pioneer days. The hookers at the *Ho*-Tel are probably direct descendants of the women that used to work in the cowboy whorehouses, right Troy?"

"Michael," Berg said in a stern motherly tone, embarrassed for herself, the Sloans, and the waitress finishing up her delivery of the evening's cuisine.

"That's okay," Troy said. "But it has nothing to do with voodoo. It's more of a generational thing. The whole Biblical concept of "sins of the father" being borne by subsequent generations. I just look at Riverton's history and see a lot of obstacles to spiritual enlightenment."

"With God, all things are possible," Darcy added, apparently attempting to encourage her husband.

"And with A-1 steak sauce, the natural flavors of this sirloin spring to life," Hanigan said, raising a chunk of sauce-drenched meat to his lips with his fork.

Chapter 19

"Jackpot!" the mustachioed deputy nicknamed Cheese shouted from a back room deep inside the basement of the florescent-green Kellogg house.

Judge Harold Sherman, the aging, good-natured state district judge with jurisdiction over Apache County capital cases, had been in a particularly chipper mood earlier that day when County Attorney Roy Peterson made his request for a search warrant, and the judge had issued the warrant without hesitation, based largely on a confidential-information affidavit from Sheriff Bill Rogge.

Steve Fletcher had since co-opted two of Rogge's deputies to assist with the search, one of whom had apparently stumbled onto an interesting find.

"Fletch, come check this out!"

The deputy was standing with his hands on either side of the door frame which led into the small, dank room, craning his neck and head out into the filthy, cluttered, roach-infested open area of the house's unfinished basement, trying to project his voice up the staircase ten feet away.

After several seconds, he saw Fletcher's scuffed tan cowboy boots hurriedly hopping down the unpainted wooden steps.

"What'cha got, Cheese?" Fletcher asked, grabbing with one hand the rusted metal support post at the base of the stairs and spinning around 180 degrees to head in the direction of the deputy.

"You ain't gonna believe this." The deputy's eyes widened as he spoke. He moved aside to allow Fletcher access into the room.

"Jesus H. Mahogany, what the hell is all this?"

Fletcher gawked around the cramped musty room at several pieces of slightly rusted, industrial-size butchering equipment, accented by all sizes and types of hand-held saws, knives, blades, and other cutting implements, some sitting on rickety make-shift plywood shelves protruding from the walls, some hanging directly on rubber wall-hooks, and some dangling from long nails driven into the cross boards of the room's low eight-foot ceiling.

"Look at the floor," the deputy pointed down at their feet, drawing Fletcher's attention to the dark smooth concrete they were standing on, which was virtually covered in reddish-brown splotches and streaks.

"Something tells me that ain't ketchup," Fletcher said, squatting down to take a closer look and running his right index finger along a section of the smooth concrete that was heavily spattered with the reddish substance.

"If we can't find the murder weapon in here, we ain't ever gonna find it," Cheese offered, as he eyed several of the knives along the wall shelves, some of which bore red spots on their blades similar in appearance to the splatter marks on the floor.

"We need to get a forensics team down here to pull samples off all this stuff," Fletcher stated.

"You want me to make a call," Cheese asked.

"Got 'em on speed dial. Thanks anyway, Cheese," Fletcher replied, as he stepped out of the butcher room to check the signal on his cell phone.

After making the necessary calls to arrange for the forensics testing, Fletcher returned to the spot he had been searching when the deputy had beckoned him to the basement – Terry Kellogg's bedroom.

The walls of Kellogg's living quarters were sponge-painted with an ominous-looking mix of black, dark metallic silver, and red colors, and there were dozens of downward-rolling streaks where the droplets of red paint had apparently rolled out from the sponge and down the wall - so many that Fletcher assumed it had to have been an intended result rather than simply a sloppy paint job. The red streaks, some longer than others, gave the appearance of dripping blood.

A number of occultic-like symbols were crudely drawn or carved over the top of the layer of paint, but were badly faded, either from the passage of time or from an attempt to rub or buff them off the wall.

Strewn atop Kellogg's badly abused wooden dresser and chest-of-drawers were a number of what appeared to be abstract, black and dark-blue melted-wax sculptures which, similar to the walls, had rolling droplets of dried wax streaking down them.

Fletcher took a step towards the dresser for a closer examination of the sculptures, kicking aside with his boot a small pile of candy wrappers and Mountain Dew cans clustered in that particular area of the uncarpeted, unstained wooden floor.

As he looked up from the trash, Fletcher noticed for the first time the head of a mannequin perched atop a small triangular shelf high in the corner of the bedroom to Fletcher's left. The mannequin was wearing a magician-style black top-hat and a black and yellow checkered scarf around its neck. It appeared to have two small Christmas-tree light bulbs jammed inside its eye sockets, one red and one a bluish or greenish tint.

Intrigued, Fletcher walked around Kellogg's stripped-down, badly stained single mattress and into the corner where the mannequin head was situated. A black power cord extended down from the back base of the mannequin's neck and into an electrical wall socket several feet below the triangular shelf. The cord had not been visible from Fletcher's prior vantage point, as it was perfectly camouflaged by the dark sponge-painted backdrop of the wall and the wall socket cover, also painted black.

Fletcher reached up to roll the switch on a small black box located halfway up the power cord. As he did, red and blue light shot from the eyes of the mannequin.

"That's different," Fletcher thought to himself.

Juxtaposed against these dark, bizarre items of decor was an 8½ by 11 inch soft-light color portrait of the face of Jesus Christ, tacked to the wall next to Kellogg's nightstand. The eyes of the painting serenely gazed in the direction of the bed, as if prepared to watch over its occupant.

On top of the nightstand was an open Bible, with crisp white pages, suggesting it was of relatively recent vintage. One of the two pages to which the book was open bore an extra-thick blue ink-pen line under one of the passages.

Fletcher dropped his eyes down to read the underlined verse from the Book of Job: "She treats her young harshly, as if they were not hers; she cares not that her labor was in vain."

Fletcher picked up the Bible and shuffled through the pages using his right thumb.

He noticed a number of other underlined passages and decided it was worth seizing the book as possible evidence.

Fletcher cradled the book in his left hand and walked out the door into the hallway. As he did, he glanced back over his shoulder for one last look at the bedroom.

With its strange mix of occultic and Christian adornments, the room had a very schizophrenic feel to it.

Having failed to turn up any hard evidence from the bedroom, aside from what little circumstantial value there was in Kellogg 's apparent fascination with decapitated mannequin heads,

Fletcher sauntered out into the dining area on the first floor of the house.

He spied a messy collection of papers atop a dusty antique roll-top desk, which appeared to be bank statements and check ledgers. The bank documents were in the name of Terry's mother, Bernice.

Fletcher was aware that Bernice Kellogg had worked as an office assistant in the Riverton Post Office most of her adult life. He presumed that she had provided the only steady stream of income to support the hordes of albino progeny who called the glowing green house their home, since Henry, the family patriarch, was less than stable mentally.

Fletcher picked up a bank statement from the pile and began perusing it. He recognized that Ms. Kellogg's financial records were outside the scope of the search warrant and that he would be unable to seize any of the documents, but he saw no harm in at least looking.

The statement reflected bi-weekly deposits into the account, like clockwork, in the amount of $1,288.67, from the U.S. Treasury, which Fletcher rightly assumed were for Bernice's postal employee wages.

Fletcher flipped through the succeeding pages of the bank statement, quickly scanning the contents, until he reached the July entries, when an entry on July 13 jumped out and grabbed his attention.

The entry reflected a deposit into the account in the amount of $8,000.00 even. Next to the amount was a reference to a "Nathan Reynolds, VIP."

Fletcher wondered what Bernice possibly could have done or sold to garner such a sizeable payday.

He pulled the notepad from his shirt pocket and set it down on the rolltop desk, next to the bank statement, and he quickly jotted down the date, amount, and name into his case notes.

Chapter 20

"Do you wanna try my latest drink concoction?" Mike Hanigan called to Jenny Berg, as he stood in front of an open refrigerator in the kitchen of his downtown Omaha apartment. "I call it Vanilla Vice."

"What's in it?" Berg answered, from her spot on the off-white cashmere love seat in the open living area of Hanigan's apartment.

"Vodka and Vanilla Coke," Hanigan replied.

"Eww. No thanks. Do you have any V-8?" Berg asked.

"You know, at the risk of jinxing our relationship, I did actually pick you up a six pack of it on my last grocery run," Hanigan responded.

"That was thoughtful of you."

"But you can't break up with me until it's all gone. Otherwise, it will be in my fridge until the next millennium."

Hanigan peered over the bar-style kitchen counter, out into the living area, holding a Vanilla Coke in one hand and a V-8 in the other.

As he kicked the refrigerator door closed with his right foot, he lifted the hand which held the vegetable drink.

"How do you drink this garbage?" Hanigan asked.

"It's an acquired taste. Do you know that in every eight-ounce can of V-8, there is 40% of your daily Vitamin A and 100% of your Vitamin C?"

"All I know is it tastes like a celery smoothie and causes an automatic gag reflex the second it hits my taste buds?" Hanigan offered, as he poured the drinks into short, clear square glasses.

"That's lovely," Berg replied.

Hanigan strolled back into the living area, drinks in hand, and slid into the love seat next to Berg.

The screen of Hanigan's laptop computer, sitting on the coffee table directly in front of him, had gone dark for want of activity.

In order to convince Berg to make her Monday-evening visit to the apartment, Hanigan had reluctantly agreed that he would work on some court-related matter, while Berg finished her own after-hours work project. Berg wanted assurance that she could complete her work that evening and assumed that if Hanigan was engrossed in his work project, she could make that happen.

However, Hanigan had never before worked at home during non-business hours, and he was seemingly trying to find as many diversions as possible, either to make the experience more palatable or perhaps to avoid doing the work altogether.

"We need some music," he said, pulling a quick first sip from his mixed drink and standing back up again.

"It has to be something mellow, and preferably instrumental only, so I can focus on my work."

Berg was staring intently at the screen of her own computer, which was positioned squarely on her lap.

"Sorry to disappoint, but I think I left my Yanni disc in the car," Hanigan cracked, as he made his way to the apartment's state-of-the art sound system.

Judging by her non-response, Berg obviously was doing her best to ignore Hanigan's sarcastic attempt at humor.

Hanigan crouched down to eye the hundreds of CD's in the spiral-shaped metal rack beside his stereo.

"How about some Dizzy Gillespie?" His query went unacknowledged. "Hello."

"That's fine. Whatever."

Berg's attention was locked into the document on her computer screen, and the shortness of her reply was intended to convey a clear message to Hanigan about his incessant interruptions of her train of thought.

Hanigan carefully placed the disc into the sound system and, realizing his guest would not be indulging him in any further conversation for awhile, resigned himself to actually trying to get some work done.

He nestled back into the love seat, took another drink from his glass, and leaned forward slightly, turning his attention to the laptop on the coffee table.

The two silently pecked away at the keys of their laptops for nearly fifteen minutes, with the only sounds in the room being the jazz horn melodies emanating from the stereo speakers and the occasional rattling of half-melted ice cubes in Hanigan's cocktail.

Surprisingly, it was Berg who broke the conversational fast.

"You know, I really enjoyed dinner last night," she said, in reference to their outing with Troy and Darcy Sloan.

"I told you Troy was a cool guy," Hanigan replied, without looking away from his computer screen. "Once you get him off the topic of his kooky church stuff."

"You know what I liked most about him?" Berg asked.

"That he picked up the check for dinner?" Hanigan said as he continued to type.

"No." Berg reached out and put her right hand on Hanigan's left shoulder, as if bracing him for some kind of blow. "He was passionate about what he does."

"Well sure, saving a bunch of ignorant redneck kids from eternal hellfire and damnation is pretty weighty stuff. It's easy to be passionate about that," Hanigan said, seemingly without guilt for mocking his good friend's life-work.

"All I do is help decide how worldly treasures get divided up between the heartless, overreaching creditors and the lazy, dead-beat debtors of the world. Where's the passion in that?"

"I agree," Berg replied, taking Hanigan's facetious comments and using them as a springboard to discuss the theme that seemed to recur whenever she and Hanigan were alone together for more than a half hour.

"You need a much bigger challenge than that," she urged. "You need something that gets your juices going and gives you whatever it is that you're trying to get from that glass of Vanilla Vice."

"A soothing buzz?"

"You know what I mean."

Berg removed her hand from Hanigan's shoulder. Seemingly satisfied that she had made her point, she returned the discussion to the couple's dinner with the Sloans.

"I do think you really crossed the line when Troy was talking about that guy from his church," Berg said.

"What guy?" Hanigan's eyes darted momentarily over in Berg's direction and a puzzled look crept onto his face.

"The guy Troy said was being questioned about the Anna Springer murder."

"Oh, Mr. Albino Amphetamino? What'd I say?"

"You honestly don't remember?" Berg asked, her voice thick with doubt. "You didn't have *that* much to drink."

"I certainly don't remember any line-crossing taking place," Hanigan responded.

"Here he is, telling us that the other minister feels like the guy really made a breakthrough recently and how they can't believe he could have been involved in something so heinous . . .," Berg dropped the tone of her voice into a mock baritone, in an attempt to imitate Hanigan, repeating verbatim his line from the previous night's dinner conversation – "Well, you know what they say Troy, there's nothing like a ritual beheading to bring you to Jesus.'"

"Troy thought it was funny," Hanigan said smiling, partly in remembrance of his off-color remark and partly in response to Berg's comical stab at impersonating him.

"I don't think so," Berg responded. "And I could tell Darcy was mortified."

"Oh, she needs to lighten up," Hanigan said.

Berg pursed her lips, closed up her laptop and placed it deliberately on the coffee table. She then lifted her right leg onto the love seat, turning her body toward Hanigan and looking earnestly at his profile, while he continued to eye the words on his monitor.

"Mike, I've noticed you seem to have real difficulty discussing a serious topic for any significant amount of time."

"That's not true. Remember the serious conversation we had at dinner last night about Carl Talbot and how Ted Sloan's bank had to bail out his businesses to save them from foreclosure?"

"And as I recall," Berg responded, "that whole conversation started because you had to mention the rumor about him making prostitutes available at his motel?"

"In my book, those are *serious* allegations. I wasn't making light of it."

"And, of course, it was necessary to repeatedly mention that the place is known as the *Ho*-tel," Berg said sarcastically, shaking her head as if she was done listening to Hanigan's attempts to rebut her point.

"Honestly, Mike, I can't believe you're not spending more time trying to figure out why that guy is involved in your Cayman car case."

"I only do what's necessary to dispose of the matters that are *actually pending* before the court. I'm not like you, I don't run out and conduct my own independent factual investigation of every case that comes in. It's the lawyers' job to make the factual record. It's our job to research the law and apply it to the facts in the record *as it is*. Not as it should be. How many times has Judge Bartlett chastised you about trying to play Nancy Drew with the facts?"

"But aren't you just a little curious? I mean the guy is from your hometown."

"Yeah, I'm a little curious. As a matter of fact . . ." Hanigan paused as he used his right index finger to direct the computer cursor to a different document minimized on his screen,

"I was just doing some research on how the Board of Directors for the Cayman company was appointed."

Hanigan ran his finger down the screen, looking for the language he had read earlier that evening.

"Let 's see . . . there it is. One third of the Board's twelve members were nominated and appointed by the car dealerships who are part of the risk retention group. The pool that appointed Carl Talbot to the Board is made up of mostly Trianta and Hirabishi car dealers in the Omaha metro area."

"Why would reputable car dealerships nominate a guy with a struggling small-town motel and restaurant business who might be involved in illegal activities?" Berg asked thoughtfully.

"Maybe it was some form of barter transaction like . . . oh, I don't know . . . Hirabishis for hookers."

"There you go again, taking a serious conversation and trying to derail it."

Hanigan shrugged his shoulders, as if admitting guilt as charged, and swallowed the last of his drink from the square cocktail glass. "Or Triantas for tricks," he added.

"Let's run a Google search on him," Berg said, ignoring Hanigan's comment, as she dropped her foot back down to the floor for leverage and leaned hard into Hanigan, bumping him with her hips, in an attempt to make room for herself.

She reached over to type on Hanigan's laptop keyboard.

"Carl Talbot. Trianta. Hirabishi. Let's try that." Berg spoke the words as she typed them. She hit the Enter key and waited.

Within seconds, the results of the search appeared on the screen.

"A-ha. We got three hits," she said, as she clicked open the first selection. "That's nothing."

She ran her finger along the mouse pad, up to the "Back" button, clicking once, then clicking again on the second selection. "This one references a Richard Talbot. Isn't that the brother?" Berg asked.

"That would be him," Hanigan replied in the affirmative.

"The one who got the head honcho position at the tree place because his mom donated a ton of money," Berg recalled.

"So the story goes." Hanigan gestured toward the computer screen.

"Look, this article talks about the Trianta Motor Corporation making a substantial grant to Trees Are Forever last year," Berg said. "Interesting. So the car manufacturer is giving money to one brother's non-profit foundation and the car dealerships are putting the other brother on the board of a private company that insures car repair claims. What's in it for Trianta?"

"I won't repeat my theory," Hanigan said gently, his mouth only a few inches from Berg's right ear, "for fear of being lectured again." He planted a soft kiss on her neck.

Berg tilted her head slightly away from Hanigan, in a half-hearted attempt to resist his affections and to continue reading the article.

"It looks like this grant was timed to coincide with the release of the Trianta Envi, because it says Trianta gave the Foundation a brand new Envi, one of the first ever manufactured, in addition to the grant money. Isn't that supposed to be an environmentally-friendly vehicle? One of those hybrids? Mike, let's think about this."

"I won't get to see you for five days," Hanigan said, in reference to Berg's impending departure to North Platte, where her judge was to preside over a medical malpractice jury trial. "Let's think about it later."

Hanigan shifted around to face Berg, and moved his lips in for a long, slow deep kiss on Berg's now-parted mouth.

Chapter 21

Mike Hanigan waited at his courtroom table with an unusual amount of eagerness for the morning's court session to begin.

His review of Tuesday's docket sheet had revealed that the only hearing scheduled for that morning arose in the case of the Cayman corporation Hanigan had been researching and featured a match-up of two attorneys whose last meeting in bankruptcy court had been the courtroom equivalent of a back-alley Mexican cock fight. Two proud, strutting roosters figuratively pecking each other to the death, with little regard for any notions of civility or fair play.

The size of the two attorneys' monstrous egos was surpassed only by their seething dislike of one another.

Vince Fiala, the eloquent, lazy-eyed attorney on one side and, on the other, Bartholomew Townsend, the distinguished-looking Yale-educated senior partner in Omaha's oldest, most prestigious law firm, who was deemed by many to be the preeminent authority on creditors' rights and bankruptcy issues in the state.

The prior courtroom exchange between the two had been highly-charged, laced with venom, and thoroughly entertaining to watch.

As Hanigan observed the two attorneys arranging documents at their separate tables, with Townsend talking quietly with a youthful-looking associate seated by his side, Hanigan pulled to mind the fascinating information the judge had shared with him since the attorneys' last courtroom confrontation, regarding the circumstances which led the two to despise each other.

Fiala, some twenty years earlier, had worked as a summer law clerk at Townsend's firm, but had been rejected for an associate attorney position, perhaps due to Fiala's quirky personality, unconventional style, and maybe even his lazy eye.

Townsend, then a young partner at the firm, had chaired the recruiting committee which made the decision to take a pass on Fiala.

It had been that rejection which had fueled Fiala's drive to build his own successful firm, essentially from the ground up, at first handling criminal defense cases, divorces, and any type of bankruptcy matter that walked in the door, but eventually garnering a reputation which permitted him to pick and choose the matters he would undertake, usually significant bankruptcy matters and high-profile criminal defense cases.

Fiala, fully aware of his adversary's Ivy League credentials, went out of his way to demonstrate that his own legal mind, though trained at a second-tier Midwestern law school, was equal, if not superior, to Townsend's.

Fiala discounted Townsend's career success as a byproduct of working at a large, historically-significant firm, and thereby inheriting a deep base of ready-made institutional clients, simply handed to him from the prior generation of creditors' lawyers in the firm. From Fiala's perspective, Townsend never could have succeeded under the circumstances dealt to Fiala.

Hanigan surmised that Townsend's naturally condescending tone and intrinsic air of superiority only served to further stoke Fiala's extreme dislike for his adversary.

Townsend's mutual disdain of Fiala stemmed primarily from Fiala's overt refusal to give Townsend the deference his resume suggested was due him. Other attorneys, judges, and even academicians humbly sought out Townsend's insights on legal issues arising in the creditors' rights area.

Yet Fiala had the gall to hold himself out as Townsend's equal in the area - likely an untenable notion from Townsend's perspective.

On one occasion in the distant past, Townsend had underestimated Fiala's ability and had suffered a humiliating defeat at Fiala's hands, which had eaten bitterly at Townsend in his innermost parts and had provoked him to pull absolutely no punches in all his subsequent dealings with the lazy-eyed attorney.

In conversations with other lawyers, Townsend was always quick to point out that Fiala did not make the cut at Townsend's firm, conveniently failing to mention that nearly twenty years had since passed, like a middle-aged former high school homecoming king passing judgment on a former classmate, condemning him as a life-long loser on the basis of his lack of teenage popularity two decades before.

Ironically, it was Fiala's ability to evoke such nastiness from Townsend which perhaps bothered Townsend more than anything, since he was otherwise a fairly even-tempered man with unflappable self-control. Each time he would "sink to Fiala's level," as he called it, he would vow to never again do so. Yet, when the opportunity would arise again, he would nevertheless find himself exchanging barbs and pointed unpleasantries with Fiala.

As the judge entered the courtroom and the lawyers began with their formal appearances, Hanigan conjured in his mind's eye additional details to further explain the personal animosity between Fiala and Townsend.

Perhaps while clerking for Townsend's firm, Fiala, then a fearless second-year law school student, had made an inappropriate advance at Townsend's lovely young wife at a firm social function. Perhaps during that same time period, Townsend had singled Fiala out with some biting criticism during a law clerk evaluation session, the words of which had never ceased echoing in the chambers of Fiala's mind all these years.

Hanigan's attention was drawn back into the proceedings when Townsend, with his healthy, perfectly-combed head of silver hair and chiseled features, entered his appearance, not only on behalf of Jerry Remlinger, the former University of Nebraska football player and current chairman of Automotive Services Risk Retention, Inc., but also on behalf of Townsend's own law firm – Bradshaw, Evans, Hargrove & Jones, LLP.

Hanigan could not recall ever seeing an attorney appear as a representative of his own firm. That novelty only added to Hanigan's already keen interest in the hearing.

"Mr. Fiala," Judge Centers said, turning his head in the direction of the lazy-eyed attorney, "the provisional liquidators have filed a motion seeking turnover of property allegedly located in this jurisdiction. Is that correct?"

"Yes, Your Honor," Fiala replied forcefully, as he rose to his feet, shooting a quick glare at Townsend.

"Eighteen days before the liquidation proceeding was commenced in the Cayman Islands, Mr. Jerry Remlinger, the President and Chairman of the Board of the debtor company, purportedly acting on behalf of the company, transferred $1.4 million of the company's cash reserves to Mr. Townsend's law firm," Fiala asserted. "We have reason to believe that those funds remain on deposit in the firm's trust account."

Fiala removed his reading glasses with his right hand and continued with his argument.

"At the time the transfer was made, the corporation was insolvent. Under the governing Cayman law, which derives from the British common law, because the company was insolvent, the directors of the company owed a fiduciary duty to creditors of the company to manage the assets of the corporation in the best interests of the creditors."

Fiala took a step out from behind the table, towards the center of the courtroom, and pointed firmly with his left hand in the direction of Townsend's table.

"Mr. Townsend's client and the other directors of the corporation, breached that fiduciary duty by transferring these funds to advance their own personal interests. The funds are clearly property of the liquidation estate and should be disgorged by Mr. Townsend and his firm and returned to the estate's account in the Cayman Islands."

"Mr. Townsend?" the judge said, without facial expression, looking towards the table where the distinguished bankruptcy attorney was seated.

"Yes, thank you your honor," Townsend replied, fastening the top button of his jacket, as he stood to address the Court.

"What Mr. Fiala neglected to mention is that, pursuant to a provision in the company's bylaws, the directors and officers are entitled to indemnification from any suits commenced against them in their official capacities. Because the company never acquired an errors and omissions insurance policy to cover that expense, it is required to self-insure the obligation."

Townsend cleared his throat before continuing.

"Several months before the liquidation proceeding was commenced, the entire Board of Directors of the corporation passed a resolution authorizing the establishment of a defense fund to cover litigation expenses incurred by the directors, officers, and other key employees of the company, arising from the performance of their official duties for the company. The subsequent transfer of the funds to my firm's trust account was simply carrying into fruition the will of the Board, as expressed in the prior resolution."

Townsend cleared his throat yet again.

"Mr. Fiala surprisingly was right about at least one thing. The funds are on deposit in my firm's trust account. They are intended to cover anticipated attorney's fees and costs to be incurred by the directors and officers, including Mr. Remlinger, in defending a number of lawsuits commenced against them in their individual capacities in various state and federal court proceedings in this jurisdiction and elsewhere."

The distinguished lawyer paused momentarily, as he flipped over the page of notes sitting atop the counsel's table.

"And my clients are prepared to argue the merits of this matter. But before doing so, we believe there are a number of procedural defects with this proceeding that must be addressed."

"Mr. Fiala's clients, while maintaining the ruse of ongoing negotiations, and with full knowledge that my client's Cayman Islands' attorney had departed on a three-week vacation, initiated this litigation by a quote 'emergency' motion, rather than following the prescribed procedure of commencing an adversary proceeding and serving my client with a summons and complaint."

"On that issue, Your Honor, we would offer the Affidavit of Nigel Crumb, my client's Cayman counsel, who had been representing Mr. Remlinger in his negotiations with the provisional liquidators regarding the defense fund."

As the affidavit was being marked as an exhibit by the judge's court reporter, Hanigan pulled up an electronic copy of the document on his courtroom computer screen and quickly scanned the content.

Reading the affidavit, he chuckled quietly, as he could almost audibly hear a high-brow British barrister making the pronouncement contained in the document that, when the attorney left for his three-week vacation, he assumed that "everything was rosy in the garden" concerning his negotiations with the liquidators over the defense fund.

"Your Honor," Townsend continued, "with respect to the merits of this matter, we would additionally offer the Affidavit of Marilyn Beecham, the corporate secretary of the company. Attached to Ms. Beecham's Affidavit is a copy of the corporate resolution which authorized the creation of the defense fund."

Fiala jumped to his feet.

"Judge Centers," he barked, "the provisional liquidators object to the Beecham Affidavit on foundational grounds and as to the authenticity of the purported Resolution."

Fiala raised the volume of his voice even higher as he continued.

"We have reason to believe that the Resolution was actually back-dated in an attempt to avoid the determination that the transfer was made while the company was insolvent."

"Your Honor," Townsend responded indignantly, "in anticipation of Mr. Fiala's unfounded objections, we are prepared to put on live testimony from the corporate secretary, as to the foundation and authenticity of the document. Ms. Beecham is available by telephone from the Grand Caymans."

"Very well," Judge Centers stated calmly. "Let's take a short, five-minute recess, and I'll have my courtroom deputy make the necessary phone connection."

Hanigan was grateful for the break in the action, as it afforded him a much-needed opportunity to empty his coffee-filled bladder.

Chapter 22

Steve Fletcher's truck was having difficulty deciding which gear to settle on as it churned up the incredibly steep grade of Carnegie Hill, in the easternmost section of Riverton.

Fletcher had never been to San Francisco, but he imagined this hill could hold its own with any that city had to offer. He also surmised that, with the possible exception of certain regions of Appalachia, this part of Riverton had to be unrivaled in its percentage of homes which sported old, beat-up household appliances and rusted, junked-out vehicles in their yards.

As the truck chugged to the crest of the hill, Fletcher pulled over to the side of the street and reached over for the small stack of documents clipped together on the passenger seat, which had been handed to him that morning by the office secretary at the Apache County Sheriff's Office.

The first document on the stack contained the address for Jackie Howell's residence and an internet map pinpointing its location. Fletcher held the map one way, then the other, tilting his head in the opposite direction each time he did so.

Though he had been to this area before, it had never dawned on him that none of the streets ran due east and west or north and south, but rather were all running at forty-five degree angles, most likely parallel to the sharp southeasterly bend of the river. Fletcher wondered if that was the reason for the streets' designations as Terraces and Rues. He peered out through the windshield, looking in vain for a street sign upon which to fix his bearings.

Fletcher glanced again at Howell's address on the sheet of paper - 719 6th Terrace.

He tossed the documents back down on the passenger seat and drove forward slowly, craning his neck to the right in search of a street sign, finally spotting a skinny green sign with white letters, advising him that he was on 4th Terrace.

He hung the next available right and made his way two blocks southwest to Howell's street.

Using only his right index finger, Fletcher guided the steering wheel to the left, guessing that the 700 block of 6th Terrace was in a southeasterly direction.

On the next block, Fletcher's guess proved correct and he parked the truck on the curb in front a small, well-kept ranch-style gray home bearing the number 719.

Fletcher set his sunglasses in the center console of the truck, and his eyes caught a glimpse of the very top portion of the second document in the stack, sticking up from behind the Carnegie Hill map and bearing the familiar fax transmission line of the State Patrol headquarters in Lincoln.

He pulled the document out from under the map. It had been faxed to the Sheriff's Office late on the previous afternoon by his assistant in Lincoln and contained the biographical information Fletcher had requested on Nathan Reynolds, the generous benefactor identified in Bernice Kellogg's bank statement.

According to the information in the document, Reynolds was a retired, independently wealthy Omaha resident who had the good fortune of buying a fair number of shares of stock in Warren Buffett's corporation, Berkshire Hathaway, in the early 80's and, as a result, had been able to retire at a relatively young age from his management position with a food wholesale business.

The document indicated that, in the fifteen years since his retirement, Reynolds had been deeply engrossed in state and local Republican party politics, providing financial backing for countless successful campaigns.

Certainly $8,000 would not be a big hit to a guy like this, Fletcher thought.

"But why Bernice Kellogg?" he wondered.

The timid postal worker wasn't exactly a mover and shaker on the political scene.

Fletcher believed this tidbit of information certainly warranted some follow-up. He decided to carry the documents with him up to Howell's place.

As Fletcher stood on the small porch area waiting for an answer to the doorbell he had just rung, he took a quick appraisal of the surroundings.

He noticed two mid-size sedans parked in the small home's open-air carport, one of which had several "Riverton High Trailblazers" bumper stickers plastered on its rear.

A row of neatly-organized clay flower pots adorned the ledge in front of a large picture window of the house, each pot with its own distinctive type and color of flowers.

Fletcher glanced down at his watch. He had made arrangements with Howell to meet at this designated time, so she should have been expecting him.

Just as Fletcher started to lean to his right for a quick peek inside the picture window, Jackie Howell opened the front door, wearing the same official Pizza Hut gear from their last visit, sans the white pouch in the front.

"Mornin' Ms. Howell. Say, you got some good-looking flowers out here."

Howell took a step out onto the porch and started pointing at the pots one at a time.

"Those are blue sage, the yellow ones are sawtooth sunflowers, and those over there are white aster."

Howell's tone was noticeably more cordial than during the encounter at the restaurant.

"Come on in," she said.

As Fletcher followed Howell into a tidy, nicely decorated living room, he saw she had another guest. A short-haired woman in her early-40's, wearing a long-sleeved navy blue jogging outfit with double white stripes running down the sides, was seated in an easy chair with her legs crossed in front of her, reading the newspaper.

She looked up at Fletcher from her paper, eyeing him from head to toe with little expression.

"This is my friend, Mikki Buckhalter," Howell said, introducing her guest.

"Hello," the woman said, without getting up.

"Howdy," Fletcher replied. "You're the Riverton volleyball coach, right?"

"And communications-slash-debate instructor, that's right," the guest stated, in a tone that smacked of "yeah, what of it?"

"How's the team looking for this fall?"
Fletcher had never so much as seen a high school volleyball game, and asked the question in a feeble attempt to begin to win the guest over.

"We have four returning starters from last year, two who were all-conference last season. I like our chances." As she spoke, the coach was turning the page of her newspaper.

"Good deal. I'll have to see if I can catch some of your games this year," Fletcher lied, before turning back towards Howell.

"You mind if I have a seat?"

"Go ahead," Howell replied, herself choosing to remain standing.

Fletcher planted himself on Howell's velvety purple couch. "I'm just doing some follow-up on the Anna Springer investigation and . . ."

"I heard you're charging that skinny little asshole with the Doberman," Howell interrupted.

"Actually, Jackie, no formal charges have been filed. We're still pursuing a number of leads." Fletcher said.

"I meant to ask you this last time we talked, but I got sidetracked. Anna's vehicle was parked outside your house at the time her, uh, remains were discovered. If she had left for D.C., do you know why her vehicle would have been left here?"

"She must have driven the TAFF car," came Howell's curt reply.

"The TAFF car?"

"Yeah, the company car she used when she traveled for work."

"Do you know what the make and model on that was?"

"It was a silver Envi. It supposedly got great gas mileage, so they let her use it when she would make her donor visits."

"Donor visits? Anna would visit people who donated to the Foundation?"

"And people they wanted to become donors, yeah, all the time. Especially on weekends."

"That's interesting," Fletcher began, "because when I met with her supervisor at TAFF, she didn't mention anything about that."

"She was making a ton of money doing it, too," Howell continued. "The last few months especially. She was flush with cash."

"Is that right?" Fletcher asked rhetorically. "But you're sure she would drive the silver Envi. The H.R. director and the vehicle-maintenance guy both denied that Anna would have had access to it."

"Well, they're full of shit, because she definitely drove that vehicle. Like I said, especially on weekends."

"Do you know whether she was driving it on July 20?"

"When was that?"

"That was the last day she worked at TAFF."

"I don't know. All I know is, she left her car here, so I assumed she drove the Envi to the airport. Maybe she caught a ride with somebody, I don't know. Probably whoever it was she was screwing."

For the first time during this visit, the sound of emotional agitation had worked its way back into Howell's voice.

"Jackie," the coach stated, in an apparent attempt to calm Howell before her hostility escalated.

"So, Ms. Howell, when was the last time you saw Anna?" Fletcher asked.

"The night before she was supposed to leave for Washington."

"Any idea what date that would have been?"

"It was a weekday, that's all I know. I want to say a Wednesday or Thursday. It was a Wednesday, because it was one week after my birthday."

"What do you remember about that night?"

"She was being real quiet. Not saying much." Howell closed her eyes tight, apparently intent on not allowing Fletcher to see her cry again.

"Does the name Nathan Reynolds mean anything to you?" Fletcher inquired, opening up the manila folder he had brought with him, just wide enough to confirm that he had the right name.

Howell shook her head in the negative, but kept her eyes shut. Not wanting to be the cause of another emotional meltdown, Fletcher turned to Howell's house guest.

"Coach, did you know Anna Springer?" Fletcher asked.

"Sure. She was on my debate team her junior and senior year. She wasn't a particularly gifted orator, but I think her mother really wanted her to learn the art of debating."

"Bitch," Howell interjected, in reference to Phyllis Springer, finally opening her eyes, then looking up towards the ceiling.

The coach flung her newspaper on the coffee table and uncrossed then re-crossed her legs.

"Actually, Jackie met Anna through me, but that's kind of a touchy subject with us."

"Can you tell me a little about that?" Fletcher asked with some trepidation, glancing furtively at Howell, before turning his gaze back to the coach.

"Well, Anna and some of my other debate-team members were over at my house for our team's end-of-season dinner party."

As the coach started to tell the story, Howell darted quickly out of the room.

"And, anyway, Jackie was there, because she and I were dating then. Her and Anna got to know each other through that and, the next thing I knew, they were a couple."

"That had to be upsetting for you," Fletcher said, in as sympathetic a tone as he could muster.

"I was incredibly upset. I felt completely betrayed. But I got over it, and I moved on with my life."

"So, are you and Jackie back together?"

"No. We're just friends. I knew Jackie would be an emotional basket-case over this whole ordeal, and I just thought I'd take the high road, and offer to re-establish our friendship. I want to be there for her."

"That's awfully nice of you," Fletcher looked over his shoulder to see if Howell had returned to the room. She had not.

"When was the last time you saw Anna?"

"That's tough to say. It's been awhile. Probably three or four months ago. I ran into her and Jackie at the bar. It was kinda chilly out that night, so I want to say it was probably late March, early April, something like that."

"How'd that go?"

"It went fine. As soon as I saw them, I left the bar."

"And that was the last time you saw Anna?"

"I believe so."

"Well, I won't take any more of your time," Fletcher said, stretching his long legs as he stood from the couch.

"Tell Jackie I said 'thanks' for meeting with me."

"She's probably in getting ready for work. I think she has to open this morning."

"Alright, then. Well, you have a good one, Coach. And good luck to the team this year."

"Thanks," the coach said, reaching again for the newspaper, apparently expecting Fletcher to show himself out.

Chapter 23

"Vodka tonic, please," Mike Hanigan said, as he slid onto a swiveling stool in the dimly-lit bar area of an out-of-the-way bowling alley on the outskirts of Council Bluffs, Iowa.

The bar was a work-day refuge of sorts for Hanigan, to which he would flee about once a month, usually on particularly difficult Mondays, for an extended lunchtime break, during which he would essentially drink his lunch, but with a side order of deep-fat-fried cheese balls.

The spot was ideal for Hanigan's purposes – a non-existent weekday lunch crowd, a dark bar area with low-key blue lighting, cheap mixed drinks, and virtually no chance of being seen by anyone he knew.

Other than, of course, the fake-baked, bleach-blonde bar matron, whose excessively wrinkled, orangish-brown skin made her look ten years older than her 38 years, and whose low-throated scratchy voice betrayed her twenty-year smoking habit.

"You want lunch, darlin'?" the matron asked, as she stuck a swizzle stick in Hanigan's cocktail.

"If a small order of cheese balls is considered lunch, then yes, I would like lunch."

"I'll get that right in for ya."

"Thanks, hun." Hanigan couldn't resist the temptation to reciprocate with his own overly-friendly pet-name.

It occurred to Hanigan as he removed his sports jacket and draped it over the empty stool to his left, that he had not been to the bowling alley bar since he started seeing Berg.

He wondered if there was any significance to the fact that his sudden urge to spend this Monday noon there coincided with Berg's extended absence, due to her North Platte jury trial running longer than expected.

As Hanigan sucked on his drink, he imagined what Berg would have to say about his imbibing in the middle of a work-day.

Hanigan envisioned himself countering Berg's likely admonition with some clever comment about the rebirth of the three-martini lunch.

Hanigan smiled, realizing that the mere process of considering Berg's probable view on the topic had served to slow him down from the pace at which he normally consumed his liquor.

Even when physically absent, Berg was imposing her forceful will upon the situation.

Hanigan turned his attention to a small television bolted high in the corner behind the bar, just to his left. The techno-trumpet opening music for the Channel 7 News at Noon told Hanigan that he had made the drive from downtown Omaha in less than 13 minutes. To his surprise, the lead story featured fellow Rivertonian, U.S. Senator Phyllis Springer.

Channel 7's peppy, short-haired anchor woman introduced the story, then gave way to pre-recorded footage from a press conference on the footsteps of the majestic State Capitol building in Lincoln.

Standing behind a portable wooden podium, the Senator was sharply dressed in a Cornhusker-red women's business suit, and her blondish-brown hair was pulled back tight behind her head, rolled into her trademark "power bun," as Hanigan liked to call it.

Hanigan placed both of his elbows on the bar and leaned forward, straining to hear the senator's words over the noises emanating from the grill area, which included the sound of his cheese balls sizzling in a vat of hot grease.

"I want to start by thanking all of you who have sent your condolences and heartfelt sympathies to our family during this traumatic time. The level of love and support we have felt has been overwhelming and truly has sustained us through our grief, as we have mourned this terrible loss," the senator stated.

"Let me also say that I have full faith and confidence in the law enforcement officials who have been tasked to investigate this brutal crime. And I trust that they will very soon bring to justice whoever was responsible for this unthinkable and senseless act of violence against my beloved daughter."

The Senator sounded remarkably composed and strident. Hanigan listened intently, but could not hear so much as waver or crack in her voice as she addressed the crowd.

"Upon learning of Anna's tragic death," the senator continued, "my first inclination was to remove from consideration any possibility of pursuing re-election to the Senate."

"However, after many tearful and gut-wrenching hours of careful deliberation and discussion with my family members and closest advisers, I have come to the conclusion that the very best way for me to honor Anna's memory and to work through my own personal grief is to wholeheartedly pursue a third term as United States Senator for the great state of Nebraska."

With that pronouncement, the small crowd assembled in front of the portable podium burst into shouts and applause.

Senator Springer flashed her patented toothy smile and made eye contact with as many of the cheering observers as she could.

She drew closer to the microphone again and cleared her throat over the din of the crowd.

"And I will pursue it with all the vigor and zest for life that my daughter displayed in everything she did. This one's for you, Anna," she added, as she looked upward and subtly pumped her fist in an apparent showing of solidarity with her dead daughter. The roar of the small crowd crew even louder, as the footage ended and the talking-head anchorwoman reappeared on the screen.

The bar matron approached Hanigan, her bronze-colored hand wrapped over the top of a small red-and-white paper basket containing the piping hot breaded balls of cheddar.

Hanigan caught of the whiff of the food and realized he had suddenly lost his appetite.

He requested his check and a small paper bag in which to transport the greasy appetizers.

As Hanigan made his way through the bowling alley parking lot, and climbed into the Mustang for his return drive to the office, he couldn't help but reflect on the way his own mother's death four years earlier had affected him.

Her passing had effectively rendered him a zombie for the better part of three months. Hanigan skipped virtually all of his law school classes that semester, showing up only for final examinations. He rarely left his apartment, except to restock his liquor supply.

Karen Hanigan had been Mike's biggest cheerleader, his primary motivator, and his closest confidante. Those initial months following her death felt like a surreal, colorless dream, void of any real meaning or purpose. And, of course, there was the emotional devastation which continued to ravage Hanigan's father as a direct result of the loss of his soulmate.

Hanigan pondered how Phyllis Springer could muster up the inner strength, less than one month after her daughter's body was cut into pieces and dumped in the river, to begin thinking about embarking on her quest for a third term, in what promised to be a nasty, hard-fought election. He wasn't sure if such a trait was to be admired or pitied.

The thoughts lingered in Hanigan's head as he returned to Judge Centers' chambers.

He stepped inside the chambers' reception area to find the judge standing, with his arms folded in front of him, in his favorite conversation spot, leaning against the doorframe which separated that area from his office, about ten feet from Martha's desk.

Martha was seated, but with her chair turned sideways to face the judge. It sounded to Hanigan as if the two were discussing gardening secrets.

"Did you guys see Phyllis Springer's press conference?" Hanigan jumped into the conversation between sentences.

"I didn't see it, but I heard the sound bites this morning on NPR," the judge responded.

"Can you believe that?" Hanigan asked incredulously.

"Sure," the judge replied. "She's the incumbent. She'll have an excellent chance at re-election."

"I know, but her daughter was just killed, and they haven't even found who did it yet."

"People grieve in different ways, Michael," the judge said.

"That's true," Martha added, nodding her head.

"I just find it a bid odd." Hanigan removed the sunglasses from atop his head and began bending the handles in and out.

"I know you're not big into conspiracy theories, Tom, but there's been some talk in Riverton about the senator possibly having something to do with her daughter's death."

"That's absurd," the judge said, dismissing the notion out of hand.

"Oh, I can't imagine," Martha said, with a troubled look on her face, gently rubbing her hand along the side of her face and gazing up at the judge, as if to confirm to him that she agreed with his negative assessment of the conspiracy theory.

Hanigan took a step towards the judge and proffered the basis for the theory.

"Anna Springer was living an alternative lifestyle that some factions of the Republican Party vociferously oppose. I wasn't buying it at first either, but after watching the senator march through that press conference with no visible sign of emotion, like some kind of political cyborg, I'm starting to wonder."

"Mr. Hanigan, you've been reading too many tabloid articles," the judge used the tone of voice he usually reserved for attorneys who took excessive liberties in making their legal arguments to the Court.

"Well, I suggest you watch the press conference on the news tonight. And when you're watching it, ask yourself, is that how I would respond in that situation? No . . no, strike that, ask yourself, is that how a person with a normal range of human emotions would respond?"

Martha looked up at the judge with a worried expression on her face, perhaps concerned that he wouldn't appreciate Hanigan's comment.

"Touche, Michael," the judge said flatly. "Touche."

Chapter 24

As the early morning sunshine peeked through the half-open blinds in the boxy, off-white eggshell-painted office at the Nebraska State Patrol headquarters in Lincoln, Steve Fletcher looked up from his paper-covered desk, squinted, and shook his jumbo-sized, plastic Kwik Shop coffee mug tersely from side to side, to gauge how much of his breakfast beverage remained.

He noticed that the ballpoint pen he was holding in his right hand had left an inch-long line of blue ink streaked on the cup, just above the red handle. He set the pen down, wet his right index finger with his tongue and began rubbing the line, which only served to smudge it into a thicker, blurrier blue mark.

Fletcher was not so much concerned with the appearance of his 32-ounce plastic mug as he was desperate for a brief diversion from the mountain of paperwork he had been slogging his way through since 5:50 that morning.

His almost-daily trips to Riverton during the past two weeks had caused a backlog of the investigative and summary reports his position required him to complete, and he had hoped that, by coming into Lincoln early, he would be able to get fully caught up before the torrent of the day's activities swept him away.

But the location of the two black metal hands on the round, standard-issue wall clock in front of him informed Fletcher that his hope would not be realized.

Like a cuckoo popping its noisy head out of a clock precisely at the top of the hour, a red-haired, freckled-faced, boyish-looking uniformed patrolman bolted in through the door of Fletcher's office right at 8:00 a.m.

"Steve, did you hear about the body?" the young patrolman asked excitedly.

"Geez, Red," Fletcher said, genuinely startled by the sudden entry, "didn't the Academy teach you to at least identify yourself before you bust down someone's door?"

"Sorry, Steve. I just thought I better get in here and see if you heard the news."

"What news? What body? What are you talking about?" Fletcher's tone suggested that he wanted his uninvited guest to slow down and clearly explain himself.

"I heard on the radio this morning that they pulled the remains of a carved-up female torso out of the Missouri . . ."

"This was on dispatch?" Fletcher interrupted.

"No, the actual radio. A news update during Tyler & Timmo's Morning Zoo on Z-105."

"Nothing like getting your case information from a couple dope-smoking disc jockeys. Did they say where this happened?"

"I guess a state park worker pulled it out just north of Rulo."

The mere mention of the tiny town in the far southeastern corner of the State, just a stone's throw from the Missouri state line, sent a haunting chill down Fletcher's spine.

A farm compound outside Rulo had been the site of Fletcher's very first murder investigation – a double homicide perpetrated by a deranged polygamist cult leader against two of his brainwashed male followers.

The two victims, according to the leader, had fallen out of favor with "Yahweh" and thus deserved the brutal torture the leader and other elders in the cult had inflicted upon them, which included sodomizing them with shovel handles, forcing them to copulate with barnyard animals, shooting off their fingertips with a pistol, slicing off long strips of their skin with a buck knife, and ultimately stomping on their sternums, as the other cult members, including women and children, stood by and observed, at the leader's insistence.

That investigation had caused Fletcher to seriously reconsider whether he had made the right career choice in joining the Patrol. But his mentor at the time, a slow-speaking, easy-going former rodeo cowboy from Western Nebraska, then with 30 years of experience investigating violent crimes, convinced Fletcher that he would never see anything quite as gruesome and inhumane as the Rulo cult slayings.

To date, the mentor's prediction had held true.

"Can you follow up on that, Red, and see where they sent the body for the forensics?" Fletcher asked, gathering up the papers in front of him into a single stack.

"I'll get right on it."

The boyish-looking patrolman bolted out of Fletcher's office with the same sense of urgency with which he had entered.

Fletcher grabbed the black phone console from the corner of his work space and slid it over into the center of the desk, directly in front of him, as he sat in his blue, cloth-backed chair.

Fletcher was scheduled to call Mr. Nathan Reynolds at his Omaha home at 8:15 a.m., but wanted to spend a few minutes jotting down a summary of his thoughts on the Springer investigation to date.

Before Fletcher knew it, the minute hand on the clock had clicked down to the large "3".

Fletcher flipped back to the front page of the State Patrol lined-paper tablet in which he had been writing. He quickly skimmed the written entries and placed a crude three-lined asterisk next to those which had any bearing on the witness he was about to interview.

With that, Fletcher punched the speaker phone button on the phone console, causing the dial tone to blare out into his office. He preferred to have his hands free to fidget, turn pages, and play with his pen while he spoke.

Fletcher dialed the ten-digit number his assistant had provided him and waited for the ring tone. After only one quick ring, a no-nonsense, business-like masculine voice answered the call.

"Nathan Reynolds speaking."

"Good morning, sir. This is Steve Fletcher with the Nebraska State Patrol. My office had set up this interview time with you . . ."

"Yes," the voice answered, sounding eager to get on with the call.

"Is this still a good time for you?"

"If we make it quick. I have another call at 8:30."

"Alright, then. Well, let's get right to it. I was hoping you can help us out with a homicide investigation we're conducting. Do you know a woman named Bernice Kellogg?"

"That name does not sound familiar to me, no."

"Some documentation has turned up suggesting that you recently wrote a check for $8,000 to a Ms. Bernice Kellogg."

"I don't personally write any of my checks. My office has a signature seal they use. And we probably cut a dozen or more checks a day to various candidates and campaigns. I could certainly have one of my assistants look through the check ledger. When did you say the check was issued?"

"I don't believe I said, but it was around mid-July of this year."

"Hmm," Reynolds paused momentarily. "I wonder if that's one of our school-board candidates in the Millard district?"

"Ms. Kellogg is a postal employee down in Riverton, Nebraska," Fletcher stated.

"Riverton, huh? The only possible election we would get involved with there might be City Council, and I doubt that. We don't do a whole lot in the smaller communities?"

"When you say 'we,' who do you mean?" Fletcher asked.

"'We'" in the sense of myself and my organization, 'VIP,' which stands for Values in Politics. We are committed to transforming our society through the political process, by supporting, both politically and financially, candidates with a Christian world view, whose faith infuses and informs their perspective, their ideology, and their agenda. We've been doing that for over ten years now and have made some tremendous strides. We were . . ."

"Sorry to interrupt, Mr. Reynolds," Fletcher said, "but with your other call coming in, we better move this along."

"Certainly," the man answered, as if just pulled off an imaginary soapbox.

"Has your organization ever supported Phyllis Springer?" Fletcher asked.

"Oh heavens no," Reynolds replied with indignance. "From my perspective, Ms. Springer is a Republican in name only. She does not support the rights of the unborn child, she is not a strong advocate for prayer in school, and she has not lent any support to our efforts to reinforce the sanctity of marriage between a man and woman. And she spends far too much time trying to advance the agenda of the environmental extremists."

"So, is it safe to say you will not be supporting her in the next election?"

"Barring a complete transformation of Ms. Springer and her platform, yes, that's a very safe assumption. We have one or two family-friendly candidates who are strongly considering a challenge to Springer for the Republican nomination."

"Are you surprised that she is running, what with her daughter's murder and all?"

"Surprised, no. Disappointed, yes. But, political differences aside, I can certainly sympathize with her loss. My wife and I lost a teenage son to a drunk driver twelve years ago."

"I'm sorry to hear that, sir," Fletcher flipped to the next page of his tablet. "So, you don't recall writing any check to a Bernice Kellogg?"

"Kellogg. Kellogg. Hmm," the man sighed as if deep in thought.

"I think . . ." another brief pause occupied the phone line, "maybe one of the Overcomers I decided to sponsor this year was named Kellogg. But I know it wasn't a Bernice."

"Was it a Terry?"

"Terry Kellogg," the man said with certainty in his voice. "That's it. He's the one who had been involved in the occult and came to faith earlier this summer through the Overcomers program. Very powerful story."

"You're familiar then with that Overcomers deal they have at the Covenant church down in Riverton?"

"Oh I'm very familiar with the program. But it's not limited to any local church. It's a national faith-based program. In fact, I was one of the first participants in the program a number of years ago. It helped me kick a lifelong struggle with alcohol. It probably saved my life physically. And it definitely saved me spiritually."

"So the eight-grand had something to do with putting Kellogg through that program?"

"Oh, it covers a whole lot more than that. Sponsorship involves a holistic approach to recovery that allows participants of little means to get their footing under them, while they're working through their dependency issues. The goal is to replace the negatives with positives. Provide them with funds necessary to get job training, buy work clothes, go back to school, whatever the case may be. The money typically goes to a custodian or trustee of some kind. I'm not sure who this Bernice is."

"That's Terry's mother."

"Well, sometimes if the church or sponsoring agency doesn't have someone who can administer the funds, they will be given to some other responsible party. That must be what happened here. Oop, I'm getting a beep on my line. That must be my other call, a little early I guess. If you have further questions, could I ask your assistant to let my office know, and we'll get something set up?"

"I doubt that will be necessary, but we'll let you know. Thanks for your time," Fletcher responded.

"Your very welcome. Good luck with your investigation."

"Thank you," Fletcher said, but the man had already dropped off the line.

As Fletcher pressed the button to disconnect the speaker phone, he hoped the autopsy of the severed torso would yield some solid leads in the case, since most of the recent supposed leads had provided little meaningful evidence.

The interview with Mr. Reynolds certainly did not seem particularly productive.

And the floor samples taken from the Kellogg butcher room had turned out to be mostly a mix of hog, cow, and venison blood. What minuscule trace of human blood had been picked out was too degraded to produce any DNA evidence. The samples from the hand-held saws in the butcher-room likewise bore no useful evidence.

Fletcher had learned that the butcher equipment previously belonged to Terry Kellogg's uncle, a former butcher at a grocery store in Auburn, Nebraska, twenty miles south of Riverton, and that Terry's father, Henry Kellogg, had staked his claim to the equipment at an estate sale following the uncle's death.

Their lack of any training, formal or otherwise, in the art of butchering animals apparently had not stopped Henry and his eldest son from regularly carving up all sorts of livestock on their own private killing floor in the basement of the neon green home.

Oddly, the thought evoked a sudden craving in Fletcher for a side order of bacon, to satisfy a morning hunger that 32 ounces of convenience-store coffee had failed to quench.

Chapter 25

Mike Hanigan sat in the Cave, putting the finishing touches on a draft Order in the Automotive Services Risk Retention case, which would deny the provisional liquidators' motion for turnover of the defense fund located in the trust account of Bartholomew Townsend's law firm.

The denial would be based on the technical, procedural ground that the matter should have been commenced as a formal adversary proceeding, with the issuance and service of summonses and complaints on Jerry Remlinger and Townsend's law firm, as opposed to simply as an "emergency" motion.

By virtue of the procedural nature of the proposed ruling, it was not necessary for Hanigan to yet dig into the substantive issues revolving around the corporate resolution that purportedly authorized the transfer of the $1.4 million from the Cayman bank account to the Omaha law firm.

Ordinarily, Hanigan would reward himself for completing a project by taking a short coffee break or perhaps pulling out the latest edition of the Weekly World News and reading an article or two.

In this instance, however, something seemed to be compelling him to forge ahead with some independent research on the case.

Hanigan considered whether this unnatural urge was brought on by his recognition that the substantive issues ultimately would have to be dealt with in the certain-to-be-filed adversary proceeding.

Or was it spurred on by Hanigan's desire to know which of the two arrogant attorneys, Townsend or Fiala, would have the upper hand in the next chapter of their ongoing war of attrition? Or was it simply a byproduct of Hanigan's curiosity with the Riverton connection to the case?

Hanigan intentionally failed to consider the fourth and most powerful factor driving him off his normal route of procrastination and work avoidance - the ever-present sound of Jenny Berg's verbal prodding, echoing in the deep recesses of his psyche.

Mike yanked open the top drawer of his beat-up desk, which always squeaked on opening with the uneven sound of metal grinding against wood.

He had been meaning to ask someone from the General Services Administration to fix the noise, but assumed that he would be required to complete a slew of forms to properly make the request, the burden of which would outweigh the annoyance of the occasional high-pitched squeak.

Hanigan pulled out the computer disk which had been received into evidence during the corporate secretary's telephonic testimony at the last hearing in the case.

The disk supposedly contained the official minutes of the Cayman company's board meetings from the past year, plus copies of resolutions issued at those meetings.

Because the key substantive issue in the case dealt with the timing of the resolution authorizing the transfer of funds to Townsend's trust account, Hanigan decided to use an old trick he picked up from the savvy plaintiff's personal- injury attorney for whom he had worked as a law clerk after his second year of law school.

Whenever a defendant's expert witness report would be produced in electronic Microsoft Word format, the plaintiff's attorney would "mine" the report for hidden changes made in earlier drafts of the document, by accessing the secret "Metadata" trail that was often unknowingly left behind in a Word document. By doing so, the plaintiff's attorney would gain valuable insight into the thought process of the expert witness and the defense's lawyer, by seeing the revisions and suggested revisions which led to the creation of the report in its final form.

Hanigan paused briefly and smiled at the thought of his time with the plaintiff's lawyer. It was incredibly unorthodox for someone with a law school class-rank as high as Hanigan's to accept a position with a firm specializing in plaintiff's personal injury work.

However, at the time, Hanigan was still in a funk from his mother's passing and was not inclined to spend his summer chained to a desk in one of Omaha's large "sweatshop" firms, as he had done after his first summer of law school at the highly-regarded 70-lawyer firm known as Frazier Stone.

Ironically, Hanigan felt he had gained far more practical legal knowledge and experience from his time with the plaintiff's lawyer than during his three months cranking out legal memoranda at the Frazier Stone sweatshop.

In addition, the refreshing candor and comedy of the plaintiff's attorney, coupled with the freedom and flexibility the position had afforded him, was just what Hanigan had needed to pull him from the mire of his depression over his mother's death.

Hanigan popped in the disk, pulled up the resolution in question, and began the "mining" process. No prior changes to the resolution were revealed.

Hanigan wondered if the document had been created by a more-recent version of the Word software in which the Metadata glitch had been corrected. Or perhaps the preparer of the resolution was aware of the Metadata issue and intentionally "scrubbed" the document or saved it as a new, separate version, before loading it onto the disk.

Undaunted, Hanigan decided to review the corporate minutes as well.

The document loaded on Hanigan's screen and he quickly scrolled down the pages to simply get a feel for what the document contained.

His quick review revealed three sets of written minutes prepared by the corporate secretary, one for each of the three meetings of the Board of Directors during that calendar year: an annual meeting of the Board in January of that year, and two special director meetings, one on April 12, at which the transfer of the defense fund was purportedly authorized, and one on July 25, at which the decision was made by the Board to place the company into provisional liquidation.

Hanigan also noticed that Carl Talbot was dutifully present at each of the three meetings, at least according to the lists of meeting attendees which the secretary included at the beginning of each set of minutes.

"Three trips to the Caymans in seven months. Nice perk," Hanigan thought to himself.

Hanigan scrolled back up to the top of the document to review in greater detail the contents of the meeting minutes, in chronological order. As Hanigan finished his substantive review of each set of minutes, out of habit, he pulled up the Metadata information.

The fact that the information was, in fact, capable of being "mined" from the minutes, told Hanigan that his concern about the software being impervious to the Metadata issues was not warranted.

The minutes from the first two meetings reflected a few minor, innocuous changes.

However, upon pulling the Metadata on the third set of minutes, something of interest grabbed Hanigan's attention.

In the list of those present at the July 25 meeting, at which the Board had resolved to throw the corporation into a provisional liquidation, a revision had been made to remove the following language from the list of attendees at the top of the document: "Mr. and Mrs. Richard Talbot, guests of Board member Carl Talbot, entered the meeting room briefly, then departed."

The final, official version of the minutes from that special meeting made absolutely no mention of the presence of the elder Talbot brother and his banker wife.

Hanigan recalled the corporate secretary's testimony, during which she described in painstaking detail the procedure followed in the preparation of the corporate minutes: during each board meeting, she would take handwritten notes detailing the proceedings; after each meeting, she would type the first draft of the minutes and would route electronic copies of the minutes, by email, to the board members, for their review and comments; upon receipt of any such comments, the secretary would then revise the minutes and forward the newly-revised version to the Board again, for final approval; she would print a hard copy of the minutes and any resolutions for the corporate notebook; and the minutes and resolutions would be saved on a disk.

Hanigan wondered if this particular change had been made at the specific request of one of the directors. He also wondered why the executive director of a tree-planting non-profit and the vice president of a Nebraska banking institution would have been in attendance at a special meeting of the Cayman company's board.

Had they just tagged along as family members for a free trip to the Carribbean or was there some legitimate business reason that justified their presence?

And why had the reference to their names been stricken?

Hanigan decided to probe further, with an email to Troy Sloan.

While Hanigan was badly missing Berg during her now weeklong absence from Omaha, part of him was glad she wasn't around to get any satisfaction from seeing him take on some of Berg's meddlesome, overzealous research tactics.

Hanigan banged out the content of the email, ran a spellcheck, and quickly re-read the content.

Troy,
Thanks again for dinner on Sunday night. Jenny and I had good time. I felt a little guilty letting a poor downtrodden minister pick up the tab for two bigshot attorneys. But my

guilt since has been relieved by an assumption that you'll somehow find a way to raid the trust fund your old man set up for you before you found religion.

Hey, I've got a favor to ask of you. I'm doing some sleuthing on that Cayman case I mentioned during dinner. It looks like Charlotte Talbot and her hubby may have been at a board meeting in the Caymans on July 25. Would you have any way to find out why Charlotte was down there?

I know you and Ted aren't exactly on the greatest of speaking terms, but I thought you might have an "in" with some of his minions at the bank from your junior high days as a gopher over there. If not, don't worry about. Just thought I'd ask.

Take care.
Mike

Hanigan paused momentarily, trying to decide which philosopher to reference in closing out the email.

He recalled a quote that Berg had emailed him a week before, and clicked over to cut and paste it into his correspondence to Sloan:

"A man is a success if he gets up in the morning and gets to bed at night, and in between he does what he wants to do." - Bob Dylan

Hanigan thought the quote was an appropriate way to insure that his "poor downtrodden" comment was not taken by Sloan as some form of back-handed dig at his daily work in the ministry. If Sloan was happy doing it, more power to him, Hanigan thought.

Chapter 26

As the shrill ring of an old rotary-style phone pierced the darkness of Steve Fletcher's bedroom, he lurched reflexively toward the nightstand by his king size bed, mistaking the ring for the beeping of his bedside alarm.

Fletcher made several clumsy, flailing attempts to hit the alarm's snooze bar, turn the alarm off, or otherwise stop the invading noise. He was still fumbling with the alarm when he heard Connie's groggy voice.

"Hello," she said, having answered the phone, which sat on the nightstand beside her side of the bed.

Fletcher squinted at the bright red numbers on his alarm clock and made out a "12" followed by a "38."

"Yeah, hold on Bill, I'll get him."

Connie passed the phone in Fletcher 's direction as she crashed her head back down on the large black Elvis Presley pillow she had slept on as long as Fletcher had known her.

"It's Bill Rogge," she said, sounding as if she had already fallen back asleep.

"Yeah, Bill," Fletcher answered, clearing the nighttime accumulation of phlegm from his throat.

"You can close the case, Fletch," said Rogge excitedly, dispensing completely with the apology that customarily would lead off any telephone call placed at that hour of the morning.

"Kellogg confessed to someone and I just got their written statement. With all the gory details."

Fletcher could not recall Rogge being this elated since the time he pulled an 18-inch bass from a lake down in central Kansas some five years before.

"Who'd he confess to?" Fletcher asked.

"The kid's name is Cale Bates. He was in AA with Kellogg and they was walking home one night after a meeting. Kellogg spilled it all to him."

"Where you at right now?"

"I'm still at the station."

"You gonna be there a while?"

"I ain't going nowhere."

"I'm driving down. I'll see you shortly."

Fletcher rolled out the side of the bed, clad only in a pair of white Fruit of the Loom briefs. He shuffled slowly toward the closet, his arms slightly outstretched, as if anticipating a collision with something in his path.

As he felt blindly for the handle to his closet, finally pulling it open, he heard Connie in the background, thrashing in the bed.

"Where you goin', Steve?" she asked, her voice still groggy.

"We got a break in the case. I gotta head to Riverton."

"Drive careful."

Connie rolled over and buried her head in the pillow, in the general vicinity of the young Presley's trademark high cheek bones.

Upon his arrival at the Sheriff's office in Riverton, Fletcher found Rogge seated at his desk, eyeballing several stapled sheets of slightly-crumpled paper before him.

Rogge looked up, his eyes puffy and slightly red from fatigue, and handed the sheets to Fletcher.

"Here it is, Fletch. It's all in there. Everything we need."

Fletcher grabbed the sheets and, leaning the weight of his thighs against Rogge's desk, began poring over the messy, handwritten statement, replete with misspelled words, which reminded him of something his son, Jason, would have written.

The statement indicated that the author, Cale Bates, was in the Overcomers program at Covenant Community Church, for an addiction to methamphetamine, where he came to know Terry Kellogg.

Following a group meeting on an evening in mid-August, Bates accompanied Kellogg and his Doberman as they walked toward home. Seemingly out of the blue, Kellogg asked Bates if he could keep a secret.

Kellogg then told Bates that God had already forgiven him for what he was about to describe, but he wanted to tell someone as part of his recovery.

According to the statement, Kellogg proceeded to tell Bates the specifics of the crime.

At the end of a workday, Kellogg waited behind the row of tall bushes which lined the parking area reserved for TAFF's upper management. Just as Springer climbed into the company's silver Trianta Envi, Kellogg and Lucy moved in on the vehicle and forced their way into the passenger side, with Kellogg immediately placing the sharpened nail tip of his garbage poker-stick in Springer's abdomen.

He shoved Lucy up and over into the back seat, between the narrow space that separated he and Springer. Kellogg ordered

Springer to shut up and to drive the vehicle slowly down the rough, bumpy, two-track dirt maintenance road that led out the backside of the TAFF complex and connected with the gravel country roads that criss-crossed the rural part of Apache county.

At Kellogg's direction, Springer drove several miles on gravel roads until reaching the intersection of Highway 75.

After driving north on 75 for more than 10 miles, Kellogg forced Springer to pull the vehicle off into the hilly, heavily forested area about a mile south of Lake Wa-Con-Da.

With the vehicle still running, Kellogg held Springer's face inches from the exhaust pipe, forcing her to inhale a significant amount of carbon monoxide.

Having rendered Springer nearly unconscious from the fumes, Kellogg, with Lucy at his side, drug Springer further back into the dense foliage, carrying his garbage pail with him, until they reached a small dirt clearing overlooking the Missouri River.

He forced her face down onto the ground, violently ripped her pants down, and had his way with her from behind.

When he had finished, he grabbed a large, jagged rock and struck her on the base of the neck.

The statement indicated that, while Springer was unconscious, but still alive, Kellogg sawed her four limbs and head off one at a time, using a freshly-sharpened, highly serrated hacksaw he had been carrying in his garbage bucket that day.

One piece at a time, he hurled the body parts down into the river below, struggling to keep Lucy from chewing the parts to pieces before he could pick them up and throw them.

Kellogg then tossed the hacksaw into the river. Using his poker stick, Kellogg dug and stirred up all of the blood-soaked dirt in the clearing and scooped it up into his bucket with his hands, before heaving the bucketful of bloody dirt as far as his scrawny arms would allow, launching it out into the river's brown water.

Kellogg then trekked back to the Envi, made the return drive to TAFF, parked the vehicle in the same VIP spot it had previously occupied, and walked home under cover of darkness.

"Wow," Fletcher said, noting to himself that the details were consistent with much of the specific information that had been revealed by the recent autopsy performed on the torso by a hospital in St. Joseph, Missouri.

That report had revealed high levels of carbon monoxide in Springer's system and a blunt blow to the upper back of Springer, which crushed one of her cervical vertebrae. And the limbs had been severed with very rough, jagged cuts.

"Nice work, Bill," Fletcher said, he flipped back to the front sheet. "That's more than enough to get charges filed and get him booked on this. We'll take another run at Terry now that we got all these specifics, but even if he doesn't crack, we should be okay."

Fletcher paused momentarily, before continuing. "But, you know, I do have a couple other things I wanna take a look at."

"Like what?"

"You seen the forensics report from St. Joe?"

"No, I ain't seen it, but I did talk to coroner on the phone some about it. Why you ask?"

"The tox they did on her torso, it showed that Springer had a fair amount of cocaine in her system when she was killed. I wouldn't mind having a look at the arrest reports for all your recent cocaine busts. Just to get an idea who moves in those circles - see if any connections to Kellogg come up."

"To be honest, Fletch, we haven't had many coke busts these days. Almost everything's meth around here."

"I know, but I'd still like to take a look."

"I'll have Kendra see what she can find for you. But I think you're wasting your time."

"Well, you did all my work for me, Bill. I feel like I gotta do something to make myself useful."

"Oh, you were closing in on it."

"Does that Bates kid live in town?"

"Yeah, he lives with his folks in a little house up by Greggsport Park."

"Alright. Well, I'm gonna take this statement with me, so I can fill out my reports. You wanna keep a copy for your file?"

"Yeah, I better. Let me go see if I can figure out how to work the copier."

Rogge made his away around the desk, snagged the statement from Fletcher, and lumbered out of his office, in search of the department Xerox machine.

As his friend disappeared from sight, Fletcher rubbed the healthy black and gray stubble on his chin and left cheek, as if deep in thought.

Chapter 27

After the fourth ring of the telephone in The Cave, Mike Hanigan rightly assumed that Martha had departed on one of her frequent trips to the Clerk's office, which, under chambers' protocol, meant the duty of answering the phone fell upon the law clerk.

Slightly annoyed with the distraction, Hanigan grabbed the handset and shoved it between the right side of his face and right shoulder, so he could continue typing.

"Judge Centers' chambers, this is Mike."

"This is the poor, downtrodden pastor calling."

Hanigan immediately recognized the voice of Troy Sloan.

"But even *I* have a secretary who answers the phone for me," Sloan said. "What's up with that?"

"Oh, Martha's down the hall taking care of some business, so I get to play receptionist," Hanigan replied.

"And you play the part well, Mike," Sloan said. "Speaking of receptionists, I made a call over to the receptionist at my dad's bank. You ready for some choice morsels?"

"Choice morsels?"

"Proverbs 18:8 - 'The words of a gossip are like choice morsels; they go down to a man's inmost parts.'"

"Morsel me," Hanigan said, playing along.

"Marj Parker, who mans the front desk and the switchboard at the bank, she was quite the font of information. She talked my ear off in between incoming calls for 35 minutes with all kinds of dirt on Charlotte Talbot. I'm just glad I didn't ask her anything about my dad," Sloan paused.

"But I do feel a little guilty relaying some of this," he continued, "so you need to assure me that it's for a good cause."

"A good and noble cause indeed, kind sir. Let it rip."

"Alright," Sloan began. "First of all, Marj pulled up the computer calendar for July and said there were loan committee meetings at the bank all day on July 25, and that Charlotte definitely would have been at those. She didn't know anything about a trip to the Cayman Islands. And something tells me she would have known about it, based on all the other things she claimed to know about."

"Like what?"

"She said Richard and Charlotte have been having some serious marital difficulties lately. A couple times she's even heard Charlotte screaming at him on the phone in her supposedly soundproof office." Sloan continued, with some noticeable uneasiness in his voice.

"Marj wasn't sure what the fighting was about, but she thinks it may have to do with the bank getting involved in the Talbot brothers' businesses."

"The bail out of the hotels and restaurant?" Hanigan asked, recalling the previous dinner discussion with Troy and Darcy Sloan.

"Yeah. It turns out the businesses were already in pretty bad shape when Gladys Talbot passed away and left them to the brothers. And apparently, she gave all the rest of her sizeable estate to charity, mostly to Trees Are Forever and other conservation groups."

"Ouch," Mike quipped.

"I guess the family foundation she set up made a seven-figure donation to some conservation group in the upper peninsula of Michigan where Gladys grew up."

"So, was it Charlotte that talked the bank into bailing the hotels and restaurant out?" Hanigan asked.

"Marj seemed to think that Charlotte's job at the bank may have been in jeopardy a year or so ago because of a number of loan deals that went south. And it was right about *that* time that the bank got involved in refinancing the Talbot businesses."

"Okay," Mike said, pecking out notes on his computer screen.

"But Marj said that at the same time the bank closed on the refinance, a whole bunch of new deposit business came in - like almost $20 million, because of Charlotte, which basically saved her job. Apparently, most of those deposits just recently went away. The rumor is that Charlotte's position at the bank may be shaky again. Marj thinks maybe that has something to do with the marital discord."

"You buying that?" Hanigan asked.

"Well, I have done some counseling for young married couples, and money does tend to be one of the major things they fight about."

"Yeah, but the Talbots aren't a young couple, and she's gotta be pulling down six figures as a VP at the bank. With the low cost of living in Riverton, they can't be hurting too bad."

"Well, it sounds like Charlotte has some pretty expensive tastes. And they've got a lake house they use in the summer."

"But this lady's absolutely sure that Charlotte was at the bank on July 25?"

"She had no doubt about that one."

"Hmm. That's bizarre," Hanigan responded.

"Hey, Stranger," Jenny Berg said as she stepped inside the Cave, a wide pleasant grin stretching across her face.

"Jen!" Hanigan surprised even himself with the level of exuberance in his greeting.

"Troy," Hanigan said into the phone, as he started to stand up, "Jenny just walked in. She's been in North Platte the last ten days. I better let you go. Thanks a ton for digging up the info for me. I appreciate it."

"Not a problem," Sloan replied. "Say 'hi' to Jen for me."

"Will do. And Troy, if you're guilt about gossiping hasn't subsided by tomorrow, just say two Hail Mary's and call me in the morning."

"Sure thing, Doc," Sloan answered. "See ya, man."

"Later," Hanigan said, hanging up the receiver.

"Hey you," he said, turning his attention to his girlfriend, as he stepped out from behind the desk, his arms outstretched for a hug.

"Troy Sloan just said 'hi' to you."

"You been staying out of trouble?" Berg asked, lightly scratching Hanigan's lower back with both of her hands, as Hanigan hugged her around the shoulders.

"Much to my surprise, yes, yes I have. You finally got the case tried, huh?"

"Yeah, but the judge was not happy with the lawyers. It's one thing to underestimate trial length by a day or so, but three days? That's pretty bad. And all the jurors had to stick around through the weekend. It was quite a production."

Berg pulled away slightly from Hanigan's grasp, so she could look him in the eyes.

"And I did miss you," Berg's voice softened.

"I missed you, too."

With that comment, Hanigan felt he was maxing out his capacity for sappy sincerity.

"So much so that I had to ask the old Jewish woman in my apartment complex to come over and nag me twice a day, just to fill that void."

Berg feigned a frown, as if to say, "I'm not *that* bad."

"Just kidding," Hanigan responded to Berg's facial expression, leaning in to give her a quick peck on the lips, before striding back behind his desk.

"This Cayman case just keeps getting more interesting."

"I told you if you put a little effort into your own hunt for evidence, it can sometimes make a big difference," Berg replied.

Seemingly ignoring Berg's comment, Hanigan continued.

"The minutes from the company's board meeting when they voted to file the liquidation had a redacted entry about Dick Talbot and his wife being present at the meeting."

"This is the tree guy, right," Jen asked, genuinely interested.

"Yep. So I asked Troy to find out why they might have been down there. Troy calls me today and says Charlotte Talbot definitely was *not* in the Cayman Islands the day of the board meeting."

"Maybe it was the other brother's wife," Berg offered.

"Carl's a bachelor," Hanigan said. "But, you know, I think I may have a way to find out from airline information who was traveling with Richard."

"I think someone's becoming quite the eager little beaver," Berg said smiling. "But I think I like it."

"Don't get too excited," Hanigan responded. "I'm not really doing this in my capacity as a law clerk, because it has virtually nothing to do with the case. I'm acting more as a private investigator, for my own personal edification."

"Oh, okay," Berg answered mockingly.

"Hey, you wanna go grab a cup of coffee somewhere?" Hanigan offered.

"I can't. We've got a suppression hearing later this morning. But I might be able to slip away for a quick lunch. Why don't you stop up around noon?"

"I don't know . . . Judge Bartlett always seems to cop a real territorial attitude every time I come by there. Like he doesn't want *his* perfect little law clerk to be corrupted by the great sluggard menace from below."

"Don't worry about him. He'll probably be out for his noon jog anyway."

"Alright," Hanigan answered, "I'll stop up."

"Tootles," Berg gave a high, quick wave, and bounced out of the Cave.

Chapter 28

Steve Fletcher snapped his cell phone shut, just as he pulled his blue Ford truck off State Highway 2 and began traveling the paved access road into the small village of Dunbar.

Gail Thompson, the stern accountant from the Trees Are Forever Foundation had just called and indicated that Anna Springer had left a small manila folder containing what appeared to be personal financial records, at the very back of the bottom drawer of a filing cabinet in the accountant's office. Thompson indicated she would have the folder hand-delivered to Fletcher the following day.

Fletcher parked his vehicle in an open spot, caddy-corner from the town's only bar and grill, not-so-cleverly dubbed "The Dun-Bar." He was meeting wife Connie and son Jason for a late supper and was looking forward to a cold cocktail.

Fletcher removed his sunglasses, stepped casually inside the dimly-lit tavern, and made his way towards the back, in the direction of the wooden booths where those wishing to dine tended to sit. As he did, several locals congratulated him on solving the Springer case.

"The Kellogg confession hit the paper already?" Fletcher asked Connie, as he scooted into the booth next to his wife and across from his son, Jason.

"It was in this afternoon's News-Press," Connie said.

"I wonder who leaked that."

Fletcher looked over at Jason, "How are you Studley?"

"Fine," the teenager replied, not bothering to look up from the plastic drinking straw he was twisting and bending in his hands.

"Hey, Jase, why don't you go up and pick out some music for us," Fletcher said, flipping a $5 bill on the booth table.

Jason grabbed the cash and headed towards the bar area, where the large, old-style juke box sat.

Fletcher looked at Connie, "I need some advice," he said.

"On what?"

"A situation with Bill Rogge."

"Did he all-of-a-sudden remember another tip for you?"

"No. But I think he may be involved in something he shouldn't be."

"What makes you think that?"

"Several things. I was looking through some phone records from the Sheriff's department, trying to figure out where the original informant's call might have come from. And I didn't find that, but there was a couple numbers that showed up a helluva lot of times, both as incoming and outgoing to Bill's direct line and his office cell phone, and during strange hours - late nights, early mornings, that kinda thing."

"Probably Suzanne," Connie offered, in reference to Rogge's wife.

"No. One of the numbers is from the old Orchard Inn, outside of town. The one the Talbot family runs. And the other number is a cell phone in Carl Talbot's name."

"Why is that bad?"

"Well, I'm getting to that. Yesterday, I pulled up some old reports on microfiche, trying to get a feel for who's been involved in the local cocaine business lately."

"Can I get you something to drink?" a young, gum-chomping waitress with excessively curly blond hair interrupted.

"I'd love a Windsor and Squirt," Fletcher answered.

"Sure. You doin' okay?" she asked Connie, in between chomps.

"Yeah, thanks," Connie replied, before turning back to face her husband.

"Why were you looking into that?"

"Springer's autopsy showed cocaine in her system. Anyhow, about a year and half ago, there was a report about 10 kilos of coke being recovered from some guy's vehicle, just south of Union, probably on his way to Riverton down from Omaha. The guy driving the car later gave up that he was working for Carl Talbot, and that shows up in the report. But I couldn't find any follow-up reports, investigation sheets, no charges, or nothing. It just kinda died with that initial report."

"How is that Bill's fault?"

"It definitely would have been in Bill's jurisdiction and it's just strange there ain't no follow-up documentation at all. It makes no sense."

Just then, the waitress hand-delivered Fletcher's drink to their table, and he took a thirsty gulp.

"When Bill took me fishing the weekend before last, I secretly jotted down the VIN number of his new boat," Fletcher continued, "and turns out, before Rogge got it, it was titled in the name of a company called C-BAS, Inc., and the transfer document was signed by Carl Talbot, as President, and listed him at an address down in the Cayman Islands. And so I checked on Bill's new Corvette, and it also came from this C-BAS company."

"Have you asked Bill about this stuff?" Connie inquired.

"No, and I ain't sure I should. I mean, we've been fishing buddies all these years. We broke into law enforcement about the same time. The guy's kinda like a younger brother or a cousin or something. I'd feel weird accusing him of something."

"You ain't gotta accuse, you can just innocently ask some questions."

"He ain't stupid, sweetie. He'll catch the drift of where I'm coming from."

"Well, maybe you can look into it some more yourself to see if there's a good explanation. And if you don't find one, hopefully by that time things with the Springer case will have settled down, and you can talk to Bill."

"That's another thing. I ain't sure we're getting the whole picture on the murder."

Fletcher leaned forward in the booth and dropped his voice into a hushed tone.

"Keep this under your hat, but I gotta hunch that somebody else at TAFF may have been involved in Springer's murder."

"Who?" Connie said, also now speaking in a near-whisper.

"I don't know. But, Jackie Howell thought Springer may have been porkin' some guy over there. And Springer had been telling Jackie that she was working all kinds of weekends and traveling a lot for her job, which ain't true at all according to her supervisor at TAFF."

"So lesbians lie to each other too, huh?"

"Looks like it. And Springer was always driving the company car on weekends, but the property management guy who's in charge of it claimed not to know anything about Springer using it. She must have had an 'in' with someone over there. To top it off, we didn't find nothing in the company car to tie Kellogg to it. I can't believe that kid was good enough to superclean the inside of that vehicle and leave not so much as a single dog hair behind."

Jason returned to the table, just as Fletcher finished his thought.

"Good first choice," Fletcher said, in reference to the Garth Brooks song playing over the bar sound system.

"That ain't mine," Jason replied. "My first song is by Ludacris."

"Loony Crisp?" Fletcher asked, intentionally butchering the name of the hip-hop artist, in an attempt to get a rise out of his son.

"Ludacris," Jason said flatly.

"Oh yeah, *him*," came Fletcher's facetious response. "Anyways, Con, I'm gonna follow up with that Cale Bates kid tomorrow, then have another go at Kellogg."

"Cale Bates is a punk," Jason interjected.

"Why do you say that?" Fletcher asked.

"He's always hanging out in the Main Street parking lot dealin' dope."

"What kind of dope?" Fletcher inquired.

"Mostly crank and coke, I think," Jason replied.

"And just how do you know so much about this?" Connie asked, failing to catch herself before she stepped over the step-mother divide.

"Jason knows better than to mess with that stuff," Fletcher answered, saving his wife from the assuredly snide reply which would have followed from Jason.

"Do you know who Bates is working for?" he asked his son.

"Nope," Jason responded. "He can't be making much money, though, 'cause he still cruises around on that junky ten-speed."

"He deals dope from a bicycle?"

"Yeah," Jason said, chuckling as he spoke.

"Hey, this must be the Crispy One himself," Fletcher said, pointing up at the speaker suspended above his head as urban-sounding music boomed out in the bar, "'cause I can't understand a damn thing he's saying."

Chapter 29

"The Trianta Payola continues," Hanigan offered, as he sauntered into Jenny Berg's bright, tidy office which, unlike The Cave, actually had several windows.

"What are you talking about?" Berg glanced up from the open green court file into which she had been resolutely staring.

"I was going through some of the financial information that the liquidators submitted in support of their claim that the Cayman company was insolvent when the defense funds were transferred . . . ."

"Yeah," Berg replied, her tone implying that she wanted Hanigan to get to the point of his story quickly.

". . . and they included financials from six months before the liquidation was filed, which showed that a number of the reserve bank accounts for the risk retention pools that the company used to pay the warranty claims were at Ted Sloan's bank in Riverton, to the tune of almost $20 million."

"So?"

"And they just happen to be the reserve accounts for the Trianta dealerships that are members of the risk retention group."

"So, you think Trianta was throwing the Talbot guy another bone by using his wife's bank?"

"Why else would they pick a little podunk bank in Riverton to place their deposits?"

"Good question. Where's the quid pro quo?" Berg asked rhetorically.

"Exactly. And the plot thickens. I walked down to the ATF office and was pumping my slot-machine buddy down there for info on how to access flight information . . . ."

"Who's your slot machine buddy?" Berg interrupted.

"I haven't told you the story about the ATF guy?"

Seeing that Berg was shaking her head in the negative, Hanigan continued.

"Several months ago, I was playing dollar slots at Harrah's and got to talking to the guy next to me. Turns out he works in this building for ATF. He offices right below me, one floor down, but I'd never seen him before."

"Interesting," Berg said half-heartedly, glancing back down again into her file.

"Anyway, about five beers and a couple hundred bucks later, he starts railing against all the anti-gambling hypocrites in the Nebraska legislature and how I'd be shocked if I knew how often most of those state senators made trips to Vegas and Atlantic City. I asked him how he knew that, and he said he had gone to a homeland security training conference where they learned some way to research air traffic itineraries and passenger travel information on a national basis."

"So, you went down and asked him to look into the Talbot Cayman trip?" Berg asked.

"Yep. And it took some serious cajoling to get him to do it."

"But he did it for you?"

"Yeah. But now I gotta take him out for a steak dinner at Cascio's."

"Small price to pay for good information," Berg offered. "So what'd he find?"

"Neither Richard or Carl Talbot showed up on any commercial flight itineraries out of Omaha, Lincoln, or Kansas City, during the two weeks leading up to July 25. But get this, there was a private charter jet out of Omaha, leased for a week by the Trianta Motor Corporation, destined for George Town on the Grand Cayman Island, by way of Bogota, Colombia. *That's* the Talbot flight."

"That's a stretch, that's what that is."

"Oh, really? Well check this out." Hanigan handed her a sheet of paper obviously printed from an internet news story.

"The World Rainforest Movement?"

"Look down about the fourth or fifth paragraph, where it lists all the companies that participated in the summit down in Bogota on July 22-23."

"Okay, I see Trianta Motor Corporation."

"Look a little further down, for Trees Are Forever Foundation."

"Yeah, there it is," Berg commented.

"So, people from Trianta and TAFF were at a meeting in Bogota on July 22nd and 23rd. Remember when we did that Google search on Talbot? One of the collaborative projects between Trianta and TAFF was something called Rainforest Rescue. I bet they shared a flight down there."

"Could be, I guess," Berg conceded. "So, you think the lady that was with him in the Caymans was from Trianta?"

"Maybe."

"How you gonna find out?"

"*We* are going to get on a conference call with the Cayman company's corporate secretary and see what she remembers about that redacted entry in the board meeting minutes."

"We?"

"Yeah, you're calling on behalf of the Magistrate Judge before whom the major class action lawsuit is pending against the Cayman company and I'm calling on behalf of the bankruptcy judge who's handling the company's section 304 petition. We need clarification on one of the exhibits that was offered and received into evidence at the last hearing."

"You're really taking this stuff to a new, scary level. What's gotten into you?" Berg asked, half-smiling and half-frowning.

"I thought about it, and it's really not all that different from when the judge asks a witness questions from the bench, seeking clarification on something they've testified about."

"Well, the class action is stayed, so my judge doesn't have anything to do with the case right now," Berg said. "He gets mad enough at me when I investigate cases assigned to him, let alone a case that's not even on his active docket. So, keep me out of this one."

"Fine. You can just listen in on the call, and I'll do the talking. Does your speaker phone work?"

"It does, but I don't want to do it here. If you really want to do this, let's go down to the jury room in the visiting judge's chambers. No one's using that this week."

"Let's do it," Hanigan said firmly.

Hanigan and Berg stealthily made their way to the other side of the building, where the smallish chambers occasionally used by judges visiting from other jurisdictions was located.

They ducked into the jury deliberation room connected by a small hallway to the chambers on one side, and the courtroom on the other.

Berg grabbed the phone from off a side credenza and pulled it over in front of Hanigan, just as he was glancing at his watch.

"They're on Eastern time, so it's about 11 down there," Hanigan said, in reference to the British Cayman Islands, where the corporate secretary resided.

He pulled a small torn piece of yellow legal pad paper from his pocket and dialed the number appearing on it.

"Hello," a woman with a pronounced British accent answered the call.

"Is this Meredith Beecham?"

"It is."

"Good morning, Ms. Beecham, this is Mike Hanigan. I'm a judicial law clerk for Judge Thomas Centers of the United States Bankruptcy Court for the District of Nebraska. The Court has a few followup questions regarding the testimony you gave at the hearing on August 14."

"Certainly," the woman replied.

"One of the exhibits that was received into evidence at the hearing, and about which you testified, was a computer diskette with the board minutes on it." Hanigan paused to see if the woman was tracking.

"Yes."

"We found on the disk a prior draft of the minutes from the July 25 board meeting which had a reference to a Mr. and Mrs. Richard Talbot attending the meeting as guests of Carl Talbot. Do you remember that reference?"

"Vaguely, yes."

"What do you remember?"

"As I recall, there was a gentleman and a young lady that had come in the far door of the meeting room mid-way through the session, and the gentleman came up, whispered a few words to Director Talbot, then left the room with the young lady. I've been trained to always reflect anyone's presence in the meeting, regardless of how brief. So, after the meeting adjourned, I asked Director Talbot who the two people were. And he said it was his brother, Richard, and Richard's wife."

"You may know this already, but Richard Talbot's wife is a Vice President of one of the banks where some of the company's reserve accounts were previously on deposit. Were they at the meeting because those accounts had been transferred down to the Caymans?"

"There had certainly been some general discussion about the timing and logistics of getting the remainder of the company's liquid assets moved to the Caymans. But there was no discussion about any specific bank. Most of the bank-account transfers had been done several weeks before that meeting. Frankly, I have no idea why they stopped by the meeting or what this Richard gentleman said to Director Talbot."

"We've gotten some information that suggests Richard Talbot's wife was not actually in the Cayman Islands on July 25."

"As I said, my reference in the minutes was based purely on Director Talbot's statement to me. I assumed he knew who his own visitors were."

"I understand. I understand."

"But, come to think of it, Director Talbot did act a bit cheeky when he told me the girl was his brother's wife."

"Can you describe what the woman looked like?"

"Very, very young. I'd say early 20's. I remember thinking that she looked more like the gentleman's daughter than his spouse."

"Anything else you can tell us about her physical appearance?"

"She was an attractive young lady. Reddish brown hair. Average height. Oh, and she had very distinctive beauty mark to one side of her mouth."

"Beauty mark?"

"A dark freckle or mole, but fairly large. I'd call it a beauty mark."

"Ms. Beecham, why did you delete the reference to them being present in the final copy of the minutes?"

"I was subsequently told by Director Talbot to take it out. And none of the other directors voiced any objection."

"Did he say why he wanted it taken out?"

"No, he didn't. And I didn't ask."

"Ma'am, you've been a big help and the court appreciates you taking the time to talk to us."

"No trouble," the woman responded.

As Hanigan disconnected the speaker phone, he turned to Berg and smiled, "How many young, attractive mole-faced executives at Trianta can there be?"

Chapter 30

Steve Fletcher walked up the narrow, rock-covered alley which afforded the only access to the Bates residence, a tiny, cracker-box house sitting in the very middle of a city block in the Greggsport area of Riverton, a working-class neighborhood densely populated with people who spent most of their non-working summertime hours on or around the river.

Most of the dirty white paint on the home's exterior had flaked off or peeled away, giving the house the appearance from the street of an old, abandoned shed.

As Fletcher looked out over the unmowed expanse of weeds and field grass which constituted either the home's front yard or the back yard of one of the surrounding homes, a pre-teen-aged boy, with a buzz haircut, clad only in long gray shorts – white underwear waistband fully exposed, and a pair of untied, badly-worn, high-top tennis shoes, without socks, pedaled his way up the alley road and past Fletcher on a chipped chrome bicycle.

The bike, Fletcher noticed, was without a seat and simply had a metal post protruding up where the seat should have been, which explained to Fletcher why the youth stood as he pedaled.

"What happened to your seat?" Fletcher asked the boy, who had already thrown the bike to the ground in front of the Bates house.

"It fell off," the youth answered, as he scurried into the home, leaving the front door wide open, with the screen door slamming shut but not completely closing.

"Hello," Fletcher called into the tiny home through the screen door.

"Yeah," a deep, angry-sounding voice, vaguely familiar to Fletcher, replied from within.

"Nebraska State Patrol. I'm here to visit with Cale Bates."

"Cale, get out here," the grumpy voice bellowed. After several seconds, the angry-sounding man spoke again.

"There's a cop outside asking for you. Go see what he wants."

The shaggy-haired teenager with the golden brown locks and rat-tail hair braid appeared at the screen door, his hairstyle in stark contrast to the almost-shaved young boy who had earlier darted into the house.

Fletcher stepped several paces back out into the weedy yard, to allow the teenager to push open the squeaky screen door and to hopefully get out of earshot of those inside the house.

"You must be Cale," Fletcher began.

"Yeah."

"I'm Steve Fletcher, with the Nebraska State Patrol. Hey, does your dad go by the name Pudge?" Fletcher asked quietly, it just having occurred to him that the distinctive voice from inside the house perhaps belonged to the crazy-eyed gravedigger who Fletcher and two other Apache County deputies had helped restrain, some fifteen years before, during a high school kegger at the rural Riverton party spot known as Seven Sisters.

The man, who at that time was probably close to 30 years old, had been belligerently attempting to pick fights with a number of the big, strong teenaged farm boys in attendance at the party.

"Yeah. Or Pudge-Ball," Cale Bates replied.

"Thought so," Fletcher replied, taking several more steps away from the house, apparently wanting to put more distance between himself and the man whose flailing limbs and sharp, bony elbows had been so vividly etched in Fletcher's recollection.

"Hey, Cale, I read your statement about Terry Kellogg's confession . . . .."

"Yep, it happened just like I wrote it," Bates interrupted. "And it's my word against Terry's."

"So you and Terry were in that recovery program together, huh?"

"That's right."

"What made you sign up for that?"

"Somebody told me about it."

"Who was that?"

"I forget."

"You don't remember who told you about the program?"

"No, I don't. Danny Reeves told me about the church. But I can't remember who told me about the meetings. I talk to a lot of people every day."

"You workin' a summer job someplace where you see a lot of people, are ya?" Fletcher asked.

"Odd jobs, here and there."

"Word around town is that you've been dealing drugs out of the Main Street parking lot."

"Not any more."

Bates bent down, pulled a yellow dandelion from the ground, and began spinning the stem between his fingers.

"And I suppose that church program helped you see the err of your ways?" Fletcher asked, attempting to mask any sarcasm in his tone.

"Just got tired of the bullshit."

"What do you mean?"

"Being paranoid all the time. Worrying about who you're dealing with. Getting screwed by the suppliers."

"Who were your suppliers?"

"I don't know. Different people."

"Did you ever work for Carl Talbot?"

"Yeah, I've bussed tables before at his restaurant."

"What I meant was, has he ever been one of your suppliers?"

"I never said that."

"I didn't say that you did, Cale, but I'm asking you the question."

"Then, no."

"How about Terry Kellogg? Did you ever work for him?"

"Terry ain't a supplier. He just dealt. And I hardly knew Terry until that church thing."

"But you two hit it off pretty good at those meetings?"

Bates shrugged his shoulders. Getting no verbal response, Fletcher pushed forward.

"Well, he told you all about this horrible crime he committed. He must have thought you two was pretty good buds."

"He told me the stuff, I wrote it down. That's all." Bates tossed the dandelion back down to the ground.

"What made you decide to call the Sheriff with it?"

"I didn't call the Sheriff. That was –," Bates stopped himself, before continuing.

"I don't know. Just thought I should."

"Well, did you or did you not call Bill Rogge?" Fletcher raised his voice slightly.

"I can't remember if I called him or if he called me."

"Why would the Sheriff call you?"

"I don't know. I probably called him."

"Your memory ain't too good there, Cale. That troubles me. You need to understand the seriousness of what you're involved in here. We've got a first-degree murder on our hands and whoever gets nailed for it could be looking at the electric chair. So, you damn well better get your facts straight."

Fletcher paused, to see if his harsher tone had helped jog some clarifications from Bates' memory. Hearing nothing, Fletcher continued.

"Did Terry tell you why he killed Springer?"

"He didn't say nothing about that?"

"Did you ask him why he did it?"

"Nope."

"You wasn't curious?"

"Not really."

"Did you ever see Kellogg after that night he confessed to you?"

"No."

"And you walked all the way home from the church that night? That's a pretty long haul."

"I had my bike."

"But the statement said you was walking?"

"Yeah," Bates hesitated, "I was walking my bike for a while, while he was telling me all that."

"Did Sheriff Rogge tell you that you may need to testify at Terry's trial?"

"Like I said, it's my word against Terry's. And who's gonna believe him?" Bates said, seemingly oblivious to his own vulnerability on character and credibility issues.

"Well, I'm gonna talk to Terry again and see what he has to say about your statement. And after I do, I may need to visit with you again. I might also need you to re-write your statement on a State Patrol form."

"I don't want to write all that again."

Just then, the buzz-cutted young boy burst out the screen door and bolted towards his seatless bike on the ground.

"You got a seat on your bike, I hope?" Fletcher said to Cale Bates, as he watched the younger boy pedal in the upright position back down the rock alley.

"Yeah. Rocco's too stupid to fix his. And I think he likes that pole going up his butt."

"So, you don't think you could write out your statement again?" Fletcher asked, shifting back to the topic at hand.

"I could, but I don't like to write. It hurts my hand."

"Well, rest your hand up, because we may need it done."

"Whatever."

"Alright, well you stay out of trouble, Cale, and stay around."

Fletcher turned and strolled back down the rock-covered alley, fairly convinced that something wasn't right with Bates' story. He reluctantly decided he should make another trip soon to the little church on the highway.

Chapter 31

"Mikey!" came Cooter's exuberant greeting, as Mike Hanigan pulled open his front door to unexpectedly reveal Cooter, Big Chig, and Stiffy standing before him in the long, carpeted hallway of Hanigan's apartment building.

"Hey, what are you guys doing here?" Hanigan asked, his voice a perfect mix of surprise and trepidation.

"I gotta take a piss," Stiffy said, in a near panicked tone, gyrating forward and backward as if he were afflicted with Parkinson's disease.

"Come on in."

Hanigan's invitation was not without some hesitation, since Jenny Berg was inside and Hanigan was unsure how she might respond to the motley bunch of Rivertonians.

"We're up here for the Battle of the Bands at the Ranch Bowl," Big Chig explained, as he stepped inside Hanigan's apartment. "Eddy Ray and his band are in it this year."

Big Chig was slurring his words slightly and the trio wreaked of beer.

"Eddy Ray Hoyle," Hanigan stated, acknowledging his recollection of the long-haired, near-brain-dead guitar player from their high school class in Riverton.

"He's still alive, huh?" Mike asked.

"Still rockin'," Big Chig said. "And we got an extra ticket for you, since Zelm bailed on us."

"Where's your pisser, dude?" Stiffy inquired, a tortured sense of urgency still pervading his voice.

"Back there to the right," Hanigan said, pointing in that direction, "but make sure you knock, my girlfriend might still be in there."

"Ooh, a *lady* friend." A sly grin slid across Big Chig's lips. "You'll have to introduce us."

"You got any brews, Mikey?" Cooter asked, peering into the kitchen area right off the front entrance to the apartment.

"I don't think I do, Coot. I got some vodka, though."

"That'll work!" Cooter replied with great enthusiasm.

"Come on in and have a seat guys, and I'll mix us up something in a little bit," Hanigan wanted to get out to the living area before Berg stumbled upon Big Chig, with his propensity for lewd and lascivious behavior, particularly when he was liquored up.

Hanigan herded Cooter into the living area and noticed Big Chig sneaking a peek into the bedroom, apparently in search of Hanigan's female guest.

"Stiffy, what the hell are you doing, man!" Hanigan screamed, as he noticed the short, hairy man outside in the corner of the apartment's eighth-story concrete deck, facing outward, in what appeared to be a urinating stance.

"I couldn't hold it any longer and the bathroom was locked," Stiffy explained dramatically, zipping up quickly and turning around to face his accuser, who was now standing in the opening where the sliding glass deck door had been.

"Dude, this is downtown Omaha," Hanigan lectured. "You can't just whip it out and take a piss on the street."

"I checked before I went. No one was down there," Stiffy said apologetically, looking back over the deck rail, at the widely-dispersed splotches of wetness on the sidewalk below.

"You're gonna get me kicked out of here, you idiot," Hanigan said, peering back quickly over his shoulder.

"Whatever you do, don't tell my girlfriend you just did that."

"Don't tell me what?" Berg asked, bounding out of Hanigan's bathroom into the living area.

"Hello," she said to the two unknown visitors standing in the living room, Stiffy's presence being obscured by Hanigan's body in the deck doorway.

"Hello to *you*," Big Chig said, as he stepped in Berg's direction. "I'm Shawn Coates. But people call me Big Man."

Big Chig took Berg's right hand which she had extended to shake, and brought it up to his dark, oversized lips, for a gentle kiss on her knuckles.

"I like to think of myself as a tall drink of water . . . with a bunch of shit floating around in it."

He smiled at Berg, with as much charm as his inebriation would permit.

"Alright, Chig, that's enough." Hanigan stepped inside and pointed out his other guests to Berg.

"Jen, this is Cooter, and the guy on the deck is Stiffy."

"Interesting names," Berg said.

"They're old high school buddies from Riverton."

"We came up to take your boyfriend to a concert, but now that you're here, we'd much rather take you with us." Big Chig was unrelenting in his advances.

"Jenny's not into metal," Hanigan answered, before Berg could even ask who was performing.

"Everyone go ahead and have a seat, and I'll mix up a pitcher of screwdrivers. Chig, you should check out my massage chair over there in the corner," Hanigan suggested, hoping to isolate Big Chig in that spot, away from Berg.

"Killer!" Cooter exclaimed, dashing to the sleek black leather recliner, and hurling his body into it, as if he were racing the others in the room for the spot.

Realizing no one else was interested in the chair, he leaned forward, removed the gray nylon backpack he was wearing, and nestled back in, anticipating his massage.

Just then, Stiffy re-entered the room from the deck area, closing the sliding glass door behind him and holding his hands awkwardly in front of his crotch area, in a not-so-subtle attempt to keep Berg from seeing the droplets of moisture that his outdoor urination session had left on his faded, torn jeans.

"You hidin' something Stiff?" Big Chig asked, his devilish grin again resurfacing. "Was that light breeze out there enough to get a rise out of you?"

"How do you work this thing?" Cooter shouted in frustration, peering over the side of the massage chair for an on/off switch or remote control of some kind.

Big Chig ignored Cooter's question and pressed forward with his cruel prodding of the small, hairy man.

"You're probably wondering how Stiffy got his nickname," Big Chig said, as he turned his head toward Berg, but continued to look at Stiffy out of the corner of his eyes.

"Don't, Chigger," Stiffy pleaded.

"Not really," Berg answered, sensing Stiffy's discomfort over the topic.

"It is kind of a *hard* story to handle," Big Chig said.

"Chig. C'mon, man," Stiffy knew his only hope of dissuading Big Chig from sharing the embarrassing story was to appeal for mercy.

"I was talking to somebody backstage before," Hanigan interrupted, as he emerged from the kitchen, glass pitcher full of orange liquid in one hand and several plastic cups in the other, quoting an obscure piece of pre-song dialogue from an old live KISS album, "and they were telling me there's a lot of you people there that like to drink vodka and orange juice."

"Ah yeah," Cooter squealed, springing himself from the black leather chair, apparently having decided that fueling his already-strong alcohol buzz was more important than getting an electronic back rub.

"Screw me," he said, reaching to snag one of the plastic cups from Hanigan.

"Coot, you need to be careful what you say when Stiffy's in a state of arousal," Big Chig was bound and determined to humiliate his hapless acquaintance.

"Jen," Hanigan said, sliding next to his girlfriend on the couch, having sensed that she was growing increasingly uncomfortable with the conversation, "did you know these are the guys who pulled Anna Springer's head out of the river?"

"That was *me*," Stiffy said proudly, tapping his chest with his right index finger, momentarily forgetting about the pee tracks he had left on his pants.

"We were all there," Cooter offered, wiping the orange-juice remains from his upper lip with the back of his hand and swirling the contents of his plastic cup with his other hand. "Mm, that's good," he opined.

"You should have seen the head," Big Chig said to Berg. "The fish had been nibbling on her pretty good."

"They even chewed off her mole," Stiffy said, coming forward to claim his mixed drink from Hanigan.

"That's right," Hanigan replied thoughtfully. "She did have a big mole there just above her mouth, didn't she?"

Hanigan glanced over and made eye contact with Berg, wanting to see if she was thinking what he was. The widening of her eyes told him she was.

"Hey, you're not a cop, are you?" Cooter asked Berg abruptly.

Berg laughed at the strangeness of the question, before responding, "No, I'm not a cop."

With that, Cooter spun around and grabbed the backpack he had left beside the massage chair.

Recklessly unzipping the top, he pulled from within the bag a full-size, standard-issue, green U.S. Army gas mask.

"Is that a gas mask?" Berg asked, hoping more for an explanation as to why Cooter was carrying it than for a mere confirmation of its identity.

"Ever since he got it, he doesn't leave home without it," Big Chig explained. "It's his prize possession."

"Does it have some kind of historical significance?" Berg inquired earnestly, her forehead creased with wrinkles of confusion.

Big Chig glanced over at Hanigan, a glint in his eye, seemingly wanting to determine how he ought to respond to Berg's question.

"Yeah," Big Chig began, "I think General Patton smoked a bowl in it just before the Alamo got attacked by the Russians."

Big Chig snickered at himself, just as Cooter pulled a plastic baggie of marijuana from a front pouch on the backpack.

"Mike," Berg said, as she stood up from the couch, her uneasiness evident from both the tone of her voice and her body language. "Could I talk to you, please?"

Hanigan followed Berg as she paced sternly back towards the bedroom.

"Hold up with that, Coot," Hanigan said as he walked past his gas-mask-clutching friend.

"You didn't tell me your friends were druggies," Berg began, in a near-whisper, having closed the bedroom door behind Hanigan.

"They're not druggies," Hanigan replied. "They just like to have a good time."

"You're not going to let them smoke in here are you?"

"Don't worry, I'm not going to smoke any," Hanigan answered.

"Well, if you're going to let them smoke that stuff, I'm leaving. I don't need to be breathing any of that second-hand."

"C'mon babe, don't freak out over this. It's just pot."

"That's fine, Mike. Whatever. I'm leaving," Berg curtly replied, turning around to jerk open the bedroom door.

Hanigan could tell from the resoluteness in Berg's voice that he would not be able to convince her either of the innocence of his friends' actions or of the acceptability of her staying on the premises while they smoked.

"I'll call you tomorrow," Hanigan said to her back, as she stomped out into the living area.

"Nice meeting you all," Berg said, her voice devoid of any inflection or sincerity, as she marched past the three guests in the living room, looking straight ahead at the front door which was her destination.

"It was *my* pleasure," Big Chig called out in a syrupy tone, as the front door opened and slammed shut.

"She's hot. I like her," Big Chig concluded.

"Can I fire this up now?" Cooter asked expectantly, having loaded a small mound of marijuana into the make-shift tin foil bowl at the very end of the mask's long, skinny breathing hose.

"Yeah," Hanigan answered gloomily, still bothered by his girlfriend's sudden departure. "Just let me throw a towel under the door."

Hanigan emerged from the bathroom with a large bath towel under his arm. The mask was now strapped to Cooter's face, and Big Chig was holding the end of the breathing hose in one hand and a blue Bic lighter in the other, poised just above the open bowl.

Hanigan opened the towel, threw it down on the linoleum entry way and, using his bare big toe, shoved the towel into the thin gap between the floor and the bottom of the front door.

"I feel like I'm back in my college dorm room," Hanigan thought to himself.

As he returned to the living area, he could see a rotating cloud of thick white smoke enveloping Cooter's face inside the air-tight gas mask, to the point where none of Cooter's facial features were visible.

Once the contents of the tin-foil bowl had been burned up, Cooter began hungrily sucking up the smoke inside the mask, until his face was once again visible through the two large plastic eye-holes.

He yanked the mask off and began convulsing from the chest up, in a valiant attempt to hold within him the excessive volume of smoke he had just inhaled.

A short two seconds later, Cooter coughed violently, white smoke shooting from his nose and billowing from his mouth, his eyes watering from the smoke irritation. As he continued to cough, a long strand of saliva escaped from the side of his mouth and fell to Hanigan's short-napped tan carpet.

"Who's next?" Big Chig asked, looking in Hanigan's direction.

"None for me," Hanigan answered, having plopped himself on the love seat.

He waved his hand in front of his face, Berg's admonition about second-hand smoke still lingering in his mind.

"I guess it's me then," Big Chig said, grasping the mask and preparing to strap it on his large brown head.

"Are there any automatic car washes on the way to the Ranch Bowl?" Cooter asked Hanigan, his voice somewhat hollowed out from his recent fit of hacking, and his eyes still irritated and watering.

"Why?" Hanigan asked, not sure he wanted an answer to his question.

"That's his new thing," Stiffy explained. "He likes to get really stoned and drive through the car wash. You know the kind with the brushes that come up and over the car and slap the windshield?" Stiffy chuckled. "It's funnier than shit just watching Cooter freak out."

"I think there's one on 72nd Street, just north of the Interstate," Hanigan offered.

He stared blankly ahead at the large brown man kneeling on his living room with an army gas mask wrapped around his face, resembling a gigantic grasshopper, with a green head and bulging eyes.

Hanigan's mind was suddenly preoccupied with the morbid possibility that Richard Talbot's guest on the July trip to the Carribbean had been the soon-to-be beheaded Anna Springer.

Chapter 32

"You got a secretary, but you don't have someone to do your heavy lifting for you?" Mike Hanigan asked, as he walked into the sanctuary area of the Covenant Community Church in Riverton and spotted Troy Sloan dragging tall stacks of padded pew chairs over towards the far wall of the large room.

"Hey, Mike!" Sloan replied enthusiastically, sounding both genuinely delighted and surprised to see his friend at the church. "What brings you down?"

"I called your house and Darcy said I could find you over here."

"Yeah, our youth group is having a Labor Day lock-in tonight, so I need to get this place ready. This is our sanctuary for worship service on Sunday mornings, but it doubles as a multi-purpose-room the rest of the time. One of the drawbacks of a small-town church, I guess."

"Detachable pews. That's a new one."

Hanigan studied the interlocking, padded chairs which made up the church rows, and started helping Sloan stack the chairs on top of each other.

"This must be important if you came all the way down here to see me," Sloan said.

"Well, I think I've stumbled onto some pretty serious stuff, and since I got part of my info from you, I thought I better talk to you before I do anything with it," Hanigan's voiced strained slightly as he drug a heavier-than-expected stack of five chairs across the carpeted floor.

"Anybody home?" a random voice wafted into the large room.

Hanigan and Sloan both turned around in the direction of the voice, just in time to see a tall, lanky figure in a Hawaiian print shirt walk past the opening which led to the sanctuary.

"In here, Officer," Sloan called loudly, recognizing Steve Fletcher from their prior meeting.

"Officer?" Hanigan asked inquisitively.

"He's a State Trooper," Sloan answered, somewhat under his breath. "I talked to him before about the Anna Springer murder."

"You're kidding. Wow."

Hanigan scratched his head, as he watched Steve Fletcher make his way into the sanctuary.

"I don't really believe in divine intervention," he mumbled, "but I guess we *are* in a church."

"What's that?" Sloan asked, walking past Hanigan and stepping forward to greet Fletcher in the center of the sanctuary.

"What can I do for you, Officer?" Sloan inquired.

"Just had a follow-up question for you on the Anna Springer investigation, if you have a minute," Fletcher said.

"Absolutely," Sloan replied. "Whatever you need. Oh . . . uh . . . Officer Fletcher, this is Mike Hanigan, a friend of mine."

"You aren't any relation to Budweiser Donny, are you?" Fletcher asked, doubting that one of the beer distributor's relatives would be spending his evening with a fundamentalist pastor.

"Afraid so," Hanigan answered, extending his hand towards Fletcher. "I'm his son."

"Steve Fletcher, Nebraska State Patrol," Fletcher said, shaking Hanigan's hand.

"How you doin'?" Hanigan asked, releasing his grip on Fletcher's hand.

"Not bad. Not bad. So, you in the beer business with your old man?"

"Nah. I think he was afraid I'd drink up all his inventory."

"Mike's a lawyer," Sloan said, assuming Hanigan would not otherwise divulge the information.

"A judicial law clerk actually," Hanigan clarified. "No big deal."

"Well, next time you see your old man, tell him 'hi' from me."

"Sure," Hanigan responded.

"Reverend," Fletcher said, turning his attention back to Sloan, "what can you tell me about Cale Bates?"

"Cale Bates?" Sloan asked rhetorically.

"Is that Cooter's younger brother?" Hanigan inquired.

"He's come to one or two youth events at the church here recently," Sloan said in Fletcher's direction, simultaneously nodding in affirmation of Hanigan's question. "But he's not a member or anything."

"But he is in that same recovery program that Terry Kellogg is in, right?" Fletcher asked.

"Overcomers? Not that I know of. And he wouldn't be in with Terry's group. He'd be in the adolescent Overcomers program that meets on Wednesday nights. Terry's in the adult Overcomers class that meets on Tuesdays and Fridays."

"Really?" Fletcher responded. "Well, can you double check that for me? It's real important for the investigation that we button down what Bates' involvement was in that program, if any. He claims Kellogg gave him a fairly detailed confession after one of them meetings."

"You bet. I'll check with Pastor John and let you know what I find out," Sloan answered.

"You know what," Hanigan interjected, "if you're investigating the Springer case, I think I may have some information for you."

"Is that right?" Fletcher sounded intrigued, but skeptical.

"Yeah, that's the whole reason I came down here tonight. But I wanted to talk to Troy first. I guess you saved me a trip into town."

"What you got for me?" Fletcher asked.

"Well, it's a long story, but the bottom line is I think Anna Springer was with a guy named Richard Talbot in the British Cayman Islands shortly before she was killed."

"Dick Talbot from Trees Are Forever?" Fletcher asked.

"Exactly," Hanigan replied.

"Alright, tell me why you say that," Fletcher said, reaching into the breast pocket of his Hawaiian shirt to pull out his small tablet.

"Again, long story, but I talked to this woman down there who saw Talbot at a July 25th meeting and he had a younger woman with him. The physical description she gave me generally matched Anna Springer. This morning, I faxed a picture of Anna Springer to the woman down there, and she positively ID'ed her. She says it was definitely Anna Springer who was with Talbot that day."

"July 25th, huh? I'll be damned," Fletcher said. "Oh, excuse my language, Reverend."

"No problem," Sloan said.

"What were they doing in the Cayman Islands?" Fletcher asked.

"Richard's brother, Carl, is on the board of directors for a company down there, and the board was meeting on July 25th."

"So, Carl Talbot was with them, too?"

"Yep," Hanigan answered.

"Was the name of the company C-BAS, Inc., like C-B-A-S," Fletcher asked, spelling out the letters of the name one at a time.

"No. It's called Automotive Services Risk Retention, Inc. It operates kinda like an insurance company, covering warranty repair claims for car dealerships. Carl was appointed to the company's board by some Trianta and Hirabishi dealerships in the Omaha area."

"I don't think Carl has ever been in the car business. I wonder how he got hooked up with the dealerships?" Fletcher asked, hoping Hanigan would have the answer.

"I've wondered that, too," Hanigan replied. "Especially with some of the extra-curricular activities I've heard Carl's involved in."

"What kind of activities?" Fletcher peered up from his notes.

"Well, my sources on this may not be the most reliable, but I've heard Carl has some kind of two-bit prostitution ring going at one of his motels."

"The one that's just outside of town?" Fletcher asked, knowing it would be difficult to maintain such an operation at Talbot's other hotel, located in the heart of Riverton, with the frequent patrol stops made there by the Riverton Police Department.

"Yeah, the Orchard Inn. And apparently he may be involved in some elicit drug activity as well."

"Uh huh," Fletcher said, nodding his head slightly, not feeling inclined to share his inside information regarding Carl Talbot's apparent involvement in the local cocaine trade.

"We think there's some kind of connection between Trianta and the Talbots." Hanigan continued. "Trianta's been giving a bunch of grants to the Foundation ever since Richard became the executive director over there. And Carl got his board appointment on the Cayman company thanks, in part, to the Trianta dealers. And a bunch of reserve-account money from the Cayman company got deposited into the bank where Richard Talbot's wife works."

"What bank is that?" Fletcher asked.

"That's my dad's bank," Sloan interjected. "Riverton State Bank."

"Alright," Fletcher said, scribbling feverishly in his pad. "What else can you tell me about this Cayman Islands trip?"

"Well, let's see," Hanigan said, rubbing his chin. "We think they were on a private charter that left Omaha on July 21st. We're pretty sure it started out as a South American trip and that Richard was attending an environmental summit in Colombia a couple days before the Cayman board meeting. They spent a couple days in Bogota, then flew to the Caymans on July 24."

"Tell you what," Fletcher stated, having fallen behind in his note-taking, "I'm gonna want you to give me a statement with your information in it."

"We can go back into my office," Sloan offered. With that, the three men walked through the open sanctuary room and, as they exited the room, both Hanigan and Fletcher glanced up briefly at the large painting above the door, depicting Jesus Christ in a green pasture amidst a herd of sheep.

Chapter 33

"Would you like spaghetti or mostaccioli with that?"

"Let's go with the mostaccioli," Mike Hanigan said, handing his menu to the thick-armed, gray-haired bespectacled waitress taking his order at one of Omaha's old family-owned Italian steakhouses.

"You gotta love a place where you get a bowl of mostaccioli as a side order with your steak," Hanigan said to his dinner date, still trying to thaw the considerable chill which had been emanating from Jenny Berg over the past four days since the encounter with the "river rats" in Hanigan's apartment.

Berg had just received a job offer from the Kansas City law firm she most wanted to join, and Hanigan had insisted that she let him take her out for dinner to celebrate.

"So," Hanigan continued, "when do you have to let the firm know whether you're accepting?"

"They said they'd like to know by next week, so they can make other offers if they need to."

"You taking it?" Hanigan asked.

"I'm pretty sure I will," Berg answered. "But I want to go back to a couple of the other firms I just interviewed with and tell them I have this offer pending."

"How come?"

"Just to see what they will offer."

"Shrewd." Hanigan looked away from Berg as he spoke. "If one of the Omaha firms matches their offer, would you consider staying here?"

"Why do you ask?"

Berg took a drink of her ice water, but her eyes were locked onto Hanigan over the top of her drinking glass.

"I don't know. Your family's here. Most of your friends are here. The Berg name is well known in Omaha legal circles," Hanigan paused and looked down, running his finger in a circle on the starched white tablecloth. "I'm here."

"And your pot-smoking friends are here," Berg responded.

"Technically, they're in Riverton," Hanigan responded. "Honestly, I can't believe you're making such a big deal about that."

Hanigan gulped hard, before continuing with the spiel he had rehearsed in his head several times before dinner.

"Part of a relationship is getting to know the other person 's past. Those guys are part of my past. I can't change that."

"No, but you can quit hanging out with them in the present."

"I rarely see those guys any more. That was the first time they'd ever been to my apartment. Besides, don't you think you're being a little judgmental?"

"It's not about passing judgment. I'm very libertarian on those issues. They're free to do what they want. But Mike, we're professionals. Professionals don't sit around smoking pot out of old Army gas masks."

"You're absolutely right. We should have used a bong."

"Not funny," Berg said, without smiling.

"Jen, how many times do I have to say this, I didn't smoke any."

"But the point is, you shouldn't even be associating with people who do."

"Well, I obviously have a greater sense of loyalty than you do. I don't believe in jettisoning old friends just because I'm supposedly part of some elite profession now."

"Like it or not, Mike, when you get sworn into the bar, you become an officer of the court, and there are certain behaviors, activities, and even appearances that just aren't acceptable. Besides, what do you possibly have in common with those guys anymore?" Berg asked, trying to understand why Hanigan would care to maintain his friendship with the rough-edged Rivertonians.

"Big Chig thought you were hot, so we have that in common."

"Something tells me he's not terribly discerning when it comes to mate selection," Berg replied, disgust evident in her voice.

"To my knowledge, he hasn't ventured outside the realm of female homo sapiens, but within that broad category, you're right, he's not real picky,"

Hanigan was smiling in remembrance of some of Big Chig's more robust sexual partners.

"What's funny?" Berg asked.

"Nothing. Nothing," Hanigan replied, knowing Berg would not share his amusement on the topic. "Hey, you're not gonna believe what I found out from Troy Sloan today," Mike offered enthusiastically.

"What's that?"

"He talked to that Pastor John guy at his church and apparently Cale Bates was placed in Terry Kellogg's recovery group at the special request of Richard Talbot."

"Okay, slow down. Tell me again who Cale Bates is."

"Cooter's little brother. He's the kid Kellogg confessed to."

"Right, okay," Berg said nodding.

"The pastor had told Cale he couldn't be in the adult recovery group, so Talbot calls the pastor and asks, as a personal favor, that he let Cale into that group since Cale supposedly had work commitments at the times the teen program met. Talbot told the pastor that Cale worked for one of his family's businesses and that he was a good kid, blah-blah-blah."

"Yeah," Berg responded, still not entirely warming up to her dinner-mate.

"Apparently, Talbot had helped the church place Kellogg with a job at TAFF, so Richard must have figured the pastor owed him a favor. Anyway, Cale Bates ended up with Terry Kellogg in the adult group."

"And you obviously think Talbot planted him there to cop the confession out of Kellogg."

"It's just a little too coincidental, don't you think," Hanigan theorized. "Less than two weeks after Talbot's in the Caymans with Anna Springer, he's making a special call on behalf of the guy who the alleged killer ends up confessing to. Besides, I can't believe a guy like Talbot would actually care about helping some white trash kid like Cale Bates."

"Oh, I see," Berg began, "you can call them 'white trash,' but when I say negative things about them, I'm being judgmental."

"When I use it, it's a term of endearment," Hanigan replied.

"Right," came Berg's sarcastic response. "Did Troy tell the homicide investigator about all this?"

"Yep. He called that Fletcher guy right before he called me. I'm telling you, Jen, this whole thing's really getting my juices flowing. I'm thinking about taking the next couple days off work and heading down to Riverton, to see if I can get to the bottom of this."

"Hey, I want in on this," Berg said excitedly, before her face suddenly turned down. "Oh wait, I can't take off tomorrow, we have a half-day trial in one of our prisoner cases. But I might be able to join you down there on Friday."

"Cool. Any way you'd have time tomorrow to do a little computer research for me up in your office?"

"If you promise me you'll never have illegal narcotics anywhere on your premises again," said Berg, unexpectedly revisiting that topic.

"As soon as we leave here, I'll stop and pick up a couple drug-sniffing dogs to station just inside my front door."

"Mike . . .," Berg said, clearly wanting Hanigan to make a serious pledge to her.

"Alright, alright. I promise."

"Okay. Now, what do you want me to research?"

"I need you to find out as much as you can about TAFF's operations since Talbot became the executive director. I'm gonna try to meet with one of TAFF's board members tomorrow in Riverton and I want as much background info as I can get."

"I'll see what I can do," Berg replied, the warmth having fully returned to her voice. She picked up the wine list to her right, suddenly in the mood to share a glass of cabernaut with her boyfriend.

Chapter 34

Steve Fletcher sat in the last stall of the basement bathroom in the Apache County Courthouse, with his jeans bunched up around his cowboy boots, contemplating the unsavory task on his agenda for that morning.

Fletcher's stomach, which routinely withstood all sorts of visually grotesque scenes without the slightest queasiness, from mangled human bodies in head-on collisions, to deer guts splattered on the roadway, to murder victims lying in pools of their own blood, apparently was unable to handle the specter of confronting a longtime friend and fishing buddy with accusations of criminal activity.

The entire contents of Fletcher's morning breakfast had been completely liquefied in his digestive tract and were being hastily discharged into the large white porcelain toilet.

Adding to Fletcher's intestinal woes was the sickening sense of betrayal which had crept under his skin and which had continued to fester since he had first surmised that Rogge was somehow involved with the illegal activities being fronted by Carl Talbot.

It was a feeling akin to that which had overtaken Fletcher twenty years before when he finally accepted the harsh reality that his then-wife Georgette was two-timing him, or more accurately, six-timing him, with a number of other partners, a reality which had been fairly obvious to all those even remotely close to the couple, but which Fletcher had essentially willed himself to ignore.

Had he done the same thing with Bill Rogge these past few years?

He shook the question from his head as he reached over to spin a section of toilet tissue from the cast iron holder which looked as if it might have been part of the original nineteenth century construction of the building.

Having emptied the contents of his stomach and steeled his nerves for what he was about to undertake, Fletcher marched deliberately into Bill Rogge's office, manila folder in hand, shutting the door behind him, and sitting down directly in front of Rogge, who was flipping through the pages of a Lund boat catalog.

"Uh oh, he shut the door," Sheriff Rogge said. "This must be serious. Problems with the ex-wife again?"

"Nope. Everything's fine there." Fletcher wanted to steer clear of any discussion of personal issues. "Bill, I'm having doubts about whether Terry Kellogg was really involved with the Springer murder."

"What are you talking about? Bates' statement is pretty damn clear on that."

"I think it was made up. We got some new information that tells me there's no way Kellogg could have killed her on the last day she was at work. That same information puts Springer with Dick and Carl Talbot shortly before she showed up dead. I've got an interview scheduled with Dick Talbot later today and I'm getting one set up with Carl."

Fletcher was carefully observing Rogge's demeanor as he laid out the support for his theory.

"Bill, I need you to tell me everything you know about Carl Talbot."

"What do you mean?" Rogge asked.

"Bill, we got a hold of Carl Talbot's phone records and they show a fair number of calls to and from your office and cell phone, several of them real recent. I need to know what those calls were about."

"What the hell are you doing, Fletch?" Rogge protested. "You're supposed to be investigating a murder, not poking around in my nest."

"Look, Bill. I'm just going where the evidence takes me."

"Listen here, Fletcher, this may be your investigation, but I'm still the chief law enforcement officer in this County, and I don't appreciate you coming in here and implying that I might be involved somehow in this thing."

Rogge's face was reddening significantly, creating an intensely stark color contrast with his blond beard.

"I ain't saying you're involved, Bill, but I need you to explain a few things for me."

"You want me to explain? Alright," Rogge said, his face still noticeably red. "I've talked a few times on the phone to Carl Talbot. I ain't afraid to admit that."

"What were those calls about?" Fletcher probed.

Rogge let out a huge angry sigh, as if contemplating whether he actually needed to explain himself to Fletcher.

"Alright, Fletch. You remember that anonymous phone tip I told you about? Well, back in August, right after Springer's head was found in the river, I got a call from Carl Talbot. He said he knew for a fact that Terry Kellogg killed Anna Springer. And I asked Carl how he knew that. He said Kellogg worked with Springer at the Foundation and his brother had told him that Kellogg had been stalking her."

"He said Richard Talbot told him that," Fletcher asked for clarification.

"Yeah," Rogge replied. "And I told Carl we'd look into it. But he made me swear I wouldn't disclose where I got the information, and I gave him my word. And you know me, Fletch, my word is golden. That's why I didn't tell you about the call right away, and that's why I couldn't tell you it was Talbot."

"Well, Bill, there's a whole bunch of calls way before Springer's head was ever found. And what about the recent calls, here in the last week or so?"

Rogge's face tightened in frustration, before he continued. "About, oh . . . I don't know, a week ago, Carl Talbot calls me and asks how the Springer investigation is going. And I tell him it's moving along."

Rogge looked up at the ceiling and began nodding.

"Yeah, it was shortly after Springer's body was found down at Rulo, 'cause I had just talked to the coroner's office in St. Joe and they had given me the basic forensics. And I may have mentioned a few of the details to Carl when we talked."

"That must have been on August 30," Fletcher offered. "According to the phone records, Carl called you that day, then you immediately called the coroner, and then you called Carl back."

"How would a call from me to the coroner show up on Carl's phone records?" Rogge asked.

"You made that one from your office line, 'cause it showed up on the call sheet I got from Kendra," Fletcher said, in reference to Rogge's office administrator.

"I didn't tell her she could give you– ," Rogge stopped and sighed heavily again, before continuing. "I think what happened is, I mentioned to Carl on the first call that most of the Kellogg leads were kinda drying up, but that the autopsy on the body might produce something. And that must have reminded me to call St. Joe. And, yeah, I do remember at least telling Carl about the broken vertebra and a couple other things that the coroner had mentioned."

"And then the very next day, August 31, another call from Carl shows up," Fletcher added.

"I don't remember that one."

"Well, Bill, you received it at 6:05 that evening, which was about six hours before you called and woke me up about the Cale Bates confession. Does that ring any bells?"

"Oh, sure, yeah. That was just Carl calling and telling me we should go pick up Cale Bates because he's got some information on the case."

"Did you ask Carl how he knew that?"

"Nope. I was just so excited that we might be getting somewhere finally with the investigation, I didn't even think to ask. But I knew Bates had worked for Carl at his restaurant. I just assumed that Carl had talked to him about the case and the kid told him what he knew. So, we went and picked up Bates, brought him in, and he wrote out the statement."

"And you didn't have to help him at all with the statement?"

"Alright, Fletch, now you're pissing me off!" Rogge fumed. "How can you think I would do something like that? Of course I didn't help him with it. I got no reason to manufacture evidence, and I sure as hell ain't gonna jeopardize my job by doing something like that. Jesus, Fletch, I thought we was friends."

Ignoring Rogge's appeal to their friendship, Fletcher pressed forward.

"What can you tell me about C-BAS, Inc.?" he asked, shifting gears in his questioning.

"You're just full of questions, aren't you?" The agitation was evident in Rogge's voice. "What's Sea Bass Inc.?"

"According to the DMV, your new Lund boat and your Corvette were titled under that name just before you got them."

"You've been snooping around in my personal assets too?!" Rogge roared, his face again flush with blood. "I cannot believe what I'm hearing. How long have we known each other?"

Rogge was now bellowing near the top of his lungs and leaning forward out of his chair. He pointed his thick index finger at Fletcher.

"Who was it that saved your ass during that drug raid outside Palmyra back in '93? I guess all that don't mean a whole lot anymore now that you're a big-time state investigator."

"Bill, I need you to calm down."

Fletcher could feel the muscles in his neck tightening, and he raised his hands slightly, slowly motioning for Rogge to ease back in his chair and relax.

"I'd like to see how calm you'd be if the tables was turned," Rogge snapped.

"Now, Bill, did I start screamin' and hollerin' when I found out you didn't tell me about your anonymous tip? Did I get upset just now when you told me for the first time that it was Carl Talbot who tipped you off? Did I?"

Rogge looked away from Fletcher, his face revealing a hint of shame.

"No," he said, returning momentarily to a relative state of calm.

"No, I didn't," Fletcher confirmed, "'cause I didn't want to make this a personal thing and hurt our friendship. We're just two law enforcement guys doing our jobs and trying to get to the bottom of a few things. There ain't no need for shouting and personal attacks."

"You're right, Fletch. I'm sorry," Rogge answered, obvious contrition in his voice.

"Now, what can you tell me about this C-BAS company?"

"Sea Bass. Sounds like a fishing outfitter or something."

"It's C-B-A-S, all capital letters. And, according to them DMV records, it has a Cayman Islands headquarters and Carl Talbot is the President of the company."

Rogge folded his enormous arms in front of him and looked down at his desk. He was squeezing his eyes shut.

Several seconds elapsed and Rogge did not move from his position.

"Bill?" Fletcher said.

After a few more seconds of silence, Rogge began shaking his head slowly from side to side, his eyes still shut tight.

Finally, he looked up and opened his eyes. He unfolded his arms and placed his huge hands face down on his desk, one on either side of the still-open boat catalog.

It appeared to Fletcher as if tears may have been forming in Rogge's eyes, though he wasn't sure.

"I don't know nothing about it, Fletch," Rogge's voice had become surprisingly steady and serene. "I'll have to look through my records and see if I can figure it out. I think you better get outta here before I get upset again."

"Fair enough, Bill. We can talk more later." Fletcher eased up out of his chair and departed Rogge's office.

Chapter 35

"Where are you at?" came the pleasant voice of Jenny Berg over Mike Hanigan's cell phone, as he struggled to keep his patience, with his silver Mustang following just inches behind an elderly farmer's beat-up flatbed pickup truck, creeping over a narrow two-lane viaduct.

"I'm in Riverton," Hanigan replied, the tension evident in his voice. "Currently putting along at a brisk 8 miles per hour, thanks to the seed-cap-wearing corpse in front of me."

"You're already down there?"

"What do you mean 'already'? It's 9:30 in the morning."

"I just assumed that since you were taking the day off, you'd sleep in and lounge around your apartment for awhile before driving down there. When I called your apartment and didn't get an answer, I figured you were still in bed."

"Nope. I was up at 7:00. I'm telling you, I am into this investigation."

"I guess so," said Berg, obviously pleased with her boyfriend's new-found spark. "Well, you'll be happy to know that, about the time you were waking up, I was already hard at work diving into some research on the Trees Are Forever Foundation."

"Excellent," Hanigan said, his voice still strained, as he contemplated a dangerous pass maneuver on the bridge to get around the flatbed.

"What time is your meeting with the TAFF board member?" Berg asked.

"Actually, I don't have anything set up yet. I'm gonna stop by Budweiser Central and ask my dad if he has any contacts with any of the good old boys on the Board."

Hanigan quickly veered his Mustang off the highway and onto the first available sidestreet after the viaduct, hoping to re-emerge several blocks further down the road, ahead of the slow-moving pickup.

"So, what'd you find out about TAFF?" he asked.

"From all the press clippings, Richard Talbot has been an incredibly aggressive Executive Director."

"How so?"

"Lots of new ventures. Big splashes. I skimmed through all of the Foundation's online newsletters since he was appointed. He increased the number of tree supplier contracts by nearly 40%, he got all those grants from Trianta, and he started some new rainforest coffee deal last year."

"Rainforest coffee? What's that?"

"Coffee they grow in the shady areas of the South American rainforest, as opposed to the normal way of stripping the forest to make a coffee plantation area. Supposedly fits in with their tree-saving mission."

"Interesting. Anything new on the Trianta stuff?"

"No, not really. I Googled the names of all the tree supply companies that TAFF does business with. Nothing too sexy. One of them filed a Chapter 11 bankruptcy fairly recently. So, I don't know what happened to their contract with TAFF."

"What was the name of that company?"

"Arboretum something or other. Let me check."

Berg flipped through the yellow pages of the legal pad on her desk.

"Arboretum Supply Co.," she stated.

"Do you know what jurisdiction the bankruptcy was in?" Mike asked.

"Not sure. I'm assuming Nebraska."

"When you assume, you make an 'ass' out of 'u' and 'me,'" Hanigan quipped.

"Excuse me?"

"Never mind. I'll figure it out. Anything else of interest?" Hanigan asked.

"Did you know Phyllis Springer is on TAFF's board?"

"I knew she used to be years ago. 'Cause her and Gladys Talbot were both on there and couldn't stand each other. I figured Phyllis had to step down once she got elected to the Senate."

"No, she's still on there, as an uncompensated director. And did you know that she has been the co-chair of the Senate energy committee?"

"Yeah. So?"

"And did you also know that, as the co-chair of the Energy Committee, she co-sponsored an Energy Bill that promotes hybrid cars?"

"Okay, keep talking."

"And did you further know that Trianta and Hirabishi are the car manufacturers on the cutting edge of hybrid vehicle technology?"

"Trianta scratches TAFF's back, and Senator Springer scratches Trianta's. Is that what you're driving at?"

"It makes sense, doesn't it?"

"But how much good will does the Senator really get from the electorate by getting a bunch of grant money coming into Tree Huggers Central?"

"Oh my gosh, what was that terrible sound?" Berg asked, concern in her voice.

"Nothing to worry about. Just a little tire squealage. I just decided to change directions and head down to the Orchard Inn, to tap their wireless router. I'm pretty sure my dad's shop hasn't come into the wireless age yet, but I think I saw a sign outside the motel that said free wireless internet."

"Why do you need it?"

"I want to check that bankruptcy info you gave me."

"I'd offer to do it for you, but I gotta go sit through that prisoner trial the rest of the day."

"That's alright. It was Arboretum Supply Company?"

"Supply Co.," Berg corrected.

"Thanks for your help, babe. Talk to you later."

Hanigan snapped his cell phone closed and tossed it into the empty passenger seat of his vehicle, pulling into the gravel parking lot of the Orchard Inn, south of Riverton.

As Mike drove past the row of room doors for the small motel, his mind's eye conjured up the image of an aging, hard-looking prostitute stepping out into the morning daylight from one of the curbside rooms, straightening her spandex mini-skirt and struggling to walk through the gravel lot with her tacky high heels.

Hanigan positioned his vehicle to the side of the small boxy lobby area of the motel, but out of the line of sight of anyone who might have been working inside. He slid his laptop computer from out of its black case on the passenger-side floorboard and powered it up, intending to pirate the wireless signal and log onto the internet.

As the computer ran through its logon protocol, Hanigan contemplated why a run-down flea-bag motel like the Orchard would offer wireless internet, surmising that business travelers at the motel had to be few and far between.

As he clicked open the internet browser, he guessed that perhaps Carl Talbot had installed the wireless router for the sole purpose of ensuring he would have an uninterrupted feed of internet pornography into his office.

Hanigan ran several searches in vain for the Arboretum Supply bankruptcy filing on the federal bankruptcy courts' PACER electronic docketing system, first trying Nebraska, then the neighboring states of Iowa and Missouri, both of which were only a few minutes' drive from Riverton.

On a whim, he decided to search the Delaware Bankruptcy Court, based on the high percentage of companies which typically incorporate in that state.

"Yes," Hanigan said triumphantly, as his name search on the Delaware PACER site revealed the bankruptcy filing by Arboretum Supply Co.

After navigating the site for ten minutes, he whipped out his cell phone, and punched up the digits for Judge Bartlett's chambers in Lincoln, obviously failing to heed Berg's statement about her need to prepare for the prisoner trial.

"Hey," came Hanigan's nonchalant greeting, as Berg answered the phone.

"Hey," Berg replied. "Just getting ready to head into court. Can I call you back later?"

"Give me 30 seconds."

"Go," Berg said sharply.

"I found the Arboretum Supply bankruptcy in Delaware. You were right, they list a tree supply agreement with Trees Are Forever as one of their executory contracts. But they've also filed an interesting preference action to recover some consulting fees."

"What's a preference action?" Berg asked.

"It's basically an adversary proceeding lawsuit in a bankruptcy where the debtor tries to recover payments made to creditors within the 90 days immediately before the bankruptcy was filed. Anyway, this Arboretum Supply Co. filed a preference action to recover some 'consulting fees' paid to C-BAS, LLC, doing business as "Consultants – Business and Social."

"And?" Berg asked, urging Hanigan to get to his point.

"They allege that in June of this year, they wired these consulting fees to Riverton State Bank, c/o C-BAS, LLC's account. And I remember that investigator saying something about a C-BAS company when I talked to him about Carl Talbot during our meeting at the church."

"So you're thinking the Talbots are getting consulting-fee kickbacks on the new tree contracts?"

"Could be. Any way you'd have time to dig up as much info as you can on this C-BAS entity?"

"Right now, I gotta go," Berg said hastily in a hushed tone that told Hanigan that Judge Bartlett was likely standing in Berg's office waiting for her to join him in the courtroom for their prisoner trial.

"I'll see what I can do."

"You're the best, babe," Hanigan said in parting.

"Yes I am."

Chapter 36

As Mike Hanigan walked in the front door of Paul Vogler's taxidermy shop, just across Main Street from the Riverton fish market, in the oldest part of downtown, he immediately detected a subtle musty scent akin to wet dog hair and month-old human body odor.

Vogler, a lifelong Riverton resident and jack-of-all-trades, had opened the taxidermy shop eight years before, following a long and varied career which included stints as a real estate broker, an appraiser, an auctioneer, a philanthropist, and a politician, even serving two terms as mayor of the town.

Donny Hanigan had identified Vogler, from Hanigan's list of current TAFF board members, as the person with whom Donny had the best relationship, due primarily to the fact that his Budweiser distributorship had sponsored numerous charitable events over the years for which Vogler had acted as fundraising chairman.

The elder Hanigan also assured his son that Vogler would by far be the most talkative of the Foundation's board members.

"Well, hello there, young man," said a spry elderly man in a flat round white top hat with a red band, wearing a gray sweater over a wrinkled white collared shirt accented by a red, white, and blue bow tie, as he emerged from a door covered with a large rubber flap hanging from the top of the door frame, greeting Hanigan at the front counter of the shop.

"You must be young Michael Hanigan."

"Yep, that's me. But it's just Mike," Hanigan replied.

"And I'm just Paul," the old man said, grinning from ear to ear. "But don't tell my wife . . . she still thinks I'm Mayor Vogler. You know women, they're turned on by powerful men."

Vogler chuckled loudly at his own comment, momentarily displacing his upper false teeth and launching a small saliva projectile in Hanigan's direction.

"That I wouldn't know," Hanigan replied, having just ducked his head to the side to avoid the man's spit. "I've never been in a position of power."

"But your dad tells me you've taken an interest in the affairs of the Trees Are Forever Foundation?"

"Yeah, you could say that. And he assured me you were the real power broker over there," Hanigan said, wanting to flatter his way into the old man's good graces.

"Oh, I fill a chair at board meetings, if that's what you mean. And I usually tell a couple bad jokes at the beginning of each meeting. I always tell the other directors that once they stop pretending to laugh at my jokes, I'll know it's time to resign from the Board."

"How long have you been on the Board over there?"

"I don't know about you," the old man said, "but I'm damn near 85 years old and I'd just as soon sit down if we're going to visit for awhile, if you don't mind."

"Absolutely," Hanigan replied. "That's fine."

"Let's head back to my TV room," the old man offered, as he pushed open a waist-high swinging wood door to allow Hanigan behind the front counter, before turning and heading through the flap-covered door through which he had entered the room.

"You got a lot of dead critters in here," Hanigan said, gawking at the multitude of taxidermy projects occupying seemingly every part of the dank back room, as he walked slowly behind the old man at the snail 's pace his elderly gait was setting.

"There's a story behind each one, too."

"I bet," Hanigan replied. "What's this guy's story?" he asked, pointing at a good-sized mountain lion whose feet were fastened to two gray garden rocks on the concrete floor of the back room.

"That's actually a female mountain lion. She came charging out of the woods, chasing after the kid of a real estate developer pal of mine that lives out in the country north of Lincoln."

Vogel stepped toward the lion and gave it a quick stroke, before continuing with his story.

"They were having an outdoor get-together of some kind and the boy was riding a dirt bike when this feisty kitty jumped out of the trees and chased him about a quarter mile before my buddy ran out and shot her several times with a little .22 caliber rifle."

"I didn't know they had mountain lions in this part of the state?"

"This is the only one I've ever seen. And, at my age, I hope it's the only one I ever do."

"Is this the TV room?" Hanigan asked, peering into a small, even darker room at the very rear of the shop, hoping to move the process forward.

"It sure is. Go on in," Vogler replied, shuffling his feet in that direction. "I was watching the real estate channel before you got here. Once a real estate man, always a real estate man."

"So, how long have you been on Trees Are Forever's board?" Hanigan asked.

"Well, let's see. I got that appointment right after my second term as mayor. So that would have been '98, no wait, early '97, like January or February. So, what's that make, thirteen years? Something like that."

"Wow. Do have the longest tenure of anyone on there?"

"There's five of us on there. Myself, Morty, Ron, Erwin, and Phyllis Springer. And, yeah, I've been there longer than any of them."

"Pretty good group to work with?"

"Oh yeah. The Senator can be a little ornery sometimes. But we seem to handle her okay. Actually, we're usually fairly unanimous in our votes. There are only a couple occasions recently when I can remember any contention."

"What were those?"

"First was whether to appoint Richard Talbot as the successor Executive Director to Sheldon Steinhart."

"Really? That was contentious?"

"Yep. That was a 3-2 vote in favor, with myself and Erwin Kleinweber voting against. The main reason Talbot was even being considered was because of a significant contingent gift from his mother's foundation trust, which she said TAFF would only get if Richard Talbot was appointed as executive director."

"Why did you vote against him?"

"Me and Erwin didn't like it. And we didn't think Talbot had enough experience in a non-profit setting. Although, I have to admit, he's brought in a whale of a lot of money over the last 12 months."

"So, Phyllis Springer voted in favor of Talbot's appointment?" Hanigan asked.

"She sure did. The deciding vote, as it turns out. And, boy, that was a surprise. She and Gladys Talbot never saw eye to eye on anything back when Gladys was on the board. I think her and Phyllis both wanted to be the alpha-female of Riverton."

"Any guess as to why Phyllis voted the way she did on Talbot's appointment?"

"Nothing I'm willing to say out loud."

"You think her and Talbot had some kind of an arrangement?"

"I can't really say that. But it wasn't more than two months into his appointment, and Talbot brought a proposal to the Board that would have involved the sale of confidential donor information. And when the Board was behind closed doors, Phyllis Springer was very outspoken in favor of the proposal. But then, Phyllis always gets excited whenever there's a buck to be made. Every time we review the financials and she sees how much money is coming into that place, her eyes light up like a Christmas tree."

"Who did Talbot want to sell the donor info to?"

"A number of major companies wanted to use our donor lists for marketing purposes. I probably shouldn't mention any names."

"Was one of them the Trianta Motor Corporation, by chance?"

"You didn't hear it from me."

"So, how did the Board respond to the proposal?"

"We said, 'no way.' We weren't going to do that. The vote was 5-0 against, but I know Phyllis would have voted in favor had she not seen the writing on the wall that none of us were going for it."

"But Trianta did end up giving TAFF a bunch of grant money, didn't they?"

"Yes, they sure did. A whole lot of money. But Talbot told us they were willing to do it even without getting the donor information."

"Why would they give all that money if they weren't getting anything in return?"

"Good publicity, I guess. Shows they're serious about conservation issues, not just in making a buck off their electric cars."

"Do you know anything about a company called Arboretum Supply Co.?"

"That's one of our new tree suppliers, but they just went into bankruptcy," Vogler said, shaking his head, before continuing.

"Shortly after Talbot got appointed, he terminated our tree supply agreement with one of our longtime suppliers and awarded several big new contracts, including the one to this Arboretum place. And he did it without Board consultation which, incidentally, was the other bone of contention between the Board members recently. Most of us felt Talbot shouldn't have done it, or, at the very least, that he should have sought input from the Board. But Phyllis was very supportive of the move. And now look, one of the new companies is in bankruptcy."

"Are you familiar with a company called C-BAS, LLC?"

"No sir, I can't say that I am."

"How about Consultants – Business and Social?"

"Never heard of 'em," Vogler replied.

"I looked at some bankruptcy filings in the Arboretum Supply case and it looks like they were paying some consulting fees to a company by that name, which may be run by Carl Talbot, Richard's brother."

"You don't say," Vogler responded.

"Richard never mentioned anything about that to the Board?"

"Nope, not a word." Vogler removed his top hat and began to run his right index finger in a circular motion around the inner lining.

"You know, I'm not sure what this means, but now that I think about it, Phyllis was kinda down on Richard at the last Board meeting a couple months back. It was the first time she hadn't been completely supportive of his efforts."

"Did she say anything specific?"

"No, nothing specific. I just remember her bringing to the Board's attention that Richard's employment contract is subject to annual review, and that the Board should take a very hard look at his performance next time it meets."

"You don't say," Hanigan replied, unintentionally mimicking Vogler's time-worn expression. "You don't say," he repeated for emphasis.

Chapter 37

"Ironic, isn't it?" Richard Talbot asked rhetorically, as he led Steve Fletcher into Talbot's large but extremely cluttered and paper-strewn office at the Trees Are Forever Foundation, for the interview session Fletcher had requested.

"I'm the executive director of an organization dedicated to preserving trees, yet I'm surrounded by stacks and stacks of dead ones. Pretty obvious why we don't put a picture of my office on the Foundation website, isn't it?"

"Right," Fletcher answered, eyeing the numerous Ansel Adams black-and-white nature photographs framed on several of the walls, as Talbot picked up a six-inch stack of documents, bound by a rubber band, from the seat of a green leather chair in front of Talbot's desk, to clear a space for Fletcher to sit.

"Kristin," Talbot said into his telephone intercom, reaching over from the front side of his desk and holding down a button on the phone console, "Please tell Carlton that Mr. Fletcher is here."

"Carlton?" Fletcher asked.

"Yes, my brother, Carlton," Talbot replied, as he made his way around to his chair.

"He works here too?"

"No, he doesn't, but he mentioned that your office had called to set up an interview with him as well, so I thought I'd save you some time and have Carlton come sit in while we talk. I hope that's okay."

"Sure, we'll see how it goes."

Before Fletcher had finished his sentence, the door to Richard Talbot's office opened to reveal the man Fletcher presumed to be Carl Talbot.

"Investigator Fletcher, this is my brother, Carlton," came Richard's introduction.

"Call me Carl. How do you do?" Carl Talbot said, in what Fletcher thought sounded like a bad imitation of someone of Italian descent from Brooklyn.

"Carl, nice to meet you," Fletcher replied, as he shook Carl Talbot's strong but noticeably sweaty palm.

In addition to the excessive perspiration in Carl's handshake, Fletcher immediately noticed that Carl's physical appearance and wardrobe selection could not have been more opposite from his elder brother's.

Richard was tall and wiry, with distinguished features, a neatly-trimmed mustache, and a full head of salt and pepper colored hair, blow dried to perfection. He was wearing finely-pressed dark slacks, and a silky collarless lavender shirt underneath a navy blue suit jacket.

By contrast, Carl was several inches shorter, considerably thicker and more muscular than his brother, with a large, oddly-shaped head, stringy black hair greased straight back, and a heavy five o'clock shadow, though it was only shortly after 1:30 in the afternoon. Carl was dressed in what looked like black windpants and dark-colored running shoes, with a black tank top beneath an undersized black sports coat which hugged the bulky muscles of his shoulders and arms.

The only discernible clue that the two men were biological relatives were their identical cat-like green eyes.

"So, what can we do for you today, Mr. Fletcher?" Richard Talbot asked, as Carl stood against the wall to the side of his brother's desk, muscular arms folded in front of him.

"I had a few questions I wanted to ask you in connection with an investigation I'm conducting," Fletcher began.

"Alright then," Richard said through a tight-lipped smile.

"As I'm sure you fellas both know, Terry Kellogg has been arrested for the murder of Anna Springer," Fletcher said.

"Yes, yes. That whole situation is simply awful," Richard replied, looking down and shaking his head.

Fletcher glanced over at Carl, who remained motionless, his face devoid of any expression.

"Tell me how it is that TAFF came to hire Terry Kellogg," Fletcher said.

"As I recall, he was a community reinvestment hire," Richard offered. "But beyond that, I can't say that I had much involvement in his hiring."

"But you were aware that he had been hired?" Fletcher asked.

"Certainly."

"According to your H.R. director, she visited with you about Terry to get your approval for his hiring."

"Oh, sure, I discussed the hire generally with Ms.Chitwood."

"What do you remember about that?"

"Not a great deal, to be perfectly honest with you. I'm sure she told me he had been in a little trouble with the law. But that's fairly common in our community reinvestment program."

"Did she tell you what kind of trouble he'd been in?"

"Drugs I think, right?" Talbot said, as if answering a quiz question.

"Did she mention anything else?" Fletcher asked.

"Not that I recall."

"So, she didn't mention that Terry had been involved in mutilating livestock?"

"Hmm. You know, as I sit here today, I don't really remember her saying that." Richard shifted in his chair. "I know that now, but that could be because of the newspaper articles after he was arrested."

"Ms. Chitwood seemed to recall discussing that with you before Terry was hired."

"I suppose it's possible. But I don't think so."

"Did you ever hear of any problems between Kellogg and Anna Springer at the workplace?"

"Nothing real concrete, but there were certainly rumors that Kellogg had some strange fascination with Ms. Springer."

"Tell me about that."

"Oh, you know how office gossip is, people talk and it gets around."

"But, who was it that told you?"

"I have no idea. Like I said, it was nothing cut and dried. Just rumor and innuendo."

"Do you know a Riverton teenager by the name of Cale Bates?" Fletcher asked, looking first at Carl, then over at Richard.

"I believe Cale busses tables at our family's restaurant," Richard said, looking in Carl's direction for confirmation.

Carl nodded in the affirmative, but did not speak.

"And did you make a call on his behalf over to the Covenant Church?" Fletcher probed.

"As I understand it, Cale had kind of fallen in with the wrong crowd," Richard responded, "but was trying to get his life straightened out through some kind of 12-step program. Unfortunately, his work schedule at the restaurant conflicted with the only time they offered the program for kids his age. So, Carlton asked if I could make a call to the program coordinator to see if there was some way around that."

"And you knew Terry Kellogg was in that program, is that right?"

"Umm, I can't say that with any certainty. Donna may have mentioned to me that he was involved in some church activities, but I don't specifically recall her saying anything about the 12-step program."

"Was Cale Bates doing anything for either of you besides bussing tables?"

"Nope," Carl answered forcefully, before glancing furtively at his brother.

"That was awful nice of you two to take such an interest in the personal life of one of your employees like that," Fletcher said, a subtle hint of disbelief in his tone.

"From what Carlton has told me, he's a good kid. Just had a tough upbringing. His father is a bit abusive, as I understand it," Richard explained.

"I can vouch for that," Fletcher replied. "He abused me and a couple deputies many years ago when we tried to restrain him at a party. So, Carl, how did you come to decide that Cale needed help with an addiction issue?"

"He came and asked you for help, didn't he, Carl?" Richard offered.

"That's right," Carl responded, his arms still folded in front of him.

"As Carlton explained it to me," Richard Talbot began, "Cale came to him and said he was interested in getting help for a meth problem and that there was a program he had heard about at Covenant Community, but it met on a night that Carl always had him scheduled to work, so he wanted Carl to switch his work schedule. But Carl couldn't do that, so Carl called me and asked if I could place a call to the church."

"Why couldn't you switch his work schedule?" Fletcher inquired, looking intently in Carl's direction and intentionally avoiding eye contact with Richard, so as to convey his growing annoyance with Richard answering on Carl's behalf.

"Just couldn't. It didn't work," Carl answered, staring straight back at Fletcher.

"It would be helpful to my investigation if I could get copies of Cale's time cards from the restaurant for July and August, if you have them."

"I'll see what I can find," Carl said, again sneaking a quick look at his brother.

"Now, about Anna Springer. When did you first learn she had been murdered?"

"I read the newspaper account after her head was discovered. And I was absolutely in a state of shock," Richard commented.

"Carl, how about you?" Fletcher asked.

"Same."

"And when did you decide that Terry Kellogg was responsible?" Fletcher inquired.

"Again, we're relying on the news media for our information, like everyone else. We've seen the newspaper stories about Kellogg's arrest," Richard interjected.

"I was asking Carl," Fletcher said sharply.

"Newspaper," Carl responded, apparently taking his brother's lead.

"Well, Carl," Fletcher began, leaning forward, "Sheriff Bill Rogge has told me that you called him with a tip about Terry Kellogg's involvement in the murder shortly after Springer's head turned up in the river. What can you tell me about that?"

Carl frowned, and looked over at Richard, who quickly shook his head.

"Rogge told you that?" Carl asked, his large odd-shaped face turning a reddish shade, as the inflection of his voice rose.

"In fact," Fletcher continued, "Bill told me that when you called him, you mentioned that Richard here was convinced that Terry had done it."

"That son of a bitch," Carl snapped, two large veins beginning to reveal themselves near his temples.

"Carl . . .," Richard said, looking at his brother in a manner that suggested Richard wanted Carl to regain his composure, "you and I did discuss Kellogg's history of violence and the fact that he was bothering Anna at work, remember? You must have reported that to the Sheriff, right?"

"I thought you weren't aware of his violent history," Fletcher interrupted.

"That's not what I said," Richard sniped. "I said I didn't think I had discussed it with Ms. Chitwood before Terry was hired. I certainly found out about it later."

"What was your relationship with Anna Springer like?" Fletcher asked suddenly, hoping to catch Richard off guard.

"Purely professional," Richard responded coolly. "But I did a few things to look out for her, since her mother is on the Board here."

"Like what?"

"She was having car troubles, so I let her use one of the company cars."

"The Trianta Envi?"

"Right."

"Did you know the Terry Kellogg confession indicates that Springer was driving that vehicle the night she was murdered?"

"I did hear that, yes."

"Had you authorized Anna to drive the vehicle that day?"

"She had my ongoing permission to use it. I didn't need to authorize her on a daily basis."

"But you're saying you had no personal relationship with Anna?"

"Define personal," Richard stated. "I'd talk to her from time to time."

"Can you tell me where you were on July 25?"

"Investigator Fletcher, I'm not sure where you're going with this interview, but I must say, I don't care for your accusatory tone."

"I'm simply gathering information, Dick."

"It's Richard. And if this line of questioning continues, Carlton and I will be in contact with our legal counsel."

"I have information that puts you in the Cayman Islands on that date," Fletcher offered.

"Your information is correct," Richard said, looking again at his brother.

"I went with Carlton on a business trip down there."

"Anyone else go with you?" Fletcher asked.

"What does this have to do with your investigation?" Richard asked, growing increasingly annoyed with Fletcher's questioning.

"I also have information suggesting that Anna Springer was with you," Fletcher stated.

"That's it," Richard said, rising from his chair, "this meeting is over. You can deal with our attorney. Carl, please show Mr. Fletcher the exit."

"I can find my own way out," Fletcher said, also coming to his feet, and looking first at Richard, then Carl. "But I gotta lot more questions for you fellas. So, you ain't seen the last of me."

Carl stepped forward and attempted to grab Fletcher by the arm, but Fletcher yanked it away and began backing out of Richard's office, all the while continuing to stare at one brother, then the other, until he was through the door.

Chapter 38

"How did I let you talk me into this?" Troy Sloan asked, as he quietly turned the key in the lock of the back-door entrance to his parents' palatial Riverton estate.

"Just like old times, huh bud?" Mike Hanigan responded. "Let's just hope your old man's computer isn't locked down as tight as his liquor cabinet used to be."

It had taken every bit of Hanigan's considerable talent in the art of persuasion, but he had convinced Sloan that the moral high ground required them to access the account database of Riverton State Bank via Ted Sloan's private, password-protected home computer, to review the recent financial activities of C-BAS, LLC, with an eye toward cracking the case against the Talbots.

Hanigan had reasoned with Sloan that, if proper legal channels were actually followed to obtain the information, the Talbots and their lawyers would find ways to delay the process long enough to enable them to somehow cover their tracks.

Sloan knew that both of his parents were out-of-town and that Cin, the Sloan family's heavy-sleeping, live-in housekeeper, would not pose much of an obstacle to a stealth late-night visit to the mansion.

Sloan's willingness to aid Hanigan in the covert operation had surprised not only Hanigan, but Sloan himself. Something about being around Hanigan seemed to throw Sloan back to a more care-free, mischievous time in his life.

"Remember my secret room, right off the loft area upstairs?" Sloan was now whispering since the two were inside the darkened home. "Dad turned it into his own little banker's war room. Made me turn over my keys to it. But I kept one back for good measure."

"Good thinking," Hanigan replied in a hushed tone. "Let's do this."

Hanigan and Sloan tiptoed down the long cold corridors of the old residence en route to the spacious front room, with its winding spiral wooden staircase leading to the mansion's upper floors.

The sight of the winding stairs evoked memories in Hanigan of climbing them in one state of mind and descending them several hours later in a far different, vastly less coherent one.

As they now mounted the staircase, the considerable creaking which accompanied their upward ascent caused the duo to stop every few steps, silently listening for any rustling from the vicinity of Cin's sleeping quarters.

Upon arrival at the top of the stairs, Sloan led Hanigan down the hallway several paces to another, shorter flight of stairs, which led to the mansion's loft area.

Sloan climbed the steps and pushed open the antique wooden door to the loft area, the hinges of the door groaning loudly from old age and lack of adequate lubrication.

"Shh," Sloan said sharply, holding the doorknob in his hand but leaning back down the small staircase and perking his ears for any downstairs movement in response to the unwelcomed noise from the door.

Hearing none, he motioned with his hand for Hanigan to ascend the final few stairs and enter the loft area.

From inside the loft, Sloan quickly and discretely closed the wooden door, pleased that its closing motion did not elicit the same wretched noise as upon opening.

He flipped on the loft's small overhead light and walked Hanigan over to what appeared to be a large bookshelf on the far wall of the loft, which Hanigan remembered as the entrance to the secret room he and Sloan had used as a drinking place during their adolescence on those occasions when Cin was vigilantly patrolling the otherwise empty home.

Sloan reached for the far right side of the middle shelf and slid a large, leather bound Webster's thesaurus to the side, revealing a tiny plastic black keyhole.

He removed from his front pocket a single silver ring, bearing one small black key. With one easy motion, Sloan inserted the key, turned it clockwise one-half rotation, and pushed the right side of the would-be bookshelf forward, revealing the interior of secret room.

"Thar she blows," Sloan said, in a slightly louder tone, pointing at the computer desk in the cramped room and the PC atop it.

"Do we want this closed?" Hanigan asked, in reference to the bookshelf-turned-secret-door.

"No," Sloan answered, "I don't want to get locked in here."

"You sure you know the password?" Hanigan asked, as he watched Sloan reach down to turn on the computer.

"It's been the same for years – BANKBOSS1."

"Doesn't one of his Cadillacs have a vanity plate that says that?"

"Yep."

"Sounds more like a trucker CB handle," Hanigan cracked. "Breaker 1-9, this here's the BankBoss1, we got a truckload of overdrawn negotiable instruments, and there's a bank examiner in the air."

"Shh, keep it down, would you?" Sloan snipped sharply, nervousness apparent in his voice as he shakily typed in what he hoped was still his father's computer password.

"He's nothing if not predictable," Sloan said as the password took hold and the computer began to log into the Riverton State Bank account database.

"Alright! You are the man . . ." Hanigan said, leaning forward, just behind Sloan's right ear, "of God," he added, wanting to remind Sloan that his otherwise deceitful act was serving a higher purpose.

"Do you have an account number?" Sloan asked.

"No I don't. Can't you search by account holder?"

"We can try it."

"Try C-BAS, LLC."

Sloan typed the appropriate characters and pressed the Enter key.

"Nothing," he said.

"Okay, try Consultants Business and Social."

"Yeah, that's it," Sloan said, eyeing the information popping up on the screen before him.

"Account number 5433018266. It's a preferred checking account showing Carlton Talbot as the lone authorized signator, as Manager of the LLC."

"Can we look at the recent account entries?"

"How recent?"

"I don't know – last six months maybe."

"I'll just pull up everything from the first of this year forward."

"That works."

Hanigan leaned still closer to the screen and squinted intently to read the text inside the narrow rows and columns of the table. "Okay, what do we got?"

He placed his right index finger at the top of the screen and slowly began moving it down the rows of green-lettered entries. "Tree Heaven. There's Arboretum Supply Co. Arabica Coffee Wholesalers. Seedlings and Sapplings, Inc. Orchard Inn. All these entries are deposits into the Consultants' account, right?" Hanigan asked Sloan.

"Yeah, those entries are," Sloan replied, "but the ones with numbers in this column are outgoing payments." Sloan was gesturing toward a series of figures on the screen. "The W over here indicates wire transfer."

"What's this set of letters and numbers to the right of the dollar figures?"

"Looks like a SWIFT Code," Sloan replied.

"What the hell is a SWIFT Code?"

"Kinda like an ABA routing number, only it's for foreign banks. Basically an identification code that tells you what bank you're dealing with."

"So, we could use that code to identify the bank that received these wires?"

"Should be able to."

"I'm gonna write that down," Hanigan reached in the breast pocket of his shirt for a pen that wasn't there.

"Troy, you know more about bank practices than I thought you would." Hanigan said, now looking around on the computer desk for a stray pen.

"Hey, I grew up with BankBoss1, what do you expect? And my two years at Wharton didn't hurt either. Let's just print this page," Sloan offered, using the computer's mouse to move the cursor up to the program's print icon.

"Can we take a quick look back at last year's entries?" Hanigan asked.

"Very quick. We need to get out of here."

Sloan typed in an extended date range, to reveal the previous year's account activity.

"Look at that," Hanigan said. "All those same companies -- Tree Heaven, Arboretum Supply, the coffee place, Seedlings, Orchard Inn – have been making regular payments to C-BAS, going back to around the time when Talbot got the director job at TAFF. I'll bet you anything those are the companies that Richard awarded contracts to, and they're all paying consulting fees to C-BAS."

"Why would TAFF need a contract with the Orchard Inn?" Sloan asked.

"The Foundation's got that huge hotel lodge as part of its conference center."

"That one may not be an actual TAFF contract, but it's got to be something screwy. Otherwise, why would Carl Talbot's own motel be paying Carl for consulting services? Maybe that's the

'Social' part of 'Consultants Business and Social' – Carl consulting with his flock of dirty motel hookers on how best to ply their trade," Hanigan quipped, still staring at the computer screen.

"Look at this, Troy. With the exception of fairly modest monthly salary payments to Carl, most of this money coming in from these other companies turns around and gets distributed by wire transfer to that other bank account, wherever it is."

"Mr. Sloan? Is that you?" The faint familiar voice of housekeeper Cin, fraught with trepidation and concern, was wafting into the secret room, emanating from what sounded like the area at the bottom of the small loft staircase.

"Holy Sheep Dip," Sloan said, reaching down to power off the computer.

"Cin, it's just me – Troy," he shouted, standing and moving towards the entrance of the secret room, before continuing. "I'm planning to surprise Dad with some software for his computer for his birthday next month, so I needed to check something out up here."

"You scared me to death," Cin replied, her voice trailing off, as if she was satisfied with Sloan's answer and was eager to crawl back into her bed.

"Sorry, Cin. Please don't tell Dad I was up here. I want it to be a surprise," Sloan yelled.

Hanigan and Sloan stood in the secret room staring at one another for several seconds, both of their hearts still racing, wanting to ensure that Cin had made her way back to her room, before saying another word.

"Good to see seminary didn't dull your keen ability to lie under pressure," Hanigan finally whispered after an extended period of absolute silence.

"The worst part about that is now I actually have to buy a birthday gift for Ted," Sloan responded.

"How about some software to keep unwanted intruders from hacking into his personal computer?" Hanigan said, smiling.

Chapter 39

Steve Fletcher stood on the deck of his country home, hands on the wood railing, looking out over the many well-aged oak and maple trees on his three-acre lot, the leaves of which would soon be splashed with their early autumnal hues.

Fletcher now believed he had enough information to obtain a warrant to search Richard Talbot's homes in Riverton and at Lake Wa Con Da.

The pilot of the Trianta charter plane which had departed Omaha on July 21, destined for the Cayman Islands via Colombia, had been located. From a review of photographs, the pilot had identified his three passengers - Carl Talbot, Richard Talbot, and Anna Springer. He indicated that Richard Talbot and Springer had been openly affectionate during the flights.

This confirmed in Fletcher's mind his suspicion that Springer had been dating an upper level management person at TAFF. And, upon reflection, it made sense to Fletcher that Springer would be attracted to Talbot on some subconscious level. Talbot was essentially an older version of the type of man Phyllis Springer had always been pushing her daughter to date – politically savvy, active in the community, and from an affluent, well-connected family.

And what better way for the daughter to add to her meddling mother's angst than by dating a married man whose family matriarch had been Phyllis Springer's chief civic adversary.

Since the inception of the investigation, Fletcher had questioned how committed Anna Springer could have been to the lesbian lifestyle, in light of her repeated forays into casual heterosexual dalliances.

Perhaps the Howell relationship was purely experimental in nature.

Or maybe Anna dove into it for the shock value, to further disturb and irritate Phyllis Springer.

Or could it be that Anna was merely filling a deep-seated need for the female attention she never received from her mother?

Fletcher was no psychologist and he had no immediate answers to these questions. But one thing seemed abundantly clear to him – Anna Springer and Richard Talbot had been having a highly secretive relationship which apparently had gone undetected by their co-workers at the Foundation or perhaps had been intentionally hushed-up by Talbot.

As Fletcher pulled a long draw of cigar smoke into his mouth, he noticed a silver Ford Mustang making the turn onto the long, winding gravel driveway leading to his house.

The vehicle pulled up onto the wide cement slab in front of Fletcher's two-car garage, and from it, emerged Mike Hanigan, wearing his customary Wayfarers and clad in a pair of loose-fitting khaki cargo pants and a faded navy blue t-shirt emblazoned with the yellow "SPAM" logo of Hanigan's favorite non-perishable mystery meat.

"This isn't the easiest place in the world to find," Hanigan said, looking up at Fletcher and walking towards the wooden stairs leading up to Fletcher's elevated deck.

"My directions weren't good?" Fletcher asked.

"I think I turned right one gravel road too early."

"Oh, you probably turned into the Beltenspergers' private drive, instead of the county road."

"It was definitely someone's house," Hanigan said. "There were two crusty-looking farmhands outside and they didn't have the most welcoming looks on their faces when I pulled up and whipped a U-ey in front of their barn."

"They don't get many visitors over there," Fletcher replied.

"The big wood sign in their yard is a classic, though," Hanigan said, in reference to a 4X6 piece of old plywood that marked the entrance into the neighboring farm, with the words "Deer Killin' HQ" scrawled on it, in what appeared to be animal blood.

"They give me deer steaks and jerky every year, so I can't complain," Fletcher replied.

"Nice deck," Hanigan said, staring at the vast expanse of Fletcher's wooden deck, as he finished his ascent up the flight of stairs.

"Thanks. Built it myself. It's actually got more square footage than the main level of my house."

"Wow," Hanigan said, his eyes catching sight of the two tall maple trees shooting up through the holes intentionally cut into the floor of the deck.

"Can I get you a beer?" Fletcher asked.

"Sure," Hanigan responded.

"You gonna be offended if all I have is Miller?"

"What my old man doesn't know, won't hurt me," Hanigan replied.

"I'll go grab us a couple. Have a seat." Fletcher motioned towards the padded wood deck chairs just to Hanigan's right. But Hanigan instead walked over near the deck-encased maple trees for a closer look.

"You like that?" Fletcher asked, sauntering back up the wooden stairs moments later, carrying the two golden bottles of brew he had retrieved from his garage refrigerator.

"It's definitely unique," Hanigan answered, still standing near the two engulfed trees. "How'd you come up with the idea?"

"Me and my brother just kept building the deck further and further out, and we didn't want to cut the trees down, so we built around 'em."

"That's pretty cool," Hanigan said, tilting his head back to gaze up towards the top of the two trees. "The Trees Are Forever Foundation would be proud."

"So, you got some more info for me on that?" Fletcher asked.

"I think so," Hanigan replied.

"Well, if it's as good as the information you gave me last time, I'm gonna have to deputize you right here on the spot."

"That'd be fine with me. I've really enjoyed looking into all this."

Hanigan twisted off the top of his Miller High Life and took an initial swig, before continuing to speak.

"I talked to Paul Vogler, who serves on the Board of Directors at Trees Are Forever. I got some nice background information on the Foundation."

"I'm all ears," Fletcher said.

"There's five board members including Phyllis Springer, and the vote in favor of appointing Richard Talbot as executive director was only 3-2. Phyllis Springer voted in favor, which is highly unusual in itself if you know anything about the longstanding animosity between her and Talbot's mother."

"Gladys, sure," Fletcher said, nodding.

"Then, after his appointment, Talbot started making some fairly drastic changes. He cancelled one of the Foundation's major tree supply contracts, and entered into several new ones with different companies. He also started a new rainforest coffee venture down in South America. All these new companies that TAFF contracted with started paying consulting fees to C-BAS, LLC which, as it turns out, is a Carl Talbot endeavor."

"You mean C-BAS, Inc.?" Fletcher asked.

"No, I'm pretty sure it's a limited liability company. It's registered with the Nebraska Secretary of State as an LLC and has a Nebraska-registered tradename of 'Consultants - Business and Social,' which must be where they came up with the C-BAS letters."

"Well that's strange, 'cuz this C-BAS, Inc. company I'm talking about is based down in the Caymans," Fletcher said, still standing. "They gotta be related somehow. So, Carl's doing some kind of consulting work on the side?"

"I don't how much actual consulting is going on. I suspect the payments are probably kickbacks on the Foundation awarding the contracts to those companies."

"You sure about that?" Fletcher asked.

"Not 100%, but doesn't it strike you as odd that every company TAFF has awarded a major contract to since Richard took over, just so happens to hire Carl's consulting firm?"

"So, you got confirmation that these companies have made the payments?"

"Seen the bank records myself," Hanigan said, his voice trailing off slightly, apparently realizing that his unauthorized entry into Ted Sloan's secret room may not garner this law enforcement officer's approval.

"So, you think the kickbacks somehow tie into the murder?" Fletcher asked.

"To be honest, I don't know that they do," Hanigan answered.

"Well, Anna was working with the financial records over at TAFF," Fletcher began. "I suppose there's a chance she figured out what Richard was up to. Hell, since he was banging her, he might have even told her himself. If she decided she wanted to blow the whistle on old Dick, that would definitely give him a motive for killing her."

"That makes sense," Hanigan agreed.

"Hey, let me show you something I got from Anna Springer's supervisor at the Foundation."

Fletcher placed his bottle of beer on the deck railing and dashed back down the wooden stairs towards his blue truck, parked next to Hanigan's Mustang on the concrete slab below.

He returned with the manila folder which had been given to him a week before by Gail Holcomb, the internal accountant at Trees Are Forever.

"I got some documents that Springer left behind at her work," Fletcher said, flipping hastily through the pages contained in the folder, "and there's these sheets in here that talk about uncertificated non-voting shares and lists a whole bunch of people - like nine-hundred and seventy-some."

Fletcher pulled the slightly wrinkled papers from the folder. "At the top of each page, it has Shareholder Name, Number of Shares, and Dividends Paid, but it doesn't say what company it's for. I've had my research people running the names, and I just found out this morning that all these people are employees of Trianta Motor Corporation, in all different places across the country. So, I'm thinking maybe this is a partial shareholder list for Trianta. Employee-owners or something."

"Trianta's publicly traded," Hanigan said. "I would think they'd have way more shareholders than that."

"Anyhow," Fletcher continued, "it looks like each of the non-voting shareholders on here got a one-time dividend of $2,400. But towards the bottom of the last page, there's a block of 243 shareholders who are crossed out, and Anna's name is handwritten in pencil in big letters over the top, with an arrow from her name towards the bottom of the dollar amount column, where someone has added up the dividends for the people who were crossed out and circled the total amount."

"$583,200," Hanigan read aloud, glancing over at the bottom of the wrinkled page in Fletcher's hand. "Pretty nice chunk of change. Wait a minute. You see those letters and numbers written handwritten under the $583,200?" Hanigan asked.

"Yeah, what about em?"

"That first one there is the SWIFT Code for a bank down in the Caymans."

"SWIFT Code?" Fletcher glanced at Hanigan for further explanation.

"Like an identification code for a bank. And it's the same bank that CBAS, LLC has been wiring money to. I bet that other handwritten number below the SWIFT Code is an account number."

"What about these?" Fletcher asked, pointing to two additional series of letters and numbers to the right of the SWIFT Code Hanigan had pointed out."

"Probably another SWIFT Code and account number. I wonder if this half a million was being transferred from the Cayman bank to some other bank. If you figure out whose account this is at the Cayman bank and what the other bank and account are, you may just crack this mother wide open."

"You ready to be deputized?" Fletcher asked jokingly.

"No, but I'm ready for another beer," Hanigan said, draining the last of his Miller High Life in one enormous gulp.

"You don't mess around," Fletcher commented.

But before he could head down the stairs toward the garage to retrieve another beer for Hanigan, Fletcher's cell phone rang.

"Fletch here."

"Steve, it's awful! You gotta get down here." The woman on the other end of the line, who Fletcher recognized to be Bill Rogge's office administrator, was completely hysterical.

"Bill shot himself!" she wailed.

Chapter 40

As Steve Fletcher sat in the waiting area of the tiny law office on Riverton's Main Street, from which the Apache County Attorney operated his private legal practice, Fletcher mindlessly thumbed his way through a month-old Newsweek magazine he had pulled from the stack of periodicals piled up on the brass end table to his right.

Fletcher could do little more than simply glance blankly at the photos as he flipped from page to page. He was still reeling from the events of the past sixteen hours.

Etched in his mind was the devastating sight of his old fishing buddy's lifeless corpse, in full uniform, splayed out on the floor of his Sheriff's Department office, with his face virtually blown off, blood splattered over the wall and ceiling behind him, sprinkling many of the prized fish that Bill Rogge had hung with such pride.

The burly Sheriff had placed his service revolver under his chin and jerked the trigger, but not before authoring two separate handwritten letters and sealing them in marked envelopes – one addressed to his wife Suzanne and the other to Fletcher.

Upon Fletcher's arrival at the scene of the suicide, he had immediately ripped open the envelope bearing his name. He had read it at least five times since.

Fletch –

I'm writing this to clear my name of any connection to Anna Springer's death.

A couple years back, I got myself in a real bad financial jam and damn near lost everything. But Carl Talbot offered to help me out, if I would do some favors for him. So I looked the other way a few times on some things Carl was doing out there at his motel. And he helped me out financially.

I don't feel good about what I done, Fletch, but you gotta believe me when I say - I had nothing to do with Anna Springer getting killed.

When I got the tip from Carl about Terry Kellogg, I thought it was legit. But I didn't want to mention it to anyone because it was from Carl. I had no reason to suspect that Carl or his brother were involved in the murder. I really believed that Kellogg done it. And I had no reason to doubt Bates' statement.

Fletch – I'm trusting you, as a friend, to keep my name clear of anything to do with Springer's death, especially for my family's sake. I ain't no murderer.

Sorry for everything.

Your friend,
Bill

Fletcher was fighting hard to keep his personal sadness over Rogge's death from clouding his ability to focus on the investigation at hand. His mind had gone round and round debating whether to believe Rogge's dying proclamation of innocence.

Fueling the debate was Connie's insistence that the suicide was proof positive that Rogge had played a role in the Springer murder.

"Otherwise, why would he have killed himself?" Connie had asked repeatedly.

But Fletcher had now convinced himself, if not Connie, that the suicide made perfect sense even if Rogge had no involvement in the murder.

As Fletcher saw it, Rogge had spent his entire adult life in law enforcement and had staked his reputation – and his ability to continually get re-elected by the County's populace – on being a straight-shooting, no-nonsense Sheriff, above reproach. The thought of being exposed as someone who could be bought off by a slime-ball like Carl Talbot would have been too much for Rogge to bear and likely was enough to cause him to take his own life.

"Fletch, come on back," said Roy Peterson, the Apache County Attorney, from behind his secretary's desk, grabbing a handful of small pink phone message sheets from his middle-aged slightly overweight legal assistant.

"You gonna get the bow out this weekend," Peterson asked Fletcher, in reference to the opening day of deer-hunting season for archers, as the two men walked the short hallway back to Peterson's office.

"I guess it depends on what happens here today," Fletcher replied. "I'd sure like to get it out."

"Well, you might be able to, after all," Peterson said, lowering his voice slightly and shutting his office door behind them. "I just got a call on the lab results from this weekend's search of Dick Talbot's place at Lake Wa Con Da."

"That was fast," Fletcher responded. "What do we got?"

Fletcher had a seat in Peterson's office, eyeing the brown-hued wall painting of a flock of pheasants flying over a brush thicket, just to his right.

"The interior cloth paneling in Talbot's boat had been scrubbed recently with an industrial strength, ammonia-based cleanser," Peterson began. "But they did find a minute trace of blood deeply embedded in the fabric of the sidewall covering near the rear of the boat. Perfect DNA match with Anna Springer."

"Boo yah," Fletcher said, obviously pleased with what he heard, before tempering his enthusiasm. "But, you know, Pete, with such a small amount, Talbot could easily admit he was seeing Springer and claim she cut herself water skiing or something. Did they come up with anything else?"

"Not really," Peterson replied, reaching over to grab the report from the corner of his desk. "But let's go over everything we got and see how strong it is from a circumstantial standpoint."

"We should probably wait for that Hanigan kid to show up."

"Tell me again who he is and how he's involved in this," Peterson said.

"Donny Hanigan's boy. He's a lawyer who works for some judge up in Omaha. He's the one who stumbled onto the lead about Anna Springer being in the Cayman Islands with the Talbots. And he's been piping me some other good info along the way."

"He knows about our meeting?" Peterson asked.

"I told him," Fletcher replied, just as a quiet knock on Peterson's office door interrupted.

"Roy," said Peterson's secretary, opening the door a slight crack. "There's a Mike Hanigan here to see you."

"Send him on in," Peterson said.

"Good timing, Kid," Fletcher said, as Mike Hanigan walked through Peterson's office door. "We was just talking about you."

"I swear, I'm innocent of all charges," Hanigan joked.

"I'm Roy Peterson," the County Attorney leaned over his desk and extended his right hand in Hanigan's direction.

"Mike Hanigan. Nice to meet you," Mike said.

"Have a seat," Peterson offered. "So what judge do you work for in Omaha?"

"Tom Centers. Bankruptcy Court."

"Oh, I try to steer clear of that place," Peterson said. "Too many rules to keep up with, and now you can't even file a pleading if you aren't hooked up to the internet."

"That's right," Hanigan replied.

"I ship all my bankruptcy work up to the Bradshaw firm in Omaha," Peterson said.

"Bart Townsend?" Hanigan asked.

"Yep. They say he's the best," came Peterson's reply.

"He does a lot of creditors' work," Hanigan responded, not willing to anoint Townsend as the state's supreme bankruptcy practitioner.

Realizing their legal dialogue had largely excluded Fletcher, Peterson gestured in the direction of the investigator.

"I was just telling Fletch that we got a DNA match on some blood found in Talbot's boat."

"Richard or Carl?" Hanigan asked.

"Richard. Up at his place on Lake Wa Con Da."

"So, you got enough to charge him?" Hanigan inquired.

"That's what we're here to talk about," Peterson replied. "We want to review everything we've got so far in terms of motive, opportunity, circumstantial evidence, everything."

"And I told Pete you might have info that could help us fill in some gaps," Fletcher interjected.

"I think I've told you everything I know, but I'm happy to help you guys out if I can," Hanigan said.

"First things first," Peterson said. "What's our evidence that Dick Talbot was having an affair with Springer?"

"All we got so far on that is the pilot's statement about them nuzzling on the plane," Fletcher replied. "Talbot denies it."

"No emails or letters between them?" Peterson inquired.

"Nothing. The TAFF email system was purged about the time this was all going down."

"That's got a fishy smell to it," Peterson opined.

"I talked to the computer guys at TAFF and they all confirmed it was a routine upgrade."

"Someone else at that place had to have known they were seeing each other," Peterson theorized. "It might be worth another run at some of the employees who worked closely with either of them. We're really solid on Springer being in the Caymans with him, right?"

"A lady named Meredith Beecham can give you that testimony," Hanigan said. "She lives down in the Grand Caymans."

"And we got the Trianta pilot on that too," Fletcher added.

"Let's talk about that Trianta angle," Peterson suggested. "What do we know?"

Hanigan looked at Fletcher, whose body language suggested that he wanted Hanigan to take the lead in explaining that issue.

"Talbot wanted to sell TAFF's confidential donor info to Trianta, the TAFF board shut him down, but Trianta for some reason still ended up opening its coffers to TAFF," Hanigan said.

"Run down those items for me," Peterson said, now jotting notes on a legal pad.

"Substantial grants to the Foundation. A free car. Collaboration on several big projects TAFF was involved in. A board appointment for Carl Talbot on the Cayman company via the Trianta dealers. Bank deposits to Riverton State Bank where Charlotte Talbot is a loan officer."

Hanigan glanced over at Fletcher for approval to continue, and Fletcher nodded.

"And we think a bunch of the Trianta grant money probably got disbursed by Richard Talbot to several new tree suppliers and coffee wholesalers, who turned around and paid substantial kickbacks to the Talbots's Nebraska company, C-BAS, LLC, in the form of consulting fees. From there, it looks like the LLC upstreamed the money, as dividends, to its parent company down in the Caymans, C-BAS, Inc."

"What's the tie-in with Anna Springer?" Peterson asked.

"We got a document from Anna's supervisor at work that's real interesting," Fletcher said. "It looks like in April of this year, about a half million bucks got diverted from the C-BAS, Inc. account in the Caymans to another Cayman bank account in Anna Springer's name."

"So the thought is that Richard whacked her for stealing from him?" Peterson asked.

"We're a little thin on that," Fletcher answered. "Could be stealing. Could be extortion. We're not sure."

"Anna was on the inside of TAFF financially and could have been threatening to narc on Talbot for all these kickbacks. The half million may have been hush money," Hanigan offered.

"Right," Fletcher stated.

"Maybe Talbot didn't like it. Or maybe she wanted even more money. So he took matters into his own hands," Hanigan said. "And I think Phyllis Springer is tied up in this somehow too."

"Whoa, time-out, Partner," Peterson said, throwing his hands up. "That's a mighty big fish. Unless you got a murder weapon with the senator's name etched in blood on it, I don't think we wanna go there."

"I'm still working on a theory there," Hanigan said.

"Theories may come in handy for writing judicial opinions, Mike, but unfortunately, I work in the real world, where evidence is all that matters," Peterson said. "No offense."

"I hear you," Hanigan replied. "I'm just throwing it out there for you to consider."

"Let's keep our focus on Talbot, for the time being," Peterson suggested.

"We got the whole frame-job angle as well," Fletcher reminded the other two.

"And that's based on Talbot getting Cale Bates into the AA class with Kellogg so he could claim to have gotten the confession?" Peterson asked, restating what had been previously explained to him.

"Right," Fletcher answered. "Oh, and we also got a couple key calls from Carl Talbot to Bill Rogge. One with the tip about Kellogg right out of the chute, and the second about Bates wanting to give his statement."

"But Bill Rogge, God rest him, obviously is in no shape to testify to those calls," Peterson said.

"We got Bill's suicide letter and his earlier statements to me," Fletcher said.

"I think there'd be a hearsay exception for that," Hanigan offered, trying to recall the specifics of the evidentiary rules which would allow such out-of-court hearsay statements to come into evidence.

"We need to hammer Bates until he breaks on this issue," Peterson stated, seemingly not satisfied with the alternatives. "We need him to admit that the Talbots put him up to the statement."

"I think he's afraid of Carl and what he'll do to him if he comes clean," Fletcher surmised.

"Well, then we need to assure him that he'll be protected," Peterson insisted. "We've built a decent case against Carl on drug trafficking and prostitution. We tell Cale we'll go easy on him and that Carl will be locked up for a minimum of 20 years."

"Bates has been in enough trouble with the law to know that Carl will get out on bail while he waits for trial," Fletcher responded. "I'd rather make a strong push against Carl. Get him charged on his other dirty deeds, and give him the chance to finger brother Dick for the murder. If Carl's only involvement was with the cover-up, maybe we can take the death penalty off the table in exchange for his testimony. And Carl ain't the sharpest tool in the shed. If we can get him separated from Richard, we might make some headway."

"If you think that's best, I'll trust your judgment, Fletch," Peterson said, rocking back and forth slightly in his chair. "But Chuck Lingelbach's representing them now and I don't think he'll let Carl say 'boo.'"

"Let's at least give it a shot," Fletcher said.

"Sound good to you, Counselor?" Peterson asked in Hanigan's direction.

"You're the pros," Hanigan answered. "I'm just along for the ride."

"Let's get her done," Peterson concluded.

Chapter 41

"Two tickets – one for you, one for me," Jenny Berg said, as she bounced toward Mike Hanigan outside the Main Street law offices of Roy Peterson, holding in her hand two printed paper tickets inscribed with black lettering.

"What are you talking about?" Hanigan asked.

"The Belle of Brownville. That replica 19th century steamboat ride I said I wanted to go on. I just got us two tickets. It leaves in twenty minutes, so we need to get down to the dock."

"You nut-job," Hanigan replied. "That old thing's liable to hit a sandbar and sink to the bottom of the river. Besides, we need to see if we can finish up that research on the Springer case."

"My computer has a built-in wireless router," Berg said, patting the black nylon case for the laptop computer she was carrying to her side with a shoulder strap. "It's a 90-minute boat trip, so we'll have plenty of time to work out on the water and for you to brief me on your meeting with the County Attorney. So, Mr. River Rat, I demand that you take me to the river."

"Like it's gonna do any good to argue with you," Hanigan replied, stepping off the curb towards his parked Mustang.

"Exactly," Berg responded, reaching for the handle to the Mustang's passenger-side door.

Once aboard the Belle of Brownville, named for the "other" oldest river town in the State of Nebraska, Hanigan and Berg chose to sit on the top deck of the craft, in a row of seats in the middle of the deck area, facing east, which would afford them a view of both the river and the Iowa shoreline.

"So, the County Attorney wasn't buying your Phyllis Springer theory?" Berg asked, Hanigan having given her the low-down on his just-concluded meeting during their brief car drive to the dock.

"It's not much of a theory, so I can't really blame him," Hanigan conceded.

"But with all that money coming in from Trianta and floating down through the Caymans, and with Phyllis being the only person in a position to do anything for Trianta, she has to be mixed up in this somehow."

"Maybe the half million that went to Anna actually got paid to the Senator," Berg offered.

"From what I've heard, those two haven't even been on speaking terms for several months. And it sounds like Anna was doing a pretty good job of spending the money on herself before she . . .."

The sudden loud toot of the boat's whistle interrupted Hanigan's comments.

"Oh, goodie, we're taking off," Berg bubbled, clapping her hands lightly in front of her, just above the keyboard of her open laptop.

"Goodie?" Hanigan said, frowning at his girlfriend. "What, are you channeling Shirley Temple or something? FYI, hun, this ain't the Good Ship Lollipop."

"I'm just excited. I've never been on one of these before."

"Well, try to control yourself," Hanigan said, his head jerking slightly as the boat pushed away from the dock. "Anyway, there's no indication that any of the money from the C-BAS Cayman account made its way to Phyllis. But, for some reason, C-BAS, Inc. has all these non-voting uncertificated shares they issued to Trianta employees."

"So, it's confirmed that the shareholder list that Springer had pertains to CBAS, Inc."

"It's not definite. But it makes sense."

"Okay, here we go," Berg said, referring to something on the screen of her laptop.

"What are you looking at?"

"It's a website that allows you to look up political campaign contributions made by major corporations," Berg answered.

"Alright," Hanigan said, leaning over for a look at the screen.

"And, during this two-year period, Trianta Motor Corporation made huge soft-money contributions to the national Republican party, which was in control of Congress then."

"So? That's ancient history," Hanigan said, dismissing any relevance to Berg's find.

"From my days as a poli-sci major, I remember there was a huge fight in Congress around that time about campaign finance reform," Berg explained. "As I recall, a new reform law got upheld by the Supreme Court towards the end of that period."

"Meaning?" Hanigan said, his attention drifting away from the conversation towards the rows of tree-covered bluffs several miles in the distance beyond the river's eastern bank.

"Meaning that if Trianta wanted to influence politicians after that law went into effect, it had to find some alternative to the big soft-money contributions it had been making. Let's think, if you're a major corporation with a lot of money to influence an election, how could you get it into the hands of the politicians, without violating the reform law?"

"Give it to a non-profit foundation that the politician sits on the board of, and hope she'll be grateful enough to advance your agenda in Washington?" Hanigan offered.

"That, or maybe you lean on your employees to donate to that politician's campaign," Berg theorized. "Kinda like what the unions do."

"Okay, but if we're talking general, soft-money donations, aren't there limits on individual donations too?" Hanigan asked.

"Yeah, it's like $2,400 per person or something. But that could add up quickly, if you have enough employees."

"Did you say $2,400?" Hanigan asked excitedly.

"That's what I remember from Poli-Sci 401 that I took senior year. It could have changed by now. I'm not sure. What?" Berg asked, sensing Hanigan had some sort of shocking revelation to unload.

"That's it!" Hanigan yelled. "You're a frickin' genius!"

"What?" Berg screamed back, drawing looks from the half dozen or so other boat riders in the top deck area.

Hanigan leaned in close to Berg, realizing that their conversation now had a would-be audience. "There were one-time dividends paid by C-BAS, Inc. to all of those Trianta employees, for $2,400 each," he whispered in Berg's ear.

"Those were probably reimbursements to the employees for making individual campaign contributions to Phyllis Springer."

"Well, that would be easy to verify," Berg said, her voice trembling slightly, as she turned her attention back to her computer, now sharing in Hanigan's excitement. "Individual campaign contributions are public record. Do you have the list of the Trianta employees?"

"No, I don't. But I got a pretty good look at that sheet. I could probably come up with a few from memory."

"Let's take a look," Berg said, typing briskly on the computer keyboard.

"And for those employees whose names were crossed off, maybe Anna nabbed the money before they could be reimbursed," Hanigan continued, as he waited for Berg to pull up the pertinent website. "Or maybe those crossed-off people never made the contribution in the first place. There's your big-time fucking motive for Phyllis to kill her daughter – she was stealing major campaign funds."

"Language," Berg said sternly, as she finished pulling up the information on Phyllis Springer's campaign contributors.

"Sorry, babe. I'm getting a little fired up."

"Okay, acer of the LSAT, let's see if that photographic memory can come through when it really matters. Hit me with a name I can search."

"Alright," Hanigan looked skyward, and began caressing his day-old chin whiskers. "I remember several Hispanic names down toward the bottom, which were part of the group that was crossed out. I wanna say Emilio Rodriguez was the last name on the list."

"Doesn't show up as a donor," Berg said, having punched the name into the website's search engine.

"How about Jorge Jimenez? J-I-M-I-N-E-Z, I think."

"Nope, nothing."

"Okay, try William Luppen. L-U-P-P-E-N. I remember that name distinctly, because my best friend in sixth grade was named Billy Luppen."

"No William Luppen," Berg answered.

"I think he also may have been one of the crossed out names. I need to come up with a name that wasn't crossed out. Think, Mike, think," Hanigan said aloud to himself.

"You know, we could always just call Steve Fletcher and ask him for the names," Berg suggested.

"Like I said, you're a frickin' genius."

"Give him a call," Berg said, looking up from her computer screen to momentarily take in the natural beauty of the river landscape around them.

Chapter 42

"Change of plans, Fletch," Roy Peterson said into Steve Fletcher's ear over his cell phone, in reference to their pre-arranged meeting with the recently-arrested Carl Talbot and his attorney, scheduled for later that afternoon.

"I got a call from Richard Talbot's new lawyer. He wants to get together right now. Are you available?"

"New lawyer?" Fletcher asked.

"Yeah, he hired some guy from Omaha, Fiala or something."

"What happened to Chuck Lingelbach?"

"Dick decided he wanted separate counsel from Carl. And I guess this Fiala guy has a conflict-of-interest that would keep him from representing Carl, anyway. Some Cayman bankruptcy deal."

"If Richard's itching to talk, I'll make time for that. What do you think prompted this?"

"I'm sure he heard that we arrested Carl. Maybe he wants to rat out his brother before his brother rats him out. His new lawyer was trying to pick me pretty hard for what our evidence is."

"What'd you tell him?"

"I mentioned the DNA results. And made some passing references to Richard's questionable activities at the Foundation."

"Let's hear what he has to say, I guess," Fletcher said.

"I'll call his lawyer and see if they'll drive over here."

"Hey, Pete," Fletcher began, "we just got confirmation that all of those non-voting shareholders in C-BAS that got $2,400 dividends, other than the ones that were crossed out, were campaign contributors to the Republican party – $2,400 each."

"Really? That Hanigan kid's good. I think he missed his calling."

"Yep," Fletcher replied. "See you shortly."

Fletcher sat next to Roy Peterson across a small conference room table from Richard Talbot and his attorney, the lazy-eyed criminal defense and bankruptcy lawyer, Vince Fiala, both wearing dark suits and ties. After exchanging introductions and awkward pleasantries, Fiala opened the serious dialogue.

"Here's the deal, gentlemen," Fiala said. "My client is prepared to come forward and identify the individual responsible for the murder of Anna Springer and to provide substantial details relating thereto. But he is only willing to do so if there is significant consideration coming his way. You tell us what your prosecutorial intent is at this time, and we will let you know what we are willing to accept in exchange for my client's information."

"Right now, counselor, your client is looking at premeditated first degree murder," responded Peterson, in a tone that suggested he didn't care for Fiala's initial posturing. "We've got substantial circumstantial evidence of Mr. Talbot's opportunity to do the crime, possible motive, and his involvement in the attempted cover-up and the framing of Terry Kellogg. And now we've got a key piece of physical evidence tying the victim to your client. There's not a whole lot of room for bargaining here, as far as I'm concerned."

"We'll see about that," Fiala replied. "Would you care to enlighten myself and my client on this mountain of evidence you claim to have garnered?"

"Where do you want me to start?" Peterson asked rhetorically, before continuing.

"We've got evidence of an elicit affair between your client and the victim. We have strong indications that your client's company was receiving improper payments on a number of TAFF supply contracts, and we know the victim certainly was in a position to have been privy to information about that – information that would have been very damaging to Mr. Talbot personally and professionally if it was ever disclosed."

Peterson peered back and forth at Talbot and Fiala, then forged ahead.

"We have hard evidence of a sizeable cash payment from your client's Cayman company to an account on which Anna Springer was a signator, evidence that Mr. Talbot was with the victim for the better part of a week before she showed up dead, and oh yes, an exact DNA match on some of the victim's blood found in your client's boat. Not to mention your client's apparent attempts to frame Terry Kellogg for this crime, by manipulating one of Carl Talbot's teenage drug runners. Do you want me to continue?"

"As I said before," Fiala said, "my client can give you the killer, but he will do so only with your assurance that he will not be charged in any way as an accomplice or accessory after the fact in the murder."

"If what your client tells us checks out, and we can confirm from the evidence that he was not involved in the planning of or carrying out of the murder itself, we may be able to work out a deal along those lines," Peterson said.

Richard Talbot leaned over and whispered in Fiala's ear, cupping his hand over his mouth to obscure opposing counsel's view of his moving lips.

"My client can also provide you with information regarding a major cocaine trafficking ring in Apache County, and possible campaign finance violations by Senator Phyllis Springer, *if* he can be assured of a satisfactory deal for himself."

"If he's talking about his brother Carl's drug dealing, we already have a strong case," Peterson said, staring back at Richard Talbot. "And, as for Senator Springer, we've uncovered some information on that issue as well, but ultimately that's something for the feds to worry about, not us. But, again, let's hear what your client has to say, and we'll see what we can get worked out."

"Very well. Go ahead, Richard," Fiala sat back slightly in his chair.

Richard Talbot cleared his throat before beginning to speak.

"I'd been seeing Anna Springer romantically for about 4 months. And, before you look down on me for sleeping with a woman half my age, let me assure you that I did everything in my power at first to resist her advances. But she was relentless. It's like she was on a mission. And basically would not take 'no' for an answer. So, I eventually succumbed."

"She wasn't a minor," Peterson offered. "It may have been immoral, but it wasn't illegal. Your sex life is your business, as far as I'm concerned."

"Thank you." Talbot exhaled before continuing. "Well, about a month into the relationship, I made the mistake of telling Anna about a certain arrangement I had with her mother that involved indirectly helping the Senator finance her upcoming re-election campaign. Anna suggested that whatever funds had been going to fund campaign efforts should instead go to Anna."

"Did she say why?" Peterson asked.

"She just wanted money, plain and simple," Talbot said. "At first, I was hesitant to go along, but the more I thought about it, the more comfortable I got with the idea. At that time, Anna was doing more for me than her mother and I knew Phyllis wouldn't be able to do anything about it, based on the somewhat secretive nature of our arrangement. Plus, to be brutally honest, I've never cared much for Phyllis."

"So you took money earmarked for campaign finance, and directed it to Anna?" Peterson asked.

"Correct," Talbot responded, reaching forward to grab a glass of water of the table.

"How much?" Peterson inquired.

"Over $500,000.00," Talbot said, raising his eyebrows as high as they would go.

"Keep talking," Fletcher interjected.

"A short time after the funds transfer to Anna, I had to inform my wife Charlotte that about $20 million in bank deposits would need to be moved from her bank in Riverton to an off-shore account, because of a liquidation proceeding that was being filed by the depositor – Automotive Services Risk something. Her job at the bank had been in jeopardy before that, and she really took it hard. We got into a nasty shouting match about it."

"Understandable," Peterson commented.

"When was that?" Fletcher asked.

"Right after the Fourth of July. Then, after the $20 million in deposits went away, Charlotte was informed by Ted Sloan that her position at the bank would be terminated at year-end. Charlotte always worries about money, and she was in a very fragile place emotionally after her conversation with Sloan."

"Where you going with this, Dick?" Fletcher inquired.

"It's Richard. And I'm getting to it. Charlotte had a working knowledge of the arrangement I had made with Senator Springer. After Ted Sloan dropped the bomb on her, Charlotte came to me and insisted that I divert some of the campaign funds to ourselves, to offset any loss of income from her bank job being terminated."

"So, you're saying Charlotte asked you to do the same thing Anna had asked – siphon campaign funds?" Peterson queried.

"Right. But of course, I couldn't tell Charlotte that I'd already sent the money to Anna, for fear of her learning of my relationship with Anna. Well, despite my best efforts, Charlotte somehow found out anyway. And, apparently with the combination of my relationship with Anna, and Charlotte finding out I gave all that money to Anna instead of her, Charlotte must have completely snapped and lost all rationale thought."

Talbot returned the glass of water to the table, before continuing.

"On August 1st, Charlotte came to me and told me that she killed Anna Springer and put her body in our boat house at Lake Wa Con Da."

"You're telling us that your wife is the murderer and that you had nothing to do with it?" Peterson asked incredulously. "How do you explain Springer's blood in your boat? I suppose your wife and your young mistress were out on a leisurely boat ride at the lake when Charlotte decided to kill her, is that it?"

"I swear to God, I had absolutely no knowledge that Charlotte was going to do it. And the boat in the blood is easily explained."

"Why did Springer go with you on your trip to the Caymans?" Fletcher asked, wanting to turn up the heat on Talbot.

"She begged me to take her. I had to be in Colombia for an environmental summit. Carl had some merchandise to pick up in Bogota and a board meeting in the Caymans. Anna just wanted to come along for the ride - to her it was like a spring-break getaway in July. And, believe me, she partied like it was spring break."

"So, when did Charlotte kill her?" Fletcher asked, probing for details to contradict Richard's story.

"Anna was planning to spend a week out at my house at Lake Wa Con Da after we got back from the Caymans. She had told everyone she was taking two weeks' vacation, going back east to interview with several lobbying firms, so no one was expecting her back at work or anywhere else. Charlotte found out somehow that Anna would be staying at the lake. I think she hired a private investigator or something."

Richard Talbot reached again for the water glass before continuing.

"Anyway, Charlotte went to our lake house in the wee hours of the morning on the night of July 31st, when she knew I wouldn't be there, backed her car into the garage, left the engine running, and waited several hours out in the boat house, until the carbon monoxide had done Anna in. She wrapped Anna's body in an old algae-covered tarp and drug her out to my boat house at the lake. Again, I knew nothing about the killing until afterwards."

"Stop right there, Richard," Fiala interrupted. "At this point, my client has identified the murderer. He is willing to testify consistent with his statement today, in exchange for immunity from any accessory or after-the-fact charges connected with the murder."

"His statement hasn't given us much to work with, aside from a possible motive for the killing. We're gonna need something more concrete than that," Peterson said. "And frankly, his story doesn't match up with the physical evidence."

Talbot leaned over and whispered in his attorney's ear. Fiala listened calmly, before leaning behind his client's head, so his mouth was out of the sight line of those across the table from them. His whispers were audible but the words he spoke to the back of Talbot's head were not discernible. Fiala turned his gaze directly back at Roy Peterson.

"Before my client will continue, we need assurance that, if his story checks out, no murder charges will be brought against him," Fiala demanded.

"Assuming he truly had no role whatsoever in the planning or carrying out of the deed itself, and we get adequate corroboration, that shouldn't be a problem," Peterson said.

"Proceed Richard," Fiala instructed.

"When Charlotte informed me of the murder, she said she wanted me to cover it up. I admit, that's where I made a mistake. I panicked and went ahead with a cover up. I remembered the stories Donna Chitwood had relayed to me about Terry Kellogg decapitating animals and I knew from what Anna had told me that Kellogg had a thing for her. So we did what we could to make it look like Kellogg had done it."

"Let's hear about that," Peterson said.

Talbot looked over at Fiala, who nodded, giving his client the green light to proceed.

"Carlton took Anna's corpse out of the tarp and used a large rock to crush the back of her neck, I guess to make sure she was dead. As if there was any question after carbon monoxide poisoning and two days wrapped in a tarp. He took her body out on my boat and trolled down the river at 3:00 in the morning. He pulled the motor up out of the boat and used the turning blade to sever Anna's body parts one at a time and chuck them into the river. And he took his Great Dane with him to chew on the body parts before he threw them overboard. But the very first limb he cut off fell in the water before he wanted it to, just south of the lake."

"The arm they found last month?" Fletcher asked.

"Right. That wasn't supposed to end up there. But Carlton did plant the decapitated head strategically under the marina dock, knowing someone would find it. After the head was found, Carlton called the sheriff with the tip about Kellogg."

"And what about Cale Bates' involvement?" Peterson asked.

"When no arrest was forthcoming, we decided we needed to help out the investigation. I asked Carlton if any of his helpers hung out with Kellogg. He said 'no.' I asked which one would be easiest to manipulate with fear. He said Cale Bates. So, Carl got Cale Bates involved to write out the confession."

"Did you have any direct involvement in that?" Peterson asked.

"Not really."

"What about your special request to the church pastor on behalf of Cale?" Fletcher offered.

"Beyond that, I had no further involvement with Cale Bates," Talbot replied.

"What can you tell us about C-BAS, LLC?" Fletcher asked.

"C-BAS is an acronym that Carl came up with – it stands for Carl's Bad Ass Syndicate, or something. And look, the drugs and the prostitutes was all Carlton. I never had anything to do with that. I was simply using the company in connection with my arrangement with Senator Springer. But I'm not going any further on this until I know what kind of a deal I'm looking at."

"Let's hear what you're willing to offer," Fiala said, looking back across the table at his adversaries.

Chapter 43

"Happy Valentine's Day again," Jenny Berg said, as she sat in a tropical-colored fabric beach chair, looking over and smiling warmly at Mike Hanigan, who was seated next to her in a matching chair, on the sugar-white sands of a Cayman Islands beach resort, laptop computers in both of their laps.

"Same to you, babe, again," Hanigan replied, smiling back at his girlfriend, before looking down at his computer screen.

"Did you know the 17th will be the six-month anniversary of our first date?" Berg asked.

"Why do you think I chose this week to surprise you with this trip?"

"Because you got some dirt cheap airfares," Berg responded.

"I mentioned that to you, did I?" Hanigan said regretfully. "Well, that was subterfuge. The real reason we're here is to commemorate the best half year of monogamous dating I've ever pulled off."

"Try not to get too romantic there," Berg said sarcastically.

"Seriously, hun, it's been a great six months," Hanigan replied.

Berg smiled and reached her hand over to squeeze Hanigan's forearm, which was poised above his laptop.

"Did you find anything about the jury verdict yet?" Berg asked, in reference to the just-finished criminal trial of Charlotte Talbot, in the Apache County District Court, some 1,200 miles from their current location in the Carribean.

"Still looking," Hanigan responded, eyeing his computer screen. "Whoa, here it is - online Omaha World-Herald," he said suddenly. "Guilty - first degree murder. Jury deliberated for only seven hours."

"So, the woman's gonna get life in prison or maybe even the death penalty for avenging a mistress, but her crooked, back-stabbing husband and his thug brother get by with slaps on the wrist?" Berg moaned. "What's wrong with that picture?"

"I think Carl got twenty-five-plus years on all the counts of drug trafficking, prostitution, and accessory-after-the-fact, which is no walk in the park. It's Richard that got the sweet deal. Pled to obstruction of justice and some criminal fraud charges. He's probably doing light duty at some Club-med prison."

"He'll be back out scamming people before we know it," Berg offered.

"If ever there was a poster-boy for Troy Sloan's spiritual oppression theory, it's Richard Talbot," Hanigan reasoned. "What kind of guy takes the person who put him in power, screws her over both monetarily and by nailing her daughter, then throws his own wife and brother under the bus, to save his own neck?"

"Definitely a scum bag. But he's obviously a pretty smart scum bag. That was quite an elaborate money laundering scheme he and the Senator cooked up. Everybody was getting something. Phyllis Springer was getting sizeable campaign contributions from Trianta, nicely laundered through TAFF, then legitimate private-sector businesses, the C-BAS companies, and the Trianta workforce. Richard got a cherry position at the Foundation, plus healthy director fees from the C-BAS Cayman company. Carl got regular trips to the Caymans, a nice way to launder his drug and prostitution money, plus frequent trips to Colombia with Richard, so he could ship back coke inside the TAFF rainforest coffee shipments."

"They had it all figured out. And they'd all still be lining their pockets if Dick hadn't started thinking with Dick Jr.," Hanigan quipped. "Sleeping with Anna really threw a major wrench in the whole deal."

"What is it with men? Sex is almost always their Achilles heel, their fatal flaw," Berg noted, shaking her head.

"It's in our genetic code," Mike reasoned. "You know, as much as I would have liked to have been right about Phyllis being involved in the murder, a part of me is glad she wasn't. Being corrupt and money-grubbing is one thing – pretty much par for the course for politicians. But to kill your own flesh and blood, that would take a special kind of evil."

"Do you realize that none of this stuff probably ever would have come out if you hadn't figured out it was Anna Springer at that meeting in the Caymans?" Berg asked thoughtfully.

"The thought has crossed my mind," Hanigan said grinning. "That Terry Kellogg dude owes me big time."

"What I can't understand," Berg began, "is how a guy like Richard Talbot is smooth enough to set this whole arrangement up and to keep a several month-long affair secret from just about everyone, but then he's dumb enough to show up at a corporate board meeting with his mistress."

"This tropical climate can make you do strange things," Hanigan said.

"Like this." Hanigan began typing quickly on his keyboard, and lifted and dropped his right pointer finger onto the final key for emphasis.

"Ooh, an instant message," Berg said, in mock astonishment. "I wonder who this could be from."

Berg pulled up the message from Hanigan and read it aloud: "What do you say if we're still dating a year from now, we get engaged?"

"Wow," Berg said, her face suddenly flushed.

She placed her right hand over her chest and breathed in, pausing several seconds before speaking.

"What about all your concerns about long-distance relationships? In a few months, I'll be working in Kansas City."

"That's another thing I've been waiting to tell you. I've decided to apply for a position with the FBI."

"What?"

"I want to be an investigator. You've always told me I need to do something that I'm passionate about, that gets my juices flowing. I think that might be the thing. And they have a Kansas City division."

"Mike, that's tremendous!"

Berg leaned over in her beach chair and threw both arms around the back of Hanigan's neck, pulling him toward her, and nearly tipping over in her chair in the process.

"I'm a little worried that some of the old skeletons in my closet might come back to bite me in the FBI screening process," Hanigan said into Berg's ear, as he returned her intense hug, "but I'm hoping the judge can exert a little influence on my behalf."

"Just tell them you've already single-handedly solved a homicide case, uncovered a high-level money-laundering scheme, and forced a two–term United States Senator to resign in disgrace over campaign finance indiscretions," Berg said, her words strained due to the tightness of Hanigan's squeeze on her.

"Never could have done any of it without you, babe. You're the catalyst for it all."

Berg released her grip on Hanigan, pulled her face back in front of Hanigan's and lifted the Rayban Wayfarers up above his eyes, staring deeply into them.

"I love you, Mike," she said.

"I love you too," Hanigan replied. "But be careful, you're about to spill my drink."

Berg looked inside the plastic glass sitting inside the cupholder in Hanigan's beach chair, which contained a thick-looking red substance.

"What is that?" Berg asked, frowning slightly. "A Bloody Mary?"

"No, it's a Bloody Veggie," Hanigan replied.

"Vodka and . . ." Berg began.

"V-8," Hanigan finished Berg's sentence for her, reaching forward to pull her into him again.

www.ingramcontent.com/pod-product-compliance
Lightning Source LLC
Chambersburg PA
CBHW031951240626
47153CB00003B/940